The Graceview Patient

Also by Caitlin Starling

The Starving Saints

Last to Leave the Room

The Death of Jane Lawrence

The Luminous Dead

Yellow Jessamine

The Oblivion Bride

The Graceview Patient

Caitlin Starling

ST. MARTIN'S PRESS
NEW YORK

This is a work of fiction. All of the characters, organizations, and events portrayed in this novel are either products of the author's imagination or are used fictitiously.

First published in the United States by St. Martin's Press, an imprint of St. Martin's Publishing Group

EU Representative: Macmillan Publishers Ireland Ltd, 1st Floor, The Liffey Trust Centre, 117–126 Sheriff Street Upper, Dublin 1, DO1 YC43

THE GRACEVIEW PATIENT. Copyright © 2025 by Caitlin Starling. All rights reserved. Printed in the United States of America. For information, address St. Martin's Publishing Group, 120 Broadway, New York, NY 10271.

All emojis designed by OpenMoji—the open-source emoji and icon project. License: CC BY-SA 4.0

www.stmartins.com

Library of Congress Cataloging-in-Publication Data

Names: Starling, Caitlin author
Title: The Graceview patient / Caitlin Starling.
Description: First edition. | New York : St. Martin's Press, 2025.
Identifiers: LCCN 2025017969 | ISBN 9781250340757 hardcover | ISBN 9781250340764 ebook
Subjects: LCGFT: Horror fiction | Novels
Classification: LCC PS3619.T3747 G73 2025 | DDC 813/.6—dc23/eng/20250513
LC record available at https://lccn.loc.gov/2025017969

The publisher of this book does not authorize the use or reproduction of any part of this book in any manner for the purpose of training artificial intelligence technologies or systems. The publisher of this book expressly reserves this book from the Text and Data Mining exception in accordance with Article 4(3) of the European Union Digital Single Market Directive 2019/790.

Our books may be purchased in bulk for specialty retail/wholesale, literacy, corporate/premium, educational, and subscription box use. Please contact MacmillanSpecialMarkets@macmillan.com.

First Edition: 2025

10 9 8 7 6 5 4 3 2 1

For Betsy

The Graceview Patient

· Chapter One ·

New nurse tonight.

She's about my age. Gentle. When Nurse Lauren did her shift change report, the new girl's fingers twitched like she wanted to be taking notes, but she'd had no paper, no pencil. No tablet. Her gloves squeaked with the movement.

Margaret Culpepper is twenty-six years old, and was admitted to Graceview Memorial seven weeks ago for inpatient management of Fayette-Gehret syndrome under the SWAIL protocol. She had an infusion this morning, and another scheduled tomorrow.

Everybody still wears full PPE around me. Face shield, gloves, N95—the works. It wasn't supposed to last this long, was it? I'm not sure what that means, except that it's bad. Of course it's bad.

Margaret, can you give your full name and date of birth?

I'm so tired of everything. I just want to go home. But—

Margaret initially tolerated treatment well, but has experienced several setbacks.

Setbacks. That's a nice way of describing it.

This room isn't as nice as the one I started out in. My body is more broken than it has ever been. The overhead PA is intermittent but loud, echoing day and night with codes, with messages, with requests I can't always understand. I'm not sure what day it is anymore, or if the whiteboard across from my bed is still accurate. My eyes blur when I try to read the clock. When my brain cooperates, I can mark the march of days by the light through the window and the coming and going of my nurses.

When my brain doesn't cooperate, I drift. Most of the time drifting is easier.

Four weeks ago, Margaret began exhibiting symptoms of tuberculosis. She is currently being treated with isoniazid INH in combination with rifampin, pyrazinamide, and ethambutol. She has been experiencing nausea, joint pain, and intermittent confusion and paranoia, as well as occasional seizures, currently understood to be caused by the interaction of her medications, the SWAIL infusions, and her underlying condition. We have been treating side effects as they emerge.

Report, twice a day, is one of my last anchors. Seven a.m., seven p.m., again and again and again. A litany of my suffering and my sins, a little different each time, but always sanitized and organized. Margaret Culpepper, burnt-out and burned down. They don't mention my stolen phone, or the nightmares, or what happened to Isobel.

They never mention Isobel at all.

All medication is being administered via a port-a-cath placed ten days ago on her left side chest, replacing a previous port-a-cath that was removed due to self-inflicted trauma.

Ten days ago? I can't remember . . .

Margaret, how is your pain right now?

I never know what number to tell them. Quantifying is something for the hospital to do; I only experience everything qualitatively. My gums are bleeding again. My breath rattles in my chest. My head swims, but I've lost track of if it hurts, or only wanders. My skin is pocked and blistering, and my stomach is the same; and yet they've both been worse many times before. I'm on the mend. I am being reorganized.

A six? That's what's circled on the board, so I must have said it. A six. Does this feel like a six? Did it earlier, however much earlier, when the new nurse first arrived?

(What's her name again? That isn't on the board. She forgot to update it. Maybe I was a six this morning, instead.)

She is voiding fine, but has not had a BM today.

I'm supposed to contribute, but it's so much easier to let them discuss me as if I'm just an object. Mostly, I've stopped caring. But it always gets me, the quick aside about the waste I produce. That's quantified, too. They need to make sure I'm giving as much as I'm taking in.

They go through a recitation of letters and numbers: my CBC, CMP, ESR, CRP. Once, I tried to sort out what it all meant. But that knowledge can't help me now, if it ever could.

My windows are dark, but the clock says . . .

No, I can't see that far today. But maybe it's still early. Ten?

Margaret is on a mechanical soft diet due to oral discomfort. Meals have been preselected and will be delivered at 2030. She is often able to feed herself, but please assess when dropping off her tray.

Dinner was mashed potatoes and chicken stewed until it was slime. I can still taste it. It can't be that late.

And bedside report still rings in my ears, infiltrating, reminding me of where I am. Who I am. How they see me.

She is a high fall risk, see her yellow wristband. Her bed alarm is on at all hours. She generally uses her call light appropriately and gets up well with an assist, but should not be left unattended in the bathroom. Although Margaret isn't currently requiring one-to-one supervision, she is considered a high elopement risk and remains on a medical hold. Notify Charge immediately if soft restraints become necessary at any point, and ensure you have a physician order within fifteen minutes.

But neither Margaret nor I anticipate that being necessary; we've had a run of good days, haven't we?

Haven't we?

· Chapter Two ·

GRACEVIEW MEMORIAL

Room:	775	Phone	XXX-XXX-2775
Date:	August 5, 2023	MON TUES WED THURS FRI (SAT) SUN	
Patient:	Margaret Culpepper	PAIN SCALE	
Doctor:	Santos	1 2 3 (4) 5 6 7 8 9 10	
Nurse:	Penelope W.	Pain medication last given:	
Charge Nurse:	Shannon L.	Next dose:	
Today's Plan! Admission, meeting with Dr. Santos.			
Diet:	Normal	Fall Risk:	Low
Activity Level:	Normal	Our goal is to have you discharged on:	September 30, 2023
Prevent falling! Call for help getting out of bed.			

My first hospital room had a perfect view of the mountains.

It was high up in the west tower, and was designed for comfort almost as much as for clinical expediency. Nothing excessive, no velvet curtains or soft mood lighting, but everything was gleamingly new, and the bed was actually soft. The linens were fresh, not laundered a thousand times. The pillows hadn't collapsed under the weight of so many other patients.

"A bit of VIP treatment!" chirped the aide who was getting me settled. "They even sprang for nicer showerheads when they remodeled this floor."

I didn't expect any VIP treatment. I wasn't sure I wanted it, either. It was—ambitious. Too confident. It said, *We know we can fix you*, and I knew that was a lie.

But I must have been hopeful, back then. I can almost remember it. A small mercy: that the memory is fading, blurring into the indistinct ebb and flow of pain. I don't think I could handle the agony of having that hope dashed. Better to lose it when I'm not looking.

I sat on the very edge of the bed, unsure of where to look, what to do. I'd brought a suitcase, but it was small. I wouldn't be wearing much besides hospital gowns for the next couple months, and all my books were on my phone. I must have read over a hundred *What to Pack When You're Admitted* lists, most of them geared toward expectant parents, and I'd dutifully packed what showed up again and again: a nice pillow, comfortable slippers, an eye mask, earplugs, a bathrobe. A little Bluetooth speaker. Pads, which I had to buy special, since my progesterone-only birth control had to be discontinued as part of the trial. While on it, I rarely bled. Without it, all bets would be off. I'd almost bought myself some hospital-cooperative pajamas, but I'd already run out of my meager budget on everything else.

And now I didn't need most of it. The pillow looked great. There were already slippers right next to the bed. I wasn't going to have a roommate, and I hated eye masks.

The aide set a bundle of fabric down next to me. "No rush, but you can get changed when you're ready," she said. "I'm going to let your nurse know you're here, and she'll be by to place your IV. Sound good?"

I nodded.

"Do you want a soda or juice while you're waiting?"

"I'm okay," I said.

Her smile was mechanical but genuine as she left the room.

I wasn't okay, of course. I was in a hospital. This wasn't labor and delivery. But there was that pesky hope thing again—I was here to be cured, wasn't I? Maybe this *was* going to be the happiest day of my life, if only in hindsight.

My condition had already taken almost everything from me. I was here to claw it all back. My gums were aching with ulcers, my skin was covered in itchy, sensitive red patches, and I'd been eating soup all week because it was the only thing I could keep down. Fayette-Gehret syndrome is rare and overwhelming. An autoimmune disorder that targets epithelial cells, sending them into a frothing overdrive, it's not life-threatening in and of itself, but the psychological and secondary physical effects are. There's not enough of us to have flourishing support groups. We have to cobble together maintenance regimens from similar diseases: psoriasis, IBD, that sort of thing. And like with so many chronic disabling conditions, there's not enough money going around for the medical care we need when things get infected or worse, let alone preventative care.

Except for this.

They found me. I'd given up looking. I'd kept up my technical writing work as long as I could, but my current flare was the worst I'd gone through yet, and I'd had to bow out of the meatier contracts. Burnt a few bridges in the process. Do you know what that feels like? To be forced to admit, *I can't take this job that buys me food because I hurt too much, I'm too exhausted, and if I push any harder it'll get worse, not better*? My parents don't. The few friends I'd managed to keep through a couple cross-country moves didn't. Sympathy and support were drying up, and I could barely get out of bed some days, my body attacking itself with all the energy I didn't have to stop it.

And then the rheumatologist I'd been seeing sporadically called. Not the office, *her*. "There's a new experimental trial being run out of a local hospital," she'd said. "You qualify."

"What?"

"Treatment. Real treatment," she'd said. "Not just playing Whac-A-Mole."

"I can't afford it." I didn't have any insurance at all at that point. I hadn't been in to see her for over half a year.

"It's covered." A rustle of paper on the other end. "Actually, it's paid."

Paid. Paid to get experimented on—and to maybe get better. Bit of an ethical minefield, being paid to be a lab rat when you're at the end of your rope, and maybe that should've been a red flag. But I looked into it. It's totally normal. They'll pay you to give you dysentery and see if their proposed treatment works.

With this, I came pre-broken.

"What's the catch?" I asked, feeling a half step to the left of my own body, a buzzing sort of numbness, embodied unreality. "I mean, besides it probably not working."

"The protocol looks promising," she said.

"If I don't get the placebo."

"No placebo. The patient pool is small enough that they're getting away without one. But it does require a long stay in the hospital." She was getting impatient; her voice had gone from pleasant and helpful to clipped.

"How long?"

"Two to three months. I'm sorry, Margaret. I have an appointment to get to," she said. "I'll have the office send you the information. But with the way your labs have been trending, I strongly encourage you to accept."

You're not going to get a better offer went unsaid.

Two to three months was unimaginable. I'd need to break my lease, or sublet my tiny studio; I couldn't afford to pay for a room I wasn't using, even with the stipend from the trial. But it was so wild, so out there, that it felt almost—magical. Impossible, and therefore enticing.

I got the email a few hours later, hours I spent pacing my apartment and trying to choke down an instant breakfast shake purely for the calories. It came with a letter on pharmaceutical company letterhead, but the signature at the bottom looked like it was real, and scanned, not just digitally applied. It was addressed to my doctor's office, and it described what I had to look forward to: a period of intensive inpatient treatment, where they'd destroy my viciously confused immune system and build me a new one. Like chemotherapy through a fun house mirror. I'd have round-the-clock nursing and a carefully controlled room to minimize the chances of getting sick while I had every last defense stripped away from me. They'd keep me safe.

All I had to do was let them have full access to my body. The letter was vague, and so was the informational packet, but I could read between the lines well enough. It wasn't going to be pleasant.

But my life was unsustainable.

And even if I didn't think it could be true, even if I didn't really believe I could be fixed, at least I wouldn't have to do this alone. Maybe they could shore up the parts of me that were failing the fastest.

So I said yes. I checked myself in. I let them take me to my room with a view, and I changed into the gown. I put on the soft socks with the grippy soles. I got into the hospital bed.

I still don't know if that was the right decision.

· Chapter Three ·

Of course, it wasn't actually that simple.

It's important to remember the before, isn't it? What life was like. What the world *is* like, outside the drifting sedative haze, the beeping of an infusion pump. My nurses go home at the end of each shift, and maybe, one day, I will, too.

But home to what, exactly?

My mother called right as I hauled my suitcase out of the trunk of my rideshare car. I remember juggling everything awkwardly, accepting the call even as I tapped in a cursory five-star rating (*thank you for a speedy delivery to the rest of my life!*), managing the curb with its flaking yellow paint.

"Oh my gosh, honey, I'm so sorry, I almost forgot. Are you there? Is it starting? How are you, are you scared?"

Or something like that. My mother's words have a tendency to pile up on top of each other into an indistinct wave of noise.

"I just got here," I said. The car pulled away. My scalp itched. My fingers ached where I had banged them against the car. I wished she hadn't called.

It would have been simpler.

I almost hadn't told her about the trial. It felt—unreal. Private, and just for me. As much as I'd been looking for loopholes and gotchas, I didn't want her to weigh in. In the end, I'd minimized it. Couldn't lie about not having a mailing address for a while, but I'd left out the *complete destruction of my immune system* bit.

She'd panicked anyway.

Where are you going to live? Can you afford a storage unit? Are you sure? I saw some bad reviews of the hospital, do you think that's normal? And on and on.

It sounded like caring, and she did care, in her own way. It just hadn't actually felt tender or supportive in years. Still, I let the sound of it wash over me, even as I tuned out the specifics and looked at my new home.

The circle I'd been let out at was an old carriageway. It was covered by a colonnaded brickwork arch that towered over me and blocked out much of the sunlight. The shadows beneath were cool and scented with car exhaust and asphalt. The road ringed around a manicured garden, just barely visible through the columns and past a delivery truck that was trying to navigate the tight space.

Graceview Memorial is old.

Old and currently well-kept, though it hasn't always been. You can see little hints of decay, inside and out. They'd kept the original facade, attached to that colonnade, the first two floors fronted by elegant red and cream bricks with cast details at various joining parts, small cement sculptures worked into the architecture. A bit of ivy clung to the brickwork, picturesque but tearing at the mortar the longer it grew there.

Behind that facade rose modern towers and a skybridge, incongruous, ill-proportioned. But functional.

Most of that was invisible from where I stood, but I'd stared at it, numb and rapt, for the slow creep forward in the drop-off line. Now, I just looked at the utilitarian WEST ENTRANCE sign above the retrofitted sliding doors, with EMERGENCY ROOM and an arrow pointing east below it.

My mother was still talking, off on a tangent about her friend Nancy, who had spent two weeks in the hospital last summer for—something. I don't remember. I don't know if my mother actually knew, either, for that matter.

"I'm supposed to check in soon," I said, interrupting the flow when it became clear she wasn't coming to any kind of point. I'd been standing at the curb for too long; somebody was finally assertive enough to honk at me. I swapped my phone to my other hand and grabbed my suitcase, heading for the doors.

Silence on the other end, and then:

"How are you feeling?" Like she'd remembered I was actually there, that she wasn't leaving a voicemail.

This was a trick question. I used to fall for it, too. I used to list off every ache and pain. And in return, I'd just get—sadness. So much sadness, and guilt, and shame, because somehow my suffering was evidence for her failure as a mother.

But I had to answer it. I couldn't lie, couldn't say, *I'm fine*, because I was walking into the atrium of a hospital. I wasn't exactly feeling *good*. "I'm managing," I said.

The atrium held some of the wonder of the facade. It was two stories tall, airy and open, and crowned with a bit of stained glass up at the windows near the ceiling. But the carpet was institutional, scuffed and worn. The benches were from the mid-eighties. The benign neglect of too much foot traffic and too little budget showed everywhere.

Signs pointed in every direction. I eyed the elevator bank,

not hopeful about the state of my room. I'd wind up being pleasantly surprised: the ward was so much nicer, so much newer, than this politely decaying entrance.

Rustling over the phone, and my mother's long-suffering sigh. I braced myself. "Look, honey," she said, "are you *sure*? Really, really sure? I know you want to feel better, but months in the hospital . . . you can catch all kinds of illnesses. MRSA! You could get MRSA."

"I'm not going to get MRSA," I said, even though that was a very real possibility. "And if I do, they'll take care of it. Mom—"

"I did look at flights this morning," she said. "They're getting more expensive every year, I swear, but I should be able to make it work. Just have to ask my sister for a loan."

"Mom. Don't do that, please."

"I'll have to get time off work, too. Betty won't like it, but she'll just have to deal with it. Although I am out of PTO—"

"*Mom*. Listen to me. Please stay home. Please keep going to work and don't ask Aunt Lisa for a fucking cent. You know she'll hold it over you for years. And I'll be *fine*."

I was met with silence. The kind of silence that was smothering, wrapping around me, threatening to stop up my nose and mouth so I couldn't breathe.

I should have let the call go to voicemail.

"I am your mother," she said.

I shut my eyes.

"And I'm your adult child."

"Do you think I can't help?"

"I never said that." We'd gone around and around on this so many times before. And all I wanted, all I *needed* in that moment, was a little shared confidence. I wanted to be able to tell her about the hospital, about what it looked like, about what I was actually afraid of. I wanted her to see through my eyes.

But they were still shut, and there was only blank emptiness.

"Look, Mom, I'm sorry. I have to go check in now. I'll call you later."

Later—days later. Or weeks. She knew it. I knew it. It would be a relief to both of us, and would simultaneously give her endless fodder for complaining to her friends and coworkers.

"Of course," my mother said, sounding so *sad*. Begging me to be drawn back in. I held firm, opened my eyes, and made myself focus on the stained glass, trying to figure out what the designs were supposed to be. "I love you, Meg."

If I'd known that would be the last time I'd hear her voice, I would have said it back.

Chapter Four

They placed my IV without issue—a first. Along the back of my arm, which was something I'd read about for those labor and delivery stays, but hadn't expected or even asked for. I peered at it as the nurse, Penelope, taped everything down.

"It should be more comfortable," Penelope said, reading my mind. Probably just long years of experience, knowing what questions patients always asked. She was a little older than me, surface-nice but with an impenetrable wall behind it. "It's also more fragile, so try not to bump it into things, but you'll be able to bend your elbow."

"Oh," I said. "Thanks." I didn't see an IV pole anywhere, but maybe that would come later. I was halfway through my admission paperwork, a clipboard balanced on my knees.

"At some point," she added, "we'll be talking about a PICC. They last longer."

And I was going to be here for a while. Still, the thought made me squirm. "That's the kind that goes..." I gestured to my arm, up to my shoulder, around to my chest.

"Yes," Penelope said.

That sort of detail hadn't been covered in the onboarding documentation. "Are there other options?" I asked. I was so squeamish back then.

"I suppose a port-a-cath," Penelope said after a moment's

thought. "We usually save that for outpatient, but we can talk about it later."

"Okay. And the doctor . . . ?"

"Will be by soon," Penelope assured me.

He wasn't.

My suitcase was unpacked. I was already in my gown. I sat on that bed for at least half an hour, wiggling my toes and scrolling on my phone, my arm feeling strange where the tape pulled at the fine hairs and where the plastic catheter snaked into my vein.

From inside my room, I could only hear some of the noise from the hallway. Overhead, announcements were muffled into unrecognizable murmurings. Dull thuds came at irregular intervals. Beneath it all, the faint beeping of a hundred different monitors and alerts.

All of it at a remove, like the roar of waves from a quarter mile away.

At least Penelope had written the Wi-Fi code on the board. I couldn't focus on any of the books I had queued up. I was just about to start an old tool restoration video when there was a knock on the door.

I jolted, shoving my phone under my leg like I'd been caught looking at porn, hoping it was the doctor.

Penelope poked her head in. "Margaret, you have a visitor," she said.

Visitor?

I stared at her blankly. For a half second of panic, I thought it might be my mother—but even if she'd been calling from the airport, a cross-country flight would be somewhere over the Midwest. My dad certainly wasn't coming. Nobody else knew I was here, but she wouldn't call a tech coming to draw my blood a visitor, surely?

With the door open, I could hear more from the hall. *"Priority page,"* a disembodied voice recited. *"Code gray. Adult. East tower. Sixth floor. Med surg. Room six-two-three."*

"Sure," I said, finally.

She smiled and opened the door the rest of the way, then ducked back out into the hall. My phone was warm beneath my thigh, actively charging.

A man appeared in the doorway, wearing an easy smile and a well-tailored suit. He was maybe mid-forties, enough older than me that he had visible smile lines and silver in his hair. He was tall, broad-shouldered. Handsome. No white coat, no stethoscope. Not the doctor, then.

"Hi, Margaret," he said. His voice was rich and resonant. "I'm Adam Marsh. I'm the representative of the team behind SWAIL."

"So... the pharmaceutical company?" That made more sense. They do know how to pick them for the hard-line sales jobs.

He covered his heart with his hand. "You've got me," he admitted. "But don't hold it against me, please. I actually started off as a researcher. May I come in?"

I glanced at Penelope.

"Dr. Santos is dealing with an emergency," she apologized. "He'll be at least an hour, I'm afraid."

(I would get used to this quickly; the doctors never arrive when they say they will, but they do come eventually.)

"Okay," I said, and they both took it as aimed at them.

Penelope left, and Adam came into the room. The door closed. The outside world receded again.

"Hospital life," he said, when we were alone. "But I can answer a few of your questions, at least. Come join me?" He motioned to the little table tucked by the window, two chairs next to it.

I levered myself out of the hospital bed, checking the belt of my robe, keenly aware of how not dressed I was now that I'd switched to hospital clothing. "Is this a courtesy call?" I asked, wary, as I sat down.

No, I imagined him saying, *unfortunately I'm here to say there's been a mistake. We're not paying you after all. You'll need to leave tonight, and you'll just need to figure out a place to stay.*

"Actually, an overdue introduction," he said, sitting down across from me. "I try to touch base with all our patients to give you more of an orientation before things get started. The hospitals we're working with are great, but their approach to customer service is a little different from ours. Understandably, of course—they're here to give care. But I'm here to make you happy."

I turned away from him, toward the window. It was late afternoon but the light was still good, good enough that I didn't have to see the ghost of my reflection in the glass. I knew what I looked like. Psoriatic patches, red and scaling across my temples and cheeks, get an immediate, *Oh my god, are you okay? What's wrong with your face?* The only makeup I was wearing, if you could call it that, was ChapStick. And I'd buzzed my hair that morning. Less to take care of while I was here, and my hair had turned thin and brittle years ago. No great loss.

Looking at the mountains was much nicer than thinking about all of that.

"They're doing a pretty good job," I said. "It's a nice room."

"We paid for certain improvements," he said.

"For, what, the twenty of us you could find with Fayette-Gehret?"

"A few more than that. And we do have trials in the works for other, related conditions." He set something on the table, and despite myself, I glanced over at it. Two small ceramic pots. "Yogurt," he said. "Full fat, real fruit, European. I thought you might like a treat."

A treat I'd actually be able to eat, maybe even enjoy. I softened by degrees.

"Thank you," I said, and accepted the spoon he offered. It was made of some kind of plastic. Not cheap plastic, but smooth and easy on my mouth as I took a few bites.

I was not going to cry. I refused to cry. There was real mango in the bottom of my cup, pureed but smooth and tart and sweet, unmistakable, that fibrous edge proving it wasn't syrup. It was just yogurt, but I'd had so little contact with other people lately, and so few kindnesses.

"I don't know if I can do this," I blurted, thinking about the PICC, about my mother's fears of MRSA, about—all of it.

"You can," he promised me, and there was a soft fervor in his voice. Confidence. I looked up, into the full brunt of his steady caring. "But," he added, "you don't have to. I hope you'll stay, but you can leave. Hell, you can still leave next week. Next month. Past a certain point, it's easier if you keep going, but we can stop whenever."

"That's not what I meant," I said, though the open door was a relief. "I just mean . . ."

I waved my spoon in the air.

"It's a lot," I said, finally. "The change. The upheaval. I almost wish you hadn't made things *nicer*."

Adam hadn't touched his yogurt beyond uncapping it, and he sat back now, folding his hands over his belly. They were nice hands. He wasn't wearing a wedding ring.

How pathetic is it, that I can remember that detail? *No wedding ring.* As if . . .

As if that mattered.

"Well," he said, after a moment, "I have two answers to that. One, the one I bet you're not going to like, is that you deserve it. Every patient does. Two, which might be more palatable given the sense I'm starting to get of you, is that soon you're probably going to be uncomfortable enough from the treatment regimen to not really give a fuck."

I laughed. I couldn't help it.

He grinned. I'm not sure if he could.

He threaded a needle I'd thought was impossible: gotten past all my armor, all my cynicism, all my fear, dodged it all like it was nothing, and said exactly what I needed to hear. Nobody else had managed that before. Some of it might have just been the good looks and the poise, tinting everything he did, but I think there was real skill there.

The question I'm still wrestling with is if he meant any of it.

"Is it really going to be that bad?" I asked after I'd had a bit to pull myself back together. He was finally digging into his yogurt. Strawberry, from the scent and the flash of arterial red on his spoon.

"At times," he said. "Chemotherapy is the closest equivalent to what they'll be doing to you, right? And chemotherapy is, at its heart, poisoning the patient and the cancer in such a way that the cancer dies first. Extreme, but effective." He stirred the yogurt; it bloomed pink. "We tried other options. Standard immunosuppressants, autologous stem cell transplants... none of those are pleasant, either, of course, but they're a little less radical. But none worked the way we wanted. We're not just killing off your immune system, we're retraining how your cells respond to certain signals and laying the groundwork for the new immune system all at the same time." He held up the ceramic pot. "Like scoring wet clay so that a new piece can be joined.

"To a certain extent, the suffering is necessary."

(*Necessary*, he'd said. Not *unavoidable*. I think about that often.)

"We're going to keep you as comfortable as we can," he reassured me, because neither of us was laughing now. "But yes. It's going to be that bad."

I finished my yogurt. It was wonderful, and I wanted to enjoy it while I still could. So I guess his speech was effective.

He watched me for a long time as I ate, the both of us silent. And then he stood.

"Why don't you come with me?" he said, and he held out his hand. "There's somebody I want you to meet."

· Chapter Five ·

Adam offered me his arm; I didn't take it. He might have meant it to be chivalrous, but it just made me feel more like an invalid than was warranted. I had him wait outside while I pulled on some leggings. I didn't have an IV pole to drag around, and with the robe on top, I almost didn't look like a patient.

(Who was I fooling? I didn't look healthy, either. I was having a decent day, but that didn't mean I wasn't still in pain, and I hadn't taken anything since I woke up, expecting I'd be taken care of.)

"We're not going too far," he assured me when I opened the door. He waved me through the small anteroom that linked my room to the hallway. Penelope was at the nurses' station, and she glanced up as we walked by, not at me but at Adam. "We'll be in seven-seven-two," he said. "Come fetch Margaret if she's needed."

She nodded. Behind her was a bank of monitors, fully populated with heart and respiration rates.

"Who else is on this floor?" I asked.

"There's a mix. The study doesn't keep the floor at full census, so any available positive pressure room gets filled with transfers from other areas of the hospital that need them," he said, steering me around a corner. The rooms were widely spaced, so mine couldn't be the only cushy accommodations.

"People with compromised immune systems, naturally occurring or otherwise?" I glossed.

He nodded. "Exactly."

There were a few other people in the hallway, all in scrubs. Voices came from the rooms with open doors. It was strange, to think of other patients, their lives contained in their own little cells in the hive.

"As for the other—what, five rooms?—Graceview fills them as they see fit. Usually with patients needing more specialized care. Here." The room he took me to was only a few doors down, and had an antechamber like mine. The door to the hallway was open, and the inner door was marked with a colored flag, green with a bar across it. He didn't reach for the handle, instead going over to a large monitor mounted on the wall above a row of paper gowns. It, like the monitors at the nurses' station, glowed with somebody's vital signs. He pressed a button beneath it.

A soft ringing sound filled the antechamber, and then the vital signs condensed to a window in the bottom right, and a woman's face appeared on the screen.

"Good afternoon, Veronica," Adam said, and her face lit up. She was maybe younger than me, propped up in her hospital bed.

From outside, that same voice from before: *"Dr. Morgenstern, please page extension three-three-two. Dr. Morgenstern . . ."*

"Adam," said the woman. Her voice was a bare rasp. She was just this side of emaciated, the bones of her face sharp, but her skin for all its exhausted sallowness was clear. Her hair was as thin as mine, but long and braided. "And who's that with you?"

"The newest SWAILer, ready to embark," he said, and

chuckled like the strained pun was funny. Veronica laughed, too. Then her gaze shifted—not to me, but to where I must have appeared on wherever her screen was.

"Welcome," she said. "Is he giving you the grand tour?"

"Something like that," I said. I still had no idea how to feel about any of this, but something about the way she looked back at us made me settle a little more. "Fayette-Gehret?" I asked, nonsensically, but it seemed wrong to assume.

She nodded. "The works," she said. "With bonus liver damage to boot."

Fayette-Gehret has a host of comorbidities. The way it had been explained to me, the cells in my body that already grow fast are in overdrive, as if trying to repair damage that doesn't exist. And in the course of that repair, my body— breaks things. It can be difficult to anticipate what will break next.

My liver numbers weren't looking so good, either.

Veronica was the first person I'd ever met in person who had FGS. My tiny world struggled against its forcible expansion. I shot Adam a look. But he was already moving toward the door. "Poke your head out when you're through," he said. "I imagine you two have a lot to talk about."

And then he was gone. The antechamber grew quiet and still.

"He's wonderful, isn't he?" Veronica almost sighed. "Always knows what to say. How much space to give. It's rare, finding people who get it, isn't it?"

Sales guy, I reminded myself. But Veronica did have a point. Knowing what to say to people like us was rare, whether it was practiced or innate. My chest tightened with a tangled mix of negative reactions: anger that Adam had perfected that skill so well that he'd gotten my guard down, disgust with myself for being so desperate that I'd noticed that lack of a wedding band, and even an ugly, sharp spike of jealousy that Veronica was doing so much better than I was. Was so clearly used to being flattered and attended to by him.

"Yeah," I heard myself say through the pounding in my ears. "Great guy." *Did he bring you imported yogurt when you were admitted?* Or had he been telling the truth, that he'd been late to get to me? Maybe he'd taken her out to lunch, before she'd ever come to Graceview. Dinner, even. Somewhere to woo her, a softer touch than dangling money in front of her.

I was being an ass. I knew I was. I rubbed at my face, robe catching on my IV and reminding me that whatever I was feeling, Veronica was in the thick of it.

"Sorry," I said. "First-day jitters, I guess. How—how is it? How has it been?"

Veronica had a hand settled against her throat. Her fingers worked at her collarbone, rolling the thin skin across it. "Bearable," she said, after a moment's thought. "They give you pain medication whenever you need it, which will probably be a lot at the start. Every symptom, they can help with. But then those medications have their own side effects... Eventually, it just got easier to learn how to manage."

That sounded about right. No easy answers in life. "How long do you have left?"

"We're just about to start rebuilding." She smiled, but it was so tired. Briefly, I wanted nothing more than to stroke her hair, hold her hand. The jealousy fell away. It was a relief, to lose that snarling weight. Veronica wasn't competition; she was my future. "They say maybe another month. A couple more weeks on total lockdown, though."

I looked again at the paper gowns, the sign on the door, the monitor we were speaking through. I'd known, but it really clicked then. "Nobody but the nurses?"

"And the occasional technician, but they try to minimize that," Veronica said. Her jaw quivered for a moment before she got hold of herself. She smiled again. This one was entirely false, but I wasn't about to take it away from her.

I'd been a shut-in for a long time, but I still went out and got coffee sometimes. Some of my meds needed to be picked up at the pharmacy. I made regular attempts at getting out into the world. I thought I'd been ready for the isolation of this whole treatment, but now, looking at Veronica, I wasn't so sure.

Again, I wished I could hold her hand. But I was poison to her. If I had even a hint of a cold, it could kill her.

And the same would go for me, soon enough.

"Reading anything good?" I asked, and I knew she could hear the pity and fear in my voice.

She looked away. "Not much," she said. "On a good day I can manage a chapter. Maybe two. It can be hard to pay attention. Or remember."

I frowned. She seemed entirely lucid, and we'd stopped by unannounced. What she was describing . . . it seemed impossible that both things could be true.

Maybe Adam checked on her before he came to get you.

That was reasonable, wasn't it? And there would have been no reason for him to mention it.

"Oh no," Veronica said. "I've frightened you, haven't I? It's not so bad—I promise. And I'm already feeling so much better. I can eat whatever I want. My skin cleared up . . . maybe last week? It's worth it." This time, her smile was pleading, but true. "Stay. Please, stay. They'll take such good care of you."

She was so desperate. Did I notice back then? Is that why I stayed? Is that why I wrote off what came next?

"What's going to happen to me?" I remember asking. "I—I know it's going to hurt. I get that, and I guess some brain fog. But what's it *like*?"

Veronica thought about it, looking down at her hands. "It's hard to describe," she said, after a long pause. "Sometimes I—sometimes it's simple. Easy. It's just waiting, or sleeping, or watching the clock. They do all the hard work for you, and all you have to do is endure."

"And other times?" I asked.

"Other times, you're just going to want to run," she said.

How many of us have there been?

How many people have been right where I am now? Because Veronica knew. I can see that clearly, now. She knew what was coming for me. I'm not special.

But we both tried to laugh it off. Me first, awkwardly, then her, as if to make me feel less alone. "Like a kid trying to duck out of the pediatrician's office before her shots," she added, trying to minimize. I latched on to that image. I was braver than a kid, wasn't I?

I'd read somewhere that pain was where physical discomfort collided with your sense of control. The more in control, the less something would hurt.

I could be in control of this.

Except then, abruptly, she stopped laughing. Her eyes widened, then darted side to side. I couldn't see her hands, but I thought I heard them clench in the sheets.

"Veronica?" I asked, confused, a little panic creeping into my own voice. She looked terrified, and with how gaunt she was, all her anxiety was magnified, turned grotesque.

What was she reacting to?

It was over as fast as it had come on. She shook her head, then smiled, sheepishly. "Sorry," she said. "I thought I heard something."

A knock, and the door behind me opened. "I'm sorry to interrupt," Adam said, stepping up to where the camera could capture him. "But your parents are here to see you, Veronica. Is now a good time?"

From the antechamber doorway, Veronica's father waved, awkwardly. Her mother stood just beside him. They were both smiling.

That damn jealousy crashed right back over me, a wall stronger than the isolation door slamming down between me and Veronica. She'd begged me to stay, but she wasn't alone. She wasn't going through this solo. I stepped aside and watched as her parents crowded around the view screen, then stepped out into the hall and tried to breathe.

Adam was right behind me. His fingertips grazed my elbow, nudging me to turn and walk back to my room.

"You look like you've seen a ghost," he said, softly.

I was so weak. Prickly, reactive, myopic. Messy. I don't know. I think I hated her then, and longed to be her, and only felt guilt, guilt, guilt about it all.

Maybe that's why I didn't mention her momentary terror.

Why I didn't ask if hallucinations were an expected side effect.

Chapter Six

Adam stayed with me until the doctor arrived, then excused himself, promising to return in a day or two. From there, the rest of the afternoon was a whirlwind of sampling. Blood draws, urine collection, skin scrapings from the worst of my plaques. Baseline imaging of the liver. A full punch biopsy at the back of my left arm, the lidocaine leaving the whole area insensate for over an hour. They catalogued every part of me.

It was the beginning of my transformation from person into patient.

They were all very kind. I remember the radiology tech warning me that the contrast dye I was being injected with might make me feel like I'd wet myself, and to not worry, that almost nobody actually did. He was right; the medicine made my skin flush, and my thighs felt hot and wet. But I came out of the CT machine dry as a bone.

Kindness, though, can't fully outweigh the dehumanization of being poked and prodded on an unpredictable schedule. I tried to read, but I'd be interrupted before I finished a page. I'd sit and wait, attentively, and nobody would arrive to retrieve me for half an hour. A more flexible person than I am might have been just fine with that; put the book down when you have to, pick it back up later, and just roll along, easy as you please. But for me, it was its own form of torture.

I bucked and fought against it, wanting to be left alone, wanting to be back in my apartment.

Not an option, I reminded myself.

Besides, what was I really missing about it? Not the dirty dishes that had been eternally piled in my sink, eventually thrown out wholesale when I had to pack the place up. Not the secondhand couch that was permanently molded into the shape of my ass. The little trinkets from a childhood I felt irreparably estranged from? The scraps of projects, crafts attempted and abandoned as my functioning got worse and worse?

My condition had all but swallowed up my past already. It happened slow at first, but by the time I reached Graceview, there was so little left. Once upon a time, there was a girl named Meg who tried and failed to knit socks, who had friends, who had goals and dreams and hopes. And then her face grew red and chapped, and she started canceling on plans. Canker sores stole the pleasure of food from her. Fatigue made everything but work pointless.

How had it gotten this far? Inch by slow, imperceptible inch.

Graceview was all I had left.

Dinner almost didn't happen, but at shift change, Penelope and her replacement realized I hadn't eaten yet. The cafeteria was closing and they wanted to make sure I got something substantial in me, so they grabbed a sandwich from the nurses' station. I don't remember what it was—something simple, ham and cheese maybe, with a little packet of yellow mustard on the side—but I remember it being a relief. Not because I was hungry (I wasn't, too anxious to be hungry), but because it wasn't exactly hospital food. No tray, no Jell-O cup, just cling wrap and white bread.

They finished up with me sometime after sunset, maybe nine, nine-thirty. Penelope's replacement (I think it was Louise that time, but it all blurs together) flushed my saline lock, but didn't hook me up to anything. "Tomorrow," she told me, "bright and early." It was almost certainly Louise; I've gotten to know her well. She's older, experienced and worn into a particular groove. Not warm or cuddly, but she knows what to fuss over and what to let go. So it must have been her, because only she would've said, "You should go stretch your legs."

Seven West had two lounges. One for families, one just for patients. Both were inhabited that evening. Veronica's parents had posted up in the family lounge, and I didn't want to talk to them; I could imagine the questions, the sympathy, the awkwardness as we both wanted something out of the other that wasn't on offer. The patient lounge—smaller, but with nicer chairs, recliners that would work well with an IV drip—held an elderly man in a face mask, watching the news.

So I went wandering.

I'd put my leggings and socks and shoes back on, but I had left the gown in place and ditched the robe. My bracelet bumped against the prominence of my wrist. Visiting hours were over; I made it obvious that I still belonged. The nurses' station on our ward was quiet now, the lights a little lower. The woman at the desk buzzed me out, probably warned by Louise that I'd be up and about.

I didn't linger, but for a brief moment, I thought of turning around, going to Veronica's room instead. Maybe . . .

But what else could she give me?

I caught the elevator and headed down, away from the comparative opulence of Seven West and into the aging body of the hospital at large.

With the lights dimmed for the evening, Graceview's benign neglect was less evident, but not invisible. I stepped out into the public lobby, onto worn carpet of a busy-enough pattern to disguise the odd stain. The wall paint was high gloss, the better to wipe down, and it looked patchy in the less consistent lighting. The windows fronting the gift shop were rimmed in sealant that was breaking apart, the glass itself growing foggy at the edges and bottom, away from where the eye was drawn to by the stacks of stuffed animals, bouquets of shiny balloons.

Without the chatter of visitors and in a long, sleepy lull between overhead announcements, I could hear a low mechanical hum. It tickled my eardrums, made my skin pebble into gooseflesh. I shook myself into motion again, the better to ignore it.

The streetlamps outside were too short to illuminate the stained glass at the top of the atrium windows. The sheets of darkened glass were illegible, hanging overhead like storm clouds. Vultures. Something poorly balanced, threatening. I kept walking, into the hall that connected this older lobby with a newer addition that squatted at the base of the east tower.

And in between the towers: a garden, manicured and gently lit, seemingly entirely out of place.

I guess I wasn't thinking, when I tried to go out to it.

"Ma'am?"

A security officer jogged over. I hadn't even noticed him lurking by the bend in the hallway. I stopped, deer in the headlights, then looked down at the band around my wrist. CULPEPPER, MARGARET, my date of birth, my identification number.

I wanted to rip it off, but that would still have left my hospital gown, my saline lock. I would've been marked, just not named. I'd wanted it that way, I reminded myself.

It felt worse than I'd expected to be put to the test.

"Sorry," I mumbled. No, I shouldn't mumble, not even with my mouth feeling sorer than it had this morning. I looked up and smiled, reminding myself how to feign reasonable health. "Sorry, I guess it's closed this late at night." But the door wasn't locked; I'd felt it give against my hand.

His look told me it was closed generally to the inhabitants of Graceview. The ones who didn't get to clock out of their shifts, anyway. "Can I call you an escort?"

"Thank you, no," I said, and wondered how many dementia patients had said the exact same thing. "My nurse knows where I am," I added, and gave him my room number for good measure.

He wasn't convinced. I could tell by the way his gaze flicked to the raw patches of my skin, the shadows beneath my eyes. But I didn't have that IV pole with me, and I didn't have blood or pus oozing from my nostrils. Nothing shockingly wrong with me. "Of course," he said, and wandered a little ways away. He never fully took his eyes off me, but I tried to pretend he had as I listened to him mutter into his radio, no doubt double-checking with Louise.

He didn't follow me when I headed for the east tower lobby. No footsteps trailed me around the bends in the hallway, past darkened and shuttered outpatient waiting areas. I wasn't being chased. I scrubbed at my face with my hands; at least the quiet hum wasn't as audible in this part of the building. And it was made not for patients, but for people passing through. Less medicinal, more institutional. Photos of old medical directors and board members on the walls.

It was better than being on the ward, even if it was still impersonal, still institutional. The different flavor was refreshing. I soaked it in and considered where I'd go next. No gardens, no coffee shop, but I wasn't ready to go back, not yet. I drifted over to the directory, scanning the list of services in the east tower, looking for one that might have a little nook of cushioned benches out of the way.

I'd landed on trying the third-floor outpatient nutrition services office when my stomach cramped violently. (That's the sort of irony that stays with you, even through what happened later. *Nutrition services.*) I knew that cramping intimately, as well as the heated flush that followed it. I didn't need to hear or feel the warning gurgle to know what was about to happen.

Luckily, they don't lock the visitor bathrooms at night.

After, I sat down heavily on one of the padded benches, closing my eyes and waiting for the room to stop spinning. I was red-faced and shaking, and my legs felt like they were halfway rendered to gelatin. Stress always did bring on the worst GI episodes, so I probably should've expected this. Should have stayed in my room.

Frustrated tears welled up in my eyes, but I focused on

my breathing. In and out. In and out. My mouth hurt; there were two canker sores, both on the right side, one along my gums and the other in my throat. The skin beneath the adhesive securing my saline lock was starting to itch. I could feel it swelling. In the stop-and-start activity of the day, I'd been able to shove most of the sensations to the background, a tugging that never stopped and occasionally increased in intensity, but now it was everything. My body ached, and my intestines gave a gentle half roll, nothing urgent but nothing benign, either.

"Should I call someone?"

I opened my eyes, expecting the security officer again. Instead, an older man with an environmental services badge was looking at me skeptically from across his cart.

I waved him off. "I'm fine," I said.

He snorted. He had to be in at least his late sixties, with thinning hair and creased and wrinkled skin that, despite its roughness, didn't look like it had seen much sun. He was pale all over, and his gaze was sharp. Calculating.

There was no point in staying out, I realized then. I *wasn't* fine—and the hospital after hours wasn't what I wanted. I wanted to lose myself in the movement of the building, not be picked out again and again as somebody in distress.

I stood up, fussing with my wristband as if it were a too-heavy bangle. The smile on my face was practiced, but the practice showed through, or maybe just my exhaustion.

"Where are you headed?" the custodian asked.

"West tower," I said, and my heart sank, remembering the twists and turns in the connecting hall, the way all the labs and waiting lounges and cafeteria offshoots were tucked in and around, making the place seem cozy and private, and adding way too much distance between point A and point B. "Seventh floor."

He worked his jaw for a moment in thought, then motioned to the elevator with his chin. "Come on."

It was an east tower elevator; I assumed he meant to take me to the skybridge. I hadn't noticed what floor it was on, but it was smart enough.

"Secret shortcut," he said. "It'll shave at least half the distance off. Promise." He pushed his cart over, then slapped the DOWN arrow.

I frowned, but when the elevator arrived, I only hesitated a moment before stepping into the car with him. He hit the button labeled LL. No badge, no code; the doors slid shut, and we dropped down one floor. Simple.

"What's down here?" I asked. The answer was obvious the moment the doors opened again: the same slowly aging carpet and wall paint, but with a decidedly administrative air, and several signs pointing to various offices. I don't know what I expected. The morgue, maybe? Steam tunnels? It was like I had wanted the man to be some cryptic groundskeeper, hinting at ominous secrets. But he was just an employee, like the security guard, like my nurses.

"Extra space," he said, leading me down a much more straightforward hallway. There were arrows indicating where the west tower elevator bank was, and I thought I could see the shine of the metal.

"And it's open to the public?"

"Not really," he said. "But it's not locked, either. People just don't usually try going down. Doesn't occur to them. They assume it's off-limits, or they don't notice it at all. But it's useful for moving equipment, that sort of thing. Much quicker." We reached the west tower elevators, and he hit the UP button for me. "Seventh floor, right? Long term, isn't it?"

I nodded. "Months," I said. "Today's just the first day."

"You've got the right idea, exploring," he said. "Poke around. Settle in. You're going to live here, might as well get familiar. If there's nothing keeping you out, try going in. At the very least, it'll give you something to do."

"Thank you," I said, even though I couldn't picture myself poking around the hospital on my own, and I didn't think I'd be well enough to do so soon. I pictured Veronica and her locked room, but with me in the bed instead.

I did appreciate it, though.

The elevator car arrived, and I stepped in.

"Good luck," the man said. "That floor tends to need it."

And then the doors closed, and he was gone.

• Chapter Seven •

GRACEVIEW MEMORIAL

Room:	775	Phone		XXX-XXX-2775
Date:	August 6, 2023	MON TUES WED THURS FRI SAT (SUN)		
Patient:	Margaret Culpepper	**PAIN SCALE** 1 2 (3) 4 5 6 7 8 9 10		
Doctor:	Santos			
Nurse:	Penelope W.	Pain medication last given:		0800
Charge Nurse:	Shannon L.	Next dose:		1400
Today's Plan! *Beginning of SWAIL* ☺				
Diet:	Normal	Fall Risk:		Low
Activity Level:	Normal	Our goal is to have you discharged on:		September 30, 2023
Prevent falling! Call for help getting out of bed.				

Tomorrow, bright and early.

The first of my five a.m. blood draws, groggy and not entirely aware of the phlebotomist taking samples by a small work light. I think if they'd turned the overheads on, it would have felt more real. As it was, I have only snatches of memory, fuzzed and elided into dream: the dark blue scrubs, the soft voice, fingers on my arm, the reassurance that I didn't have to do anything at all. That I could just keep sleeping.

And then shift change at seven, which I was truly awake for, anxious and sitting prim and proper in my bed. I'd made it, after I woke up. Showered, too. I'd tried to reset everything to perfection, as if to prove I was engaged in the process, that I was taking ownership. It felt important back then.

The litany went by; I dutifully weighed in on my pain level (a little better than the day before) and otherwise found nothing to correct. Louise had me described down to the marrow in a few efficient sentences. Penelope already knew me (and I know that it was Penelope this day, for certain; I even remember she was wearing bright teal scrubs, different from the standard-issue light blue that the nurses usually wore). It was just a safety precaution.

I expected Dr. Santos to stop by before Penelope started working on me, but he didn't make an appearance. She didn't seem surprised, so I didn't ask. Instead, I watched as she placed a new IV cannula in my other arm.

"One for SWAIL, one for everything else," she said.

"They don't play nice?"

"Not always. Keep thinking about that PICC, it would make for a lot fewer needle sticks." She wrote a date and her initials on the dressing, then checked my original site to make sure it still looked good. My skin beneath the tape was a little red, but it hadn't gotten worse overnight.

Satisfied, she left the room for just a minute and returned

with a cooler. I watched her prep and hang the first SWAIL bag: innocuously clear. They wouldn't always be.

The tubing went through an infusion pump, then was connected to the brand-new cannula.

"What will it be like?" I asked as she hung another bag, this one attached to the original site.

"Hard to say. Sometimes it takes a few days to really start to feel it. But Dr. Santos okayed some pain medication for you, so just let me know if you want that. No reason for you to be uncomfortable. I've got an oral numbing gel, too, if it would help?"

Why was it so embarrassing, that she knew the canker sores were bothering me? I was there for her to take care of me, wasn't I? But I was still sheepish as I nodded, and as I let her apply the gel with a few swipes of a cotton swab.

"You might not feel like eating much today, but you should put in a breakfast order," she said, "before the kitchens close."

No more sandwiches from the nurse stash, apparently. I called the cafeteria line the next time she left the room and put in an order for oatmeal, the pump clicking softly at my side. The person who took the order said I'd have it in half an hour. Forty minutes later, the restoration of an 1800s apple peeler playing on my phone screen, I was still waiting, and Penelope, who bustled into and out of the room a few times, gave me a juice cup out of sympathy.

A soft knock came from the doorway. I looked up, expecting somebody with a cart.

But it was Adam.

He looked much the same as he had the day before, polished smooth, and he carried a riot of flowers, a lopsided, self-aware smile on his face. "May I come in?" he asked. His voice tasted like honey. *Tasted*, yes—the combination of drugs dripping into my veins was doing *something*. My eyelids fluttered, but not with intention.

"Of course," I said, listening out for slurring and not finding any.

He came all the way to my bedside, then proffered the floral arrangement for me to examine. I closed my eyes, inhaling a complex wash of scents that banished the sterility of the room despite not being overpoweringly strong. It wasn't from the gift shop, I don't think, or even from a standard florist's stock. I didn't recognize everything, but I could see sprays of yarrow, spikes of lupine and desert paintbrush, even some woody sprigs of sagebrush. A mountain meadow in a vase.

"Get well soon?" I asked, unable to help my smile.

"Get well," he agreed, and, seemingly pleased with my reaction, he set them on the dresser close to my bed. "How are you feeling?"

"They've given me the good stuff," I said, reaching over and lightly tapping the tubing. I hadn't asked Penelope for any pain medicine, so it must have been something in the SWAIL mix itself. Whatever it was, the effect was similar: I didn't care if it hurt, and I couldn't think straight.

"I'm floating a little. I'd give myself a one right now." At his perplexed look, I waved at the pain rating scale on the whiteboard.

He went over and erased the circle around 3.

I started forward. "You can—*can* you do that?"

"She left the marker in here," he said with an impish smile.

I laughed, feeling almost drunk, but also unmoored, a little freaked out. It felt wrong, that he'd changed something on the board, even if he'd been making a correction. I'd come to learn that the board wasn't sacrosanct, wasn't infallible; sometimes it didn't get updated for a day or two at a time, when there wasn't much change, and I wouldn't know who my nurse was. And sometimes—

Sometimes it told me impossible things.

But right then, right there, Adam changing it was so brazen, so confident, that it tilted me off my very uncertain axis and made me want to cling on tight. He was just a sales guy, but he'd brought me flowers, and he knew what was coming for me, better than I did. It was more intimacy than I'd had in years, I think. I pointed to a chair. "Sit, stay a while." I hoped I didn't sound like I was begging.

If I did, he was polite enough not to mention it. He drew the chair up to my bedside and sat down, hands clasped together loosely in front of him. And I just—looked at him, a little more closely than I'd looked at anybody in recent memory. I fell into him, a little.

He made it so easy.

Then he said, "I heard you made good use of your last night of freedom," and I turned away, feeling my face heat up.

"The night nurse suggested it," I said, a little too quickly, then stopped myself. He must have heard it from Louise herself, I realized. No chance of a pharma rep rubbing elbows with a random custodian, or a security guard on night shift. Of course he knew I'd had permission.

Why did I feel so caught out?

"Did you find anything interesting?"

I made myself relax into the bed and face him again. "No.

I took my walk a little too late. No cafeteria, no gift shop, no gardens." I felt out a sharp shard of vulnerability with my tongue, then added, "I did tour the downstairs restrooms, though." Then I grimaced. Vulnerability was one thing, bodily functions another.

But he took it in stride. "How do they rate?"

"Five out of five." The grimace faded. The medication haze tugged at me more strongly in the wake of my adrenaline spikes. Each one left me a little more exhausted. "Clean, unlocked, and private if you catch them at just the right time. A lot of room to stretch out."

He laughed, the sound lapping against my eardrums. I was gazing at him again. His suit looked similar to the one he'd worn the morning before, but the tie was different. A geometric pattern, green and glossy, with small black details like eyes peeking out between the regular interlock of unnamable shapes.

The thought of his other suit made me think of the day before, of yogurt I would've killed for with my oatmeal still missing, and—

"How's Veronica?"

At the time, I was sure it was the drugs I was on that made his response seem delayed. Now I'm not so sure. I don't think he hesitated, *hesitated* isn't the right word. I think it took him a beat to remember who I was even asking about.

"Oh, she's doing well," he said, resettling himself in his seat.

I think I almost asked about that moment when she'd been frightened. But it made no sense, not with how comfortable I felt around him. Everything had to be fine, didn't it? And with that soft floating feeling, I could see how maybe a stray thought could have derailed him.

So I didn't ask.

I don't remember what else we talked about that day. Whatever it was, it had nothing to do with me, or him, or SWAIL, or Graceview. Maybe we talked about the weather. It was something light and surface-level, easy, as the medication stole more and more of my ability to pay attention. By the time my breakfast arrived, I didn't even notice how bland and soggy the oatmeal must have been. And at some point, he left, and I dozed; or I dozed, and he left.

It all runs together, after a while.

· Chapter Eight ·

And then I met Isobel.

I don't want to think about this part, but I need to. For her. I owe her that much.
    It hurts.
    It hurts, *it hurts—*
    I am so sorry, Isobel.

I wasn't awake for bedside report the second night. I don't know how she looked, staring down at my insensate body, twitching and swaying under the drugs that were priming me for the next day's work. I don't know what Penelope told her about me, or if she knew Adam yet, or much of anything.
    I don't know her last name. *Nurse Isobel R.* is all it said on the progress notes I could access on my phone, back when I had it.
    The first time I saw her was when I woke up sometime after sunset. I was disoriented, and that was still a very new sensation. I didn't have the tricks I later developed to find myself in the great wash of sensory input, and with the sun set and the curtains pulled, all I knew was that I was in a bed that

wasn't my own, a narrow bed on a slight incline, with pillows that were cleaner than mine had been in a long time, an alien cleanliness. My IVs were barely noticeable, the saline and whatever else dripping into my veins room temperature and unremarkable. *Click-click-click* went the pump.

I did hurt, though. All over. My joints ached, and that's how I found my way back to my body that night. I remember that part very clearly. Counting my joints, easing my stiff muscles into movement.

The *1* was still circled on the board in Adam's hand. I was definitely closer to a five. Whatever effect SWAIL had had, blotting out my discomfort, must have worn off while I slept. Squinting in the low light, I fumbled for the CALL button.

I hesitated, unsure if I should use it. Surely my night nurse would be in soon. The pump by my bedside would start beeping, and it would need to be adjusted. But the bag of normal saline on the pole looked plump and full, and I didn't see another drip going.

She'll want to know I'm awake, I told myself, but it still took so much effort to press the button. To ask for help. Does that sound strange? I don't know. When I first started getting sick, I had this romantic idea of it. I was miserable, yes—but at least it meant I finally had permission to rest. I'd be taken care of, instead of running on empty, all alone. Like a childhood sick day; I yearned for that simplicity, that safety.

Of course, that's not how it works. There was nobody to take care of me, not in any way I could rely on, and I just had to run on worse than empty. Suffer and grind and try to pay for treatments that only had a chance of helping if I "relaxed." Year upon year, until I got the SWAIL offer. And this little desperate part of me whispered, *It's time.*

And now I was being looked after in the truest sense of the phrase. I could see my vitals on the screen by my bed, I didn't know what had happened to the day behind me, and that was just fine. All I had to do was rest. Get better. Endure the bad parts. It was like a fairy tale, a dream come true.

Adults don't get that. And maybe that's why the louder part of me kept fighting that care. No, it shouted, you need to buck up and deal with it. You don't get to press a button when you're hurting and have somebody come to the rescue.

But I did.

And she did. More or less.

"Good evening," said Isobel, entering the room and wiping her hands down with antibacterial ooze from the dispenser. Unlike some of the nurses, she didn't smile, instead going to the bedside computer and swiping in with her badge, pulling up every detail she had on me. "I'm Isobel. Can I have you confirm your name and date of birth?"

"Margaret Culpepper," I said, and rattled off the rest, fiddling with the remote to raise the back of the bed. My fingers were clumsy. It took a few attempts, and she didn't help. I appreciated it as much as I resented her for it. Either option was another little indignity: the only winning move would have been to not need help at all.

I finally managed to find the right button. I looked up and found her gazing at me with a flat expectancy.

"How can I help?" she asked, with none of Adam's warmth,

or even Penelope's. Matter-of-fact. She was wearing the standard pale blue scrubs, her pockets noticeably full, though with what I couldn't tell. Her hair was pulled back, her face scrubbed bare.

I hadn't realized until then how much Penelope and even Louise softened their appearances.

My throat clenched. *I don't need help*, I almost said, but I'd hit the CALL button, and my limbs were heavy with throbbing heat. "My pain is getting bad again," I said, fingers working at the rough weave of the hospital blanket.

Isobel glanced at the computer screen. "I'll get you some Tylenol."

So much for the good stuff.

My mouth was so dry. "Tylenol doesn't—usually do much. For me." I knew immediately that I probably sounded pathetic, or worse: like I was showing *drug-seeking behavior*. "Just ibuprofen would work better," I added, hastily. "I don't—I'm not—"

"I'll get you some Tylenol," she repeated, and left the room.

I stared after her.

My head was spinning. The drugs were no doubt making the whole situation harder to parse than it needed to be, exacerbating the whiplash. Tylenol was fine. Would be fine. I flexed my toes, wiggling in my bed, willing my body to get its shit together. This was my normal, I reminded myself.

I drank half the water in my plastic mug, which was full and still had ice floating in it. The water helped the pain, and to clear the fug from my head. But that just made it more uncomfortably obvious how long Isobel was gone for. I tried not to stare at the clock, but time marched on anyway. Fifteen minutes. Twenty.

It was almost forty minutes later by the time she returned with a little paper cup. I held out my wrist for her to scan the barcode.

"I was told," I said, after I swallowed down the two pills, "that I'd be kept as comfortable as possible." I didn't bother hiding my annoyance.

"You'll have to discuss that with Dr. Santos," she said, her own irritation creeping into her voice. "At this stage of SWAIL, Tylenol is as needed, the rest you'll need approval for."

"Well, please mark my pain down as a five," I said. I ran a hand over my scalp, swinging wildly between feeling like a tantrumming child and being certain my affront was justified. "And let Dr. Santos or whoever's on call know."

"You should consider leaving the trial," Isobel replied.

The words were a blow. I think I made some weak little sound, confused and startled. I hated her in that moment.

"Nothing that you're on should be causing discomfort," she continued, not looking at me, tapping something into the computer. "If this is your baseline, you may not be able to manage the next steps. Even with medical support."

"Shut up."

She flinched, then looked away, chest rising and falling as she took a steadying breath.

"That wasn't my place," she said, after a brief, ringing silence. "I'll let the doctor know."

And then she was gone.

I shook for a long time after that. The Tylenol did shit all, like I knew it would, but the rage was a perfect distraction. I reveled in it. I got up out of my bed, shuffled over to the board, and erased Adam's circle, replacing it with my own.

FIVE. Five, I fucking hurt, and it was *my* fucking pain. How dare she? How dare she tell me to tap out? I was breathing too fast, and I could hear the quick *beep beep beep* of my vitals rocketing up. I didn't want her back in that room, so I let the rage wash through me, mellowing out to a soft, comforting smolder.

She didn't understand how much endurance I had left in me, or how much spite.

I know now, of course, why she said what she did. And I know she was right. But at the time, I couldn't see it. I couldn't even see the burnout beneath her words, the exhaustion, the overwhelm. I didn't know what else she was dealing with, that night or any of the others.

I wish she'd told me more plainly what was coming for me.

But I don't think I would have listened.

Chapter Nine

Around two a.m., Isobel finally returned with stronger pain meds. Nothing wild, just a few tablets, but they were enough. I even slept, though with how much I'd been in and out of it during the day, I didn't sleep for long. I think something woke me up—maybe an overhead code page, or some other noise from the hall. I kept the lights off. I didn't want Isobel to know I was awake.

The phlebotomist came to take labs around five, just like the morning before. Quick, in and out, and it was simplest to act like I was half-asleep. But once she was gone, I grew restless. Both of my IVs had been disconnected while I was sleeping. I wasn't attached to any monitors. The meds were more or less out of my system, and for the first time in almost twenty-four hours, I was myself again. I eased out of the hospital bed, took care of things in the bathroom, and stared into the mirror.

Still the same. Just me.

Going back to bed seemed impossible as I eyed the few steps between me and it. Not physically, though; it was my mind that screamed, not my muscles. I grabbed my robe, found my slippers, and crept over to the antechamber door.

It opened. The hallway beyond was dim, the lights turned

down for the night shift. There was a warm glow down at the nurses' station, enough that I could see that Isobel wasn't there. Nobody was, actually, and a thrill went through me.

Louise had told me I could go wandering the night before. I'd just tell anybody who spotted me that I assumed that still held. It might even have been true.

Where to go, though? Not the lobby; I'd need somebody to buzz me out. The lounge, maybe. I hadn't given it a good look yet. But on the way was Veronica's room, and I found myself stopping at her door. The flag had been moved to the outer door, and it wasn't green anymore. The bar was still there, but the plastic behind it was a bright, clear red.

Shit, I thought, because that couldn't mean anything good.

But I didn't hear anything through the door, no blaring machines or shouted instructions. No alert was being called over the PA. No disasters in progress. She was almost certainly asleep—but maybe she wasn't, maybe I could go in and say hi. Maybe I could get a gut check on Isobel. On everything.

I tried the handle, half expecting it to be locked. It wasn't; probably a fire safety thing. I slipped inside, telling myself I'd just peek through the inner door's small window.

It had a surprisingly good view of the bed. Probably so the nurses could do exactly what I was doing now. And in that bed sat Veronica, illuminated by her bedside lamp, awake, fussing with her nails. Dark nails, which at first I thought were painted, before realizing the skin itself was discolored.

I had no idea how to turn on the video system, so I knocked.

Her head shot up, eyes wide, terrified. Her dusky hands dropped to the sheets and fisted in them. The antechamber was dark; I realized she couldn't see me through the glass. I found the light switch and flicked it on.

Relief washed over her, though she still appeared wary as she reached for a remote.

The monitor next to me sprang to life, Veronica's image looking away from the camera. At the real me, rather than my video feed. Maybe it wasn't on?

"Hi," I said, awkward and shamefaced. "Uh . . . can you hear me okay?"

"Yes, I can," Veronica said. "Good . . . morning?"

"Phlebotomy came and went," I said. "So yes?"

She smiled, experimentally. I searched for something wrong with her, some evidence of whatever had made them change the flag on her door. But she seemed . . . better. Tired, of course, and her hands looked strange, but better. Maybe a little less emaciated, maybe just more engaged. I'd thought she was fully alert when we met, but maybe I'd been wrong. For just a moment, it made me wonder how I appeared to my nurses when the meds were running.

I wonder about it a lot, now.

"Sorry," I added, needing to get some kind of response out of her. "Sorry, I just—had a bad night. New nurse, we don't get along well, I decided to stretch my legs. Your door, they changed the flag on it. Is everything okay?"

You can tell me to fuck off now, I added, silently.

But Veronica didn't look irritated. She looked . . . hungry, maybe? Something needy. I don't mean that in a bad way. Needful, perhaps? Not quite desperate, but getting there.

"We had a few setbacks, after you left," she said, after taking a moment and wetting her lips. "They say it's nothing to worry about, though. Just need to tweak the medication a little."

"They can do that?" I asked. "It's not all set in stone?"

She shrugged. "They change it pretty frequently. Adam explained it to me as medicine being as much an art as a science, and every patient is a little different. The team starts with the main version of the meds, then tailors it to fit how our bodies respond."

And that made sense. Still makes sense, actually. That was never the problem.

But she didn't sound as confident as she had two days prior. Dread pooled in my belly. Dread, not sadness, not empathy. I was still too focused on what might happen to me, soon enough.

"Actually," she said, pushing forward, trying to sound nonchalant, "since you're here—can you do something for me?"

I stepped closer to the monitor. Away from the door window. Her focus on the screen changed, shifting to her matching video feed now. "I can try, I guess?" How could I say no?

"Can you bring me some flowers?"

I blinked, certain I'd misheard. I don't know what I was expecting to hear, but probably something related to her treatment. I don't think I was paranoid enough yet to anticipate some call for help, some independent research, but maybe just asking my nurses about something. Getting another opinion.

"Flowers?" I asked.

The camera feed had a limited range of view, but no, there

weren't any flowers on her table. I couldn't remember if there had been any the last time I'd seen her, either. It hadn't stood out to me; nobody sends me flowers.

Except Adam. Adam had.

Veronica's expression had shifted, gone introspective, sad. "It's silly," she conceded. "I know it's silly. I just miss them."

"Can't you order them from the gift shop? Or ask your parents?"

That came out more bitterly than I'd intended. Maybe Isobel's gruffness rubbing off on me, multiplying with my own.

"Oh. They went home yesterday," she said. Yeah, that had hurt. I hadn't actually wanted it to, I realized, too late. "It's hard for them to get the time off work."

"Shit, I'm sorry," I said. "It's just—" But what did my objections matter? Why *shouldn't* I go get her some flowers? I could still leave my room. I wasn't stuck in bed, in isolation, wishing I had a nice bouquet to look at, to smell, to remind me of the rest of the world.

(I should have asked, *Why doesn't Adam bring you flowers?*)

I rubbed at my scalp, fingernails grazing a few raised psoriatic patches. They itched dully in response as dead skin sloughed up beneath my short nails. "I'll do it. Sorry. What kind?"

Veronica smiled. When was the last time I'd made somebody smile, not out of politeness but because I'd done something for them? And I hadn't even actually gone anywhere yet. "Oh, anything. But—" She screwed up her face a little, scrunching her nose, and when she relaxed, her smile had turned sheepish. "What side of the hall are you on? Can you see the courtyard garden from your room?"

"No, other side. I've got the mountains. But I think I know

the one. Tried to go out there the other night, security stopped me." I held up my wrist so she could see the ID band.

"They don't like us wandering," she agreed.

"Do you want me to break in?" I offered. "I don't think it'd be hard. Wear street clothes, try going out there during the day when I don't have an infusion going, I think I could still pass as healthy. Ish." The more I thought about it, the more I doubted there was even an actual rule about patients being forbidden. The security officer probably just hadn't wanted to go out and keep an eye on me while I poked around.

The hospital maybe wouldn't look kindly on every patient going down there and harvesting a handful of flowers, but just one? Just me?

Sure. No problem.

Veronica grinned, a flash of a thing, a tiny fish in a dark pool, then reined herself back in. "Oh," she demurred. "I couldn't ask."

"No, I'm serious," I said. "What kind do you want?"

It was so ridiculous I felt almost high. Childlike. For just that moment, everything seemed so much easier.

"There's this bed with all sorts of purple flowers in it, towards the east tower side," Veronica said. "Are you sure? It's so silly. They probably won't even let them in the room."

"No reason not to try," I said.

Veronica smiled, then looked away, sharply.

About to cry?

Or had she heard something again?

"It's going to be okay," I said, awkwardly. "You're almost through it, right? Just a little longer."

"Yeah," she said, looking back at the camera and swiping at one watery eye. "Yeah, you're right. Thank you. I . . ."

She trailed off.

Veronica's eyes had gone glassy. Her mouth fell slack.

"Veronica?"

No response. She was so still, it was as if the camera feed had frozen. Without motion, her vivacity faded quickly. Her skin looked so pale. Her lips were cracked. Her hand, now by her throat, was clutching tight to her collarbone, and it looked like it might break, a twig snapping beneath a silk sheet. It would punch through her flesh if it broke. I could see it now, jagged and pearlescent and—

She needed help. I looked around for a red CALL button, and when I didn't see it immediately, I flung open the antechamber door and yelled, "Help!"

Thankfully, there were people at the nurses' station now. Isobel and another nurse shot up from their seats and hurried over. I stepped aside to let them in.

They crowded around the monitor, observing, and Isobel began gowning up. She didn't even look at me.

"Another absence seizure," the other nurse was saying, low, "second in under ten hours—"

And then there was a firm, large hand on my elbow, guiding me out of the room. I spotted the CALL button then, too late. Right by the light switch.

I looked at the person pulling at me.

It was Adam.

It couldn't have been much past six in the morning, but he looked as immaculate as he had the day before. I could smell his aftershave, and the lingering scent of an abandoned coffee.

I twisted to look back in, but the nurses were sealing the hallway door. "What's happening?"

"I'm so sorry you had to see that," Adam said. "But you acted fast, that's good. Thank you."

"Is she okay?" I yanked my arm away from him. His fingers caught on my IV through my robe. It pinched, and I hissed, pulling my arm close to my chest.

He reached for my shoulders, then stopped himself. "It's a side effect of the protocol. She'll be fine, she just needs the exact balance of her medications tweaked. Let's get you sitting down. Nurse Isobel said Dr. Santos will be by soon."

I just stared at the door.

"Margaret?"

I'd never even told her my name.

"Margaret."

He took my shoulder then, and I shivered, gaze slowly lifting to him. "That's going to happen to me, too."

"It's a known side effect, yes," Adam said. And then nothing more, no attempts to convince me I'd be different, or that it wouldn't hurt, or even a reminder that it would be worth it.

I swallowed. "Did you know?"

He inclined his head quizzically. "Know what?"

"That she'd been having seizures. Is that why you're here at ass o'clock in the morning?"

Because nothing else made sense. It was like something out of a nightmare, all the necessary players on the scene at just the right moment. Why did he have to look so perfect? Why was he so *calm*?

Adam hesitated, and I thought I saw his tongue peek from between his teeth for just a moment, a dart of white and pink. Then he nodded. "Dr. Santos and I are monitoring her situation closely. I'm helping coordinate with the main development group on changes to her regimen."

It was under control. But it didn't feel like it from where I stood.

"The first time we spoke, she said she can barely read some days." We were walking again. I didn't protest, because where else did I have to go? Past the nurses' station. Back to my room, with its own antechamber, its own hooks for gowns, its own inactive screen. "That she can't remember. That there are days she wants to leave."

And I thought about my own first day of treatment, of the floating, of the pain after.

It was already starting.

"Medicine is a game of hurting in just the right way to heal," he said, and we were at the bed. I wanted to sit by the window instead, and I nearly flinched away from him. I remained standing. "The specific suffering you'll experience, I can't guess. Neither can you. But I can promise you that you will be safe here. If you don't remember, you also won't need to. Your nurses will remember for you. If you can't read, I'll read to you."

I hate myself for it now, but I did want that. Yearn for it. Him, at my bedside. Maybe that's why I got back into the hospital bed then, let him tuck the blanket up over my legs.

"Think of it," he said, "like a cocoon. A caterpillar disassembles itself into a mass of cells, then reconstitutes itself into a butterfly. But it always remembers where it started. It remembers the taste of its favorite food. It is the same individual, no matter what happened in between."

The same individual, maybe, but a different beast entirely.

· Chapter Ten ·

I couldn't go to the garden that day.

At every turn, something stopped me. Dr. Santos was delayed, and I had to sit and wait for him to round. Then there was the day's infusion, a lengthy one that, while not as disorienting as the first, kept me tethered to my bed by more than my IV tubing. Even once I was unhooked, dinner took over an hour to arrive, and before I knew it, it was shift change again. The sun was setting. A whole day, wasted.

Were they intentionally keeping me busy? Or was it just how SWAIL worked, part of the reason it required such a lengthy hospital admission and such close nurse supervision?

Or maybe it was a side effect of Veronica's decline. Maybe they were all dealing with her.

Isobel was brusque when she took over. Not unkind, but entirely businesslike, minimizing her time in my room. I appreciated it. *You should consider leaving the trial* still haunted me, sandpaper-rough in the back of my brain. So at odds with what Veronica had told me, and shouldn't she know better?

But then I'd think about how Veronica had looked, seizing in her bed, or before that, frightened by something only she could hear. How reliable of an observer was she, so deep in it? Maybe Isobel was right. Maybe—

And around and around I went.

So I got up, got dressed. It was night, yes, and I was exhausted, yes, but nobody was there to stop me anymore, and Veronica wanted those flowers.

And I wanted out and away from everything that made me think of the great unknown I was hurtling toward. No amount of ASMR-y auger restoration videos had done the job while the sun was up, but maybe some unsanctioned horticulture would.

Isobel did see me leave, I think. I have a vague memory of her sitting at the nurses' station. Somebody else buzzed me out, but she was there, head in her hands. Tired already?

Or something else?

At the time, I didn't think about it. I walked out of the ward, to the elevator bank, and hit DOWN. The mistake I'd made last time, I figured, was not looking like I knew where I was going. Like I didn't belong there, because, of course, I hadn't. But now I had a motivating, organizing purpose: get to the garden, see if the door was unlocked, and if it was, get the flowers.

It felt good, having a purpose again. Having a *simple* purpose. One task. One metric I could pass or fail by.

I did my best to ignore the fatigue trailing me. I felt like I was leaving scraps of myself behind, bits of momentum lost like flakes from my itching scalp. But the animating force of *striding*, not skulking, helped. Here was the lobby; here was the door. It moved under my hand. I wouldn't even have to prop it open to make sure I could get back in.

I was going to get Veronica her flowers. I was going to be useful.

Useful.

Maybe that was it. It had been so long since I'd been anything but a burden on anybody in my life. At least I could cut some flowers.

The garden wasn't illuminated at night. Nothing overhead, and no path lights, either. The only light was from the moon (far off), ambient light pollution largely blocked out by the hulk of the main hospital building, and faint beams cast down from lit windows above. Not pitch-dark by any means, but it took thought to navigate.

I remember being cold. Chilly, really, nothing extreme, but I hugged my arms tight to me. I couldn't tell if the weather was unseasonably cool or if I was feverish. I ignored either answer. The paths were winding, probably designed for the illusion of privacy in a densely populated place. I imagined others who had walked those paths, pre-grieving for seriously ill patients, or chasing after kids who didn't know that dad was in surgery.

It was a nice garden, for their sakes.

Tended regularly, I think. I didn't see any weeds in between the pavers or along the path. And for a moment, even in the dark, even on my mission, I felt it: the soothing remove from the everyday, the relaxation that comes from being in an orderly, curated space.

A space like my room. Like the whole ward. That thought sounded discordant, though, and I couldn't figure out why. Something was wrong, even then. Something wasn't adding up.

But there was the bed of purple flowers.

The color wasn't obvious, with the evening low and dark over them. Some of the flowers had closed up, while others were just barely visible, no sheen to their petals or leaves. But there were all sorts of purples as my eyes adjusted, as my brain became willing to tease out the subtle differences. Placards named them: monarda, monardella, borage. A pollinator's garden.

I have never been a gardener, but I've cleaned up a few gardening books.

I had no knife, no scissors. Nothing but my brittle nails. They'd notice the damage in the morning, if I didn't pick carefully, so I took my time. Full blooms, not nascent ones, not dying ones; I pinched them off, ignoring the prickle of the borage's spiny stems into my fingertips, smelling the riot of perfume that erupted as I beheaded each one.

It was so good, so perfect, so beautiful—up until the second it wasn't. I didn't count and couldn't tell you how big of a bouquet I'd gathered before I needed a break, but it wasn't much. I was just so unaccountably tired. Not in pain, no more than usual, but tired. Heavy. Stooping over that flower bed was just too much. I sat down on a bench, and I wasn't immediately sure I was going to be able to get up again.

No nurse CALL button in a garden. I hunched forward over my lap and counted breaths. My meager fistful was probably enough, wasn't it? Veronica would understand. When I thought I could manage it, I made myself get back up again and started walking toward the door, but slower this time. Trying to pay attention to how it felt, how *I* felt.

Like shit. I felt like shit.

But I didn't want to give up. I wasn't *ready* to go back.

It wasn't an issue of failing. I hadn't. The more I looked at that fistful of flowers, the larger it seemed. And yet it still felt like the tolling of some bell, to turn around.

Why couldn't I decide when I was done for myself?

Distantly, I became aware of footsteps on the path. Sneakers on pavers. Somebody just around the bend, moving toward me. I expected a security officer, or maybe even the older guy from environmental services, like they were the only two people who existed down here at night.

It was Isobel.

She stopped a short distance from me. I stared in horror, shame, anger.

How? How had she found me? "I can explain," I blurted, when what I really wanted to do was scream.

"Your next dose of Tylenol is available," was all she said, waggling a little foil packet. She had a miniature water bottle in one of her scrubs pockets.

I stared at her, searching for any sign of irritation. I'd snuck out, after all. But here she was, right on schedule, so—what? Had she known where I was the whole time? Had somebody spotted me, called around the hospital asking for misplaced patients?

My eyes dropped to my wristband. It was just paper.

Right?

"Let's go back to your room," Isobel said, and in place of any anger was a deep weariness.

"I . . ." I didn't think I could walk all the way back.

She looked at me, *really* looked at me, and I realized she'd been staring past me this whole time. Her gaze sharpened. "Sit down," she said, and disappeared back into the hospital. I sank onto the closest bench, covering my face with my hands, trying not to cry. It was all too much: the narrowing of my life now dwindling to one hospital room; the realization that even if Veronica needed me, I was useless; the humiliation of how badly I needed the wheelchair that Isobel had returned with. I was nothing on my own, it seemed, or worse than nothing, and I couldn't stop the sobs that broke from me as Isobel steered me back into Graceview, back to the elevator bank, back into Seven West.

Isobel didn't comfort me; she politely ignored me all the way back to my room, until I'd run out of tears. She let me get into bed on my own, a small mercy, and I obediently took my medication after she scanned me in. She got a small cup to put the flowers in, and I didn't tell her where to take them.

I slept through bedside report and was glad not to hear what she thought of me.

When I asked Penelope to deliver the flowers for me later that morning, her expression crumpled, just for a moment.

But she took them away all the same.

That night, Isobel was back. She was my main night nurse, reliably there each evening at seven sharp. By the fourth night of my stay, and her third on shift, I'd begun to expect her the way I expected Penelope in the morning.

Each day, I drifted a little more. I tried, at first, to hold fast. I made a show of setting up my laptop, but the Wi-Fi was terrible, and I didn't have any active jobs. Updating my portfolio took ages, ages I couldn't stay coherent for, and I gave up pretty quickly. If I couldn't even focus long enough to get through a single chapter of my book, how could I do anything for myself?

I hated that drifting, but it was so much easier to let it carry me along.

The evenings were better. I wondered at that, why they didn't give me the floaty stuff at night when I could sleep through it, but Isobel had a ready explanation when I finally, grudgingly, asked.

"You need recovery time," she said. She was kinder after the garden, less snappish, but still distant. Tired, I came to realize.

"But I'm not doing anything during the day."

"It may not feel like it, but you are. You're being worn down." She hesitated, then said, apologetically, "You'll start to really feel it soon."

I bristled, but she didn't push it any further.

"Besides," she added, "night is for sleeping. SWAIL doesn't always allow for it. No sleep can get nasty. Sometimes, people get very disoriented. So try to rest, please."

My fifth night, after shift change but before lights out, she was in and out of the room more frequently. I was feeling better than usual, and made progress on the book I was reading. I'd even started thinking about tackling my portfolio again when Isobel came back, this time with a cooler.

"Remember what I said about night being for sleeping?" she asked.

I nodded.

"Unfortunately, tonight we're breaking the rules. Time for the next step." She didn't look happy about it.

It echoed there, unrepeated, between us: *You may not be able to manage the next steps, even with medical support.* I fought back a shudder. I would not flinch, not now, not in front of Isobel.

I glanced at my board, but there was no change there from the last few mornings: just a note that we were getting started, and a cheerful little smiley face. "Now?"

"Dr. Santos made an adjustment based on your afternoon labs." She set the cooler down and popped the top open, pulling out the IV bag inside.

This bag's fluid was an unsettling yellow-green color, slightly murky, and had no label except for a barcode. Isobel scanned it, then my wristband, and tapped a few keys on her computer station while I rattled off my name and date of birth, already well-trained. Then she hung the bag on the pole and started hitching its tubing into the infusion pump and my IV.

"What is it?"

"A SWAIL compound," she said, not looking away from what she was doing. A few presses of the buttons and the pump started the new fluid moving. "I'm not really privy to the details, but in my experience, this one can hurt."

I recoiled instinctively, but I was connected to that pump; I couldn't do anything to halt the start-stop inch of green-tinged fluid up the line, closer and closer to my arm. I steeled myself for it instead. "What sort of hurt?" I asked. The not-knowing would only make it worse.

"Usually a mild stinging, but different patients react differently." She glanced at me; our eyes met, and I hoped she couldn't see how terrified I was.

Because I could manage a mild stinging. I knew I could.

The drug reached the saline lock. I counted on an inhale,

then an exhale. Nothing changed, except that I could feel the chill of the liquid; it had been kept very cold, and my skin pebbled into gooseflesh as it brought down the temperature of my arm. I stared down at it, imagining I could see into my veins as the medicine dispersed, flowing toward my heart and—

"*Shit,*" I hissed, because that's when the pain hit. It burned at the IV site, bright and unrelenting, like a hundred slender needles had been threaded into my skin and were being pulled apart, spreading my nerve endings thin. My fingers clenched into a fist. Isobel's hand dropped down to cover mine, and for a brief moment the pain receded behind the shock that she cared.

Then I realized she was just trying to ease my hand open, and that the burning was getting even worse.

"You're increasing the pressure on the vein," she said. "I know it's hard, but you need to relax. I'm going to go grab a heat pack. Sometimes the counter-stimulation helps. Breathe, Margaret."

"Meg," I whispered.

"Meg," she agreed, and then she was gone.

I counted every breath until she returned, taking them as slowly as I could. My face reddened, and I fought back tears. I wanted to thrash and scream and run away from the machine, but I sat there, hands pressed flat to my thighs, staring at the tubing. I couldn't see the flow anymore, the color suffused through evenly now, but it was better than staring at the bag, wondering how long it would take for it to be a quarter empty, watching each drip make no visible impact on the volume remaining.

The door opened. Isobel didn't rush over to my bedside, and I wanted to scream at her to hurry up, but I closed my eyes tight instead.

A snap as she cracked the heat pack, then pressed it to the IV site. She guided my free hand over it. "How does that feel?" she asked.

"Ow, shit, *fuck*," I replied, because the added heat just made everything that much more tender, more raw. I kept it in place, though, waiting, hoping, because she was the one with the experience.

"If that's not working, you don't have to force it," she said, when my jaw didn't relax. I was shaking. She moved my hand, and the heat pack dropped down onto the mattress, warm against my hip. I watched her go to the computer, swiping in and typing something. "I've asked the on-call doctor to approve some more pain medication," she said, turning back to me. "But that could take a bit."

My breath whistled through my clenched teeth, but I nodded.

"It's going to be running for a little over two hours," she continued. "And it's not going to get better on its own."

I groaned.

"Exactly. But I'm going to stay with you."

My incredulity cut through the haze of pain for one brief, blessed moment I couldn't pause to appreciate. "What?"

"I'm going to sit right here, and we can talk. Or not. But I'm not going to leave." She let out a shaky breath. "Unless you ask me to."

"Don't you have other patients?" I snapped. I didn't know what I was feeling. With one breath I was pissed, angry that she'd condescend to me, and in the next I was so desperately grateful that I didn't trust her in the slightest.

Isobel stood her ground. "I let my charge nurse know that you were going to need some extra help for a while."

Extra help. Moral support. I didn't believe in moral support. But I didn't want to be alone.

"There's nothing you can do," I said, my voice wavering. "No extra help to *give.*"

"Then tell me to go."

I stared at her, desperate, and she stared right back. Challenging. Challenging, but asking, too, inquiring, whispering, *What do you really want right now?*

"I want you to make it stop," I confessed, closing my eyes.

Adam had said I could stop at any time, hadn't he? Isobel had pushed it, had insulted me with it instead of comforting me, but they both had told me the same thing: I could cry uncle, and this would all be over. I'd be able to think again. This searing agony would end, and I'd go back to just my normal ulcers and aching joints and twisting bowels. My slowly degrading liver. The ticking of a clock as I waited for some new symptom to throw my life even more off course.

I'd learned to live with it all, or near enough. I could do it again.

"Meg? What do you want me to stop? The drip?"

"I don't know!" I shouted.

She recoiled.

"I don't know," I repeated, quieter this time, ashamed. How could there be so many ways to feel shame? To feel like a walking disaster? "I'm sorry," I added. "You don't have to put up with this, I don't . . ."

"Tell me something."

I made a helpless, confused sound.

"Anything," she said. She pulled up a chair. "What you studied in school." Her gaze flitted around the room. "About the book you're reading. Anything a little less personal. Farther away from whatever you're feeling now. Trust me."

"I don't have anything," I whispered.

"You do," she said, and she was so sure. "Tell me what you're going to do when you're better."

Maybe it was the *when* that did it. A simple word choice, and I'm sure it was intentional, but it was like a magic trick. I breathed a little easier. "I, uh. I like watching these videos on old hand tool restorations," I said, haltingly, because I didn't have plans, but I at least still had interests. "The main guy I follow, he does two versions, with and without narration. I've watched the one on a cheese-cutting calculator like six times." Either she was a great actress, or she was legitimately interested; she prompted me on when I started to trail off, she listened, she *engaged*, until one of her brief check-ins at the computer yielded gold: a morphine drip that she got started at my other IV site, that drowned out the pain I'd almost managed to ignore and sent me into a deadened sleep.

She was gone when I woke up, but there was a Post-it note on my bedside tray.

Keep an open mind. Strength can mean more than one thing. —Isobel

· Chapter Eleven ·

GRACEVIEW MEMORIAL

Room:	775	Phone	XXX-XXX-2775
Date:	August 10, 2023	MON TUES WED ~~THURS~~ FRI SAT SUN	
Patient:	Margaret Culpepper	PAIN SCALE	
Doctor:	Santos		
Nurse:	Georgia B.	Pain medication last given:	0830
Charge Nurse:	Tristan P.	Next dose:	1230
Today's Plan! *Be strong.*			
Diet:	Low Fiber Easy to Chew	Fall Risk:	Moderate
Activity Level:	Ambulate in Room	Our goal is to have you discharged on:	September 30, 2023
CALL FOR HELP.			

I didn't get a chance to ask her what she meant. She was off shift the next night, and the following day, treatment—intensified.

And my memory becomes unreliable.

There's a space between consciousness and oblivion where nightmares live. Fever dreams, hallucinations, the world warping and turning putty-soft. I don't know how much of what I remember from that week is real. More of it than I'd like. Less of it than it seems. Somewhere in that middle space.

Illness and healing can only ever be liminal, I guess.

I remember:

Throwing up in countless green plastic bags. Sometimes alone, sometimes with a nurse to take it away after. The CALL button taunting me as I lay huddled on my mattress, splattered in my own sick. The nurses coming whether I called them or not, eventually.

Singing songs I never knew the words of. Singing to my food. Singing to myself because it made the room stop spinning for just a little bit longer.

Adam, holding my hand, new flowers at my bedside. I told him about my portfolio. Or maybe he told me about his. "We're the same," he said. "We sell explanations." But that can't have happened, because a drug isn't an explanation: it's a solution.

Nobody explained anything.

I don't remember doctors. I don't remember Santos or anybody else, nobody but the nurses, the techs, environmental services, the people on the television, left on by my nurses in an attempt to orient me better. I remember my parents, but I know they never visited. I remember myself in the mirror of the bathroom, looking better, feeling worse. My memory and my imagination, though, can't be tricked into remembering a single white coat.

But the whiteboard kept on changing, and I gave numbers, ones and eights and threes, pain growing and receding and always forgotten as soon as it had passed, replaced for better or worse. My body had no history anymore. I was held together by electronic notes and bedside shift reports, the only thing ensuring I was who I'd been the day before.

Margaret Culpepper, age twenty-six, being hollowed out with a pharmaceutical melon baller, everything slated to be rearranged.

I remember so many indignities through a cotton-ball haze that gentles all the edges. Except for:

Daylight burning against my eyes, my abdomen cramping, my body shaking from the pain. Stumbling out of bed, to the bathroom. Nothing on the toilet, but I trembled with the force of that nothing.

I huddled in the shower. Water spattered across my back, weak pressure but hot, steaming hot. Inside, something gave way with a wet sucking, the creation of a vacuum, my body stretched apart, dangling, dangling. Blood, I remember blood, not a torrent but it seemed like it was everywhere, swirling into the water. My abdomen cramped again, and the vacuum broke apart with a visceral drop, and then—

Pain, pain, *pain pain pain*—

And a slick slide of tissue, a soft and meaty slap, and there, in between my feet, was a purple-brown-red clot the size of my fist. Not round, more triangular, with two horns, and I knew what I was staring at, or thought I knew, but I also knew it couldn't be real.

I screamed.

My nurse was there instantly, or perhaps she'd been there the whole time. There's no way they would have let me shower alone, not as unsteady as I was, surely? I grabbed at her, clawed at her, tried to climb her body to get away from what I was sure was my uterus, lying there on the floor, pulsing—or jittering from the shower flow. She was talking to me, low and urgent, but words didn't make sense. Nothing made sense until I was hauled over to the bed, guided onto the mattress sobbing. More bodies in the room.

Adam. Adam, watching everything.

And then nothing. Absence, long enough that when I came to myself again, I didn't remember the shower anymore, or the lump of flesh. I was dressed again. My hair was dry.

If I hadn't cut my hair before getting admitted, would it have still been damp? Clinging and choking, proof or a reminder or at least some legacy of what had happened? I don't know. But I didn't remember, except for quick snatches, flashes of nightmare. I was still cramping, and there was a pad in my underwear. But the pain was nowhere to be found.

The IV they'd been using for the SWAIL infusions had moved to just below the bend of my elbow. The space where it had been was covered by a bit of taped-on gauze. I stared at it, confused. The pump by my bedside went *click click click*.

The bag was pink that time.

I know I dreamed of flesh, pulsing and slick and tumorous, just beneath the sheets of my bed. Cradling my body, pressing up against it, fitting to every crevice of my weakened self.

It smelled sweet. Yogurt, with mango at the bottom.

When the phlebotomist came one morning, I was awake and struggling to make out the writing on the whiteboard in the dim dawn light. My teeth throbbed in my gums. I stayed motionless as he wrapped the tourniquet around my upper arm.

"Did I give birth?" I asked, knowing it didn't explain what I'd seen, unable to make any other words.

"No," he said. And maybe I started to cry, frustrated, confused, because he added, "A blood clot, the exact shape and size of your uterus. Pathology's been talking about it. Really cool, huh?"

The light grew brighter, and I made out the words:

CALL FOR HELP

· Chapter Twelve ·

Have you ever heard of *learned helplessness*?

It's pretty much exactly what it sounds like: subject a person or an animal to the same stressful stimulus, over and over and over again, and don't let them escape it. Don't let them stop it. Don't let them have any choice but to endure. Over time, they stop fighting, even if you finally let them have some say in things.

Back in college, while I was working as a TA, I proctored several sessions of an exam, all held one right after the other. During the first one, the fire alarm went off. I took all my students outside, but it was a false alarm. Once it was silent, back in we went, and they got to work while I tried to figure out how to handle the disruption to the timed computer test.

Then the alarm went off again.

The maintenance team poked their heads in. "We're still trying to fix it," they said. "Sorry, we'll just keep muting it."

But they kept not fixing it, which meant that every twenty minutes, the alarm would go off, and the students and I had to sit there, not leaving, not moving. Each test session was only fifty minutes long, so while it sucked for them, it was fine. They got the opportunity to retake the test later, if they felt like their performance had been affected. But I sat there, session after session, false alarm after false alarm. Every time it started blaring, my heart would race, and I even knew when it was about to come, I could hear this subtle change in the air—

And there was nothing I could do.

Eventually, they got the balance of my medications figured out, and I could think again. It took a little over a week. Coming back to myself was immediate and overwhelming. Before is jumbled, broken, bombed-out chaos, and after is just me, sitting in a bed, brain once more tracking everything in order. Concrete details were settled against one another in proper proportion, nothing standing out too much, nothing receding into absence from lack of attention. The clock and the pump went *tick click tick click*, and I read over the whiteboard.

Pain levels negligible, doctor the same, Nurse Louise again. And there, at the bottom, *Prevent falling! Call for help getting out of bed.*

It dispelled the half-legible memory of CALL FOR HELP like sun on fog. Absolutely mundane. It had just been my medicated mind, struggling to latch on to anything that seemed like it would help.

The door to my room opened, startling me badly enough that I could hear a little alert on the computer by my bed. Louise entered, bringing with her a meal tray. She paused when she heard the shrill little alarm, but it stopped as my heart settled in my chest.

"Good evening," she said. "Feeling a little better?"

My throat was sore. Had I been screaming? Or not talking at all? I cleared it, then said, "Yes, some." I was trembling, but I was only half-aware of it, until I tried to take hold of the insulated water cup on my little bedside tray. It rattled, plastic on plastic, and I let go of it hastily. My forearm no longer had the gauze taped to it; I couldn't even see where my original IV had been. "How did you know?"

More like, *How many times have you asked and I've given you bizarre nonanswers that were answers all their own?*

"Your numbers are looking better, so I was hopeful." She set the tray down beside the cup. Under the plastic lid was Jell-O, juice, and saltines. Coming down off liquids, I guess, but I can't remember being put *on* them. Still, the saltines in their plastic wrapper made me keenly aware of how hungry I was, something I'd missed along with the shakes.

I grabbed the cup again, both hands clutched tight. I sipped from the accordioned plastic straw. "That was—I don't—" I fumbled for the words, my mind as clumsy as my fingers. She knew how bad it had been, or at least had seen the outside of it; really, she knew *more* than me, if only in continuity of memory. How was I supposed to ask if it had really been that bad? How was I supposed to acknowledge all the chaos when I could barely remember it, could barely sort out real from imagined?

I needed somebody that wasn't her. Adam, maybe, or—or my mom, but no, she'd have been less than helpful. I needed somebody I could *choose* to be vulnerable with, instead of somebody who was paid to intrude.

(*Intrude?* She was there to help.)
(She wanted to help.)

I don't remember if I managed to get any other words out. If I did, they were more stammered fragments. I think I was probably silent, though, shell-shocked. Louise stood by my bedside, then gently took the carafe from my clawed, shaking hands.

"It's normal," Louise told me; her experience filled in all the gaps in what I couldn't articulate. "But it should get better from here on out."

Normal.

That word echoed as I chewed those crackers into paste that clung to my soft palate, washed them down with too-sweet juice. Louise stayed for a little while, taking vitals, swapping in a new bag of saline. She helped me to the bathroom; when I settled back in, I finally noticed my fall risk was now at *moderate*.

A moderate fall risk. All the lost time. The blood clot—

Normal?

Louise didn't seem concerned, and she must have seen much worse than what I was going through. I tried to be comforted by that, but instead I started thinking about burnout, desensitization, or even just transferring to this ward from some subdiscipline entirely unrelated to my care and not knowing what to be worried about.

I could feel myself beginning to panic again. I looked at the computer, reflexively, worried it would begin to alarm.

Don't notice me, don't notice me, and when was I even connected to a continuous monitor? It must have started while I was in the throes of SWAIL. Looking down at myself, I registered the small patches stuck onto my skin beneath my gown. Wires snaking out to a small box mounted to the side of the bed.

How had I missed that? Maybe I wasn't as back to myself as I thought.

But it made sense, the monitors; hadn't the screens in the antechamber to Veronica's room showed her vitals? And I had some vague memory of somebody—Adam? Penelope? Dr. Santos?—explaining the need to keep a close eye on me. This wasn't a spa stay.

Right. I had to let them help. It was okay that I didn't understand everything that was happening to me. It was *normal*. I was sick, and to fix me, they had to first make me sicker. Which meant allowing them to care for me.

But the miasma of the last week clung to me, almost tangible, hanging from my shoulders. The scent of mango, the feeling of soft, slick flesh. I couldn't shake it. It was like I'd brought something back with me from that place, and maybe it was only the knowledge of how out of control I'd been. But maybe...

Maybe...

And then it struck me: Veronica would know if this—the side effects, the emotional roller coaster I was on, the way I was being treated—was normal.

I tried to stand up, but that was still out of the question. The bedside phone was close, though, and I remembered her room number. *We'll be in seven-seven-two*, in Adam's voice, on loop inside my skull. I fumbled with the buttons until I figured out how to call between rooms, then waited, leg jittering, as the receiver rang.

And rang.

And rang.

I clutched at the plastic until the system terminated the call.

· Chapter Thirteen ·

I needed a blood transfusion.

I found that out at shift change the next morning, Louise running Penelope through a list of things they acted like I should already be aware of. I nodded along. Maybe, I thought, that would fix me right up. I'd been dizzy, and I huddled in my robe, trembling intermittently. I'd slept some, though not much, waking to stare at that phone.

I'd tried calling her two more times. I never got an answer.

Just ask. Couldn't it be that simple? Louise or Penelope could go check on her, see if maybe she was just asleep. But I couldn't bring myself to ask. That paranoia hadn't left me, not since I'd started second-guessing Louise's care.

A blood transfusion wasn't going to fix *that*.

Penelope came back maybe an hour after bedside report with another nurse I didn't recognize and a bag of packed red blood cells. They both reviewed every detail of who I was and what I was getting, attached the tubing, and let it flow.

Blood is viscous and kept cold. It sludged through the tubing into my veins, the skin around the cannula prickling into gooseflesh. I can still feel it, if I think about it too hard. My body contracted around the invasion, a frightened clenching, but there was no disaster; no adverse reaction to the blood, no fault with the line, nothing but a persistent chill that evaporated a few inches up my arm.

"It's going to take about an hour and a half to run," Penelope told me. "Then I'll be back to finish up. Can I get you anything?"

"No," I said, and only thought of Isobel's heat pack trick after she'd been gone five minutes.

I stared at the tubing snaking to what I thought of as my non-SWAIL arm. They'd moved that IV, too, I realized. Creeping up my arm, away from the original site. I didn't think I'd pulled that out. I remembered, distantly, some comment that the sites didn't stay good for long.

I knew so little about my care, I realized.

I groped for my cell phone. Before that great lost wash of time, I'd occasionally checked the portal for my medical records, but since coming back to myself, it hadn't occurred to me. Too addled, too confused. Now, I opened the app and scrolled, determined to catch myself up. I skimmed through my nurses' progress notes (Louise's were almost indecipherable, all acronyms and half sentences; Penelope's and Isobel's were more narrative, and all of them kept mentioning my lack of orientation, my distress, my pain. Had anything been done about it?), my blood panel results (fine, fine, suddenly not fine), and found the pathology report.

It was converted from a scan of a printout, the formatting wonky and hard to read.

DIAGNOSIS:

Bloody, fleshy mass, 5cm x 6cm x 1cm. Passed vaginally with no intervention.

Sample determined to be a decidual cast, wherein the lining of the endometrium is sloughed off in one piece, forming a cast of the uterine cavity; may be associated with ectopic pregnancy or exogenous progesterone.

COMMENT: Pt participating in SWAIL trial. Pt reported to have ceased oral contraceptives prior to trial. Pt diagnosed with Fayette-Gehret syndrome. Interaction of progesterone-only oral contraceptives with Fayette-Gehret syndrome, including disruption of usual medication habits, may be indicated as cause of decidual cast. Not expected to reoccur. Recommend evaluating pt for anemia.

██████████████████████████████
██████████████████████████████
██████████████████████████████
██████████████████████████████
██████████████████████████████
██████████████████████████████
██████████████████████████████
██████████████████████████████

Electronically signed by: BILAN NOOR, M.D.
08/13/2023 16:05
Pathology Services—Graceview Memorial Laboratory.

I stared at the large, blacked-out space between the end of the summary and the signature. Redacted? My pathology report was *redacted*?

I backed out of that file, telling myself it was an artifact of the poor scan. But then I clicked one of Dr. Santos's progress notes.

Everything but the date was blotted out.

I went back through his other notes. The first one or two, which I'd read out of curiosity, were fine. But once the SWAIL infusions had really gotten going, bits and pieces were replaced by black redaction boxes. There was no way to interact with the covered areas. I couldn't copy the underlying text, and the app's help section provided no instructions or explanations as to why parts of my own medical record would be inaccessible. Obviously, it had something to do with SWAIL's proprietary compounds, but—

But it felt wrong.

I had to talk to Veronica.

I unclipped my telemetry box from the bed rail and tucked it into the front pocket of my gown, then eased myself out of bed. The blood hung on the same pole as the bag of normal saline I wasn't currently hooked up to. There wouldn't be an infusion today; something about a risk of interference from the blood products, even though they'd be going into different arms. That made it easier to maneuver.

My head spun a little as I got to my feet, but it settled quickly. Desperation can do that.

I was already in my robe. My slippers took a minute to find, put up on the seat of one of the chairs by the window. It gave me practice maneuvering with the pole. I stopped in the bathroom, half out of need and half to give myself an excuse if Penelope poked her head in after the unavoidable change in my heart rate, and paused in front of the mirror.

My lips were almost gray, but my cheeks had bright pink spots, like a doll's face. Blood, anonymized and bringing me back to life. Modern medicine at its finest.

I shuffled out to the hall. Nobody had *told* me to stay in my bed, though it was undoubtedly implied. The blood on my pole was damning. I rotated it away from the nurses' station. Penelope wasn't there, but the other nurse to sign off on the transfusion was, head down, eyes on a screen I couldn't see, along with a few other people in scrubs that I hadn't interacted with. It was midmorning, and the ward was as busy as I'd ever seen it. Nobody paid me any mind.

I walked away from my room as confidently as I could, glad for this ward's special funding; the wheels on the pole didn't squeak at all.

For all my disorientation to myself and my life, I remembered exactly where to go. Except both doors to Veronica's room stood open. There was no flag, green or red, barred or not. I slipped into the antechamber.

Somehow, I was still surprised when the monitors were all blank. Somehow, I still didn't understand what I was going to find.

I stepped into her empty room. I stared at her empty bed. There were no flowers.

It had been too long for my bouquet to still be good, I told myself. She'd been taken to imaging, I told myself.

There was a knock on the doorframe behind me. I turned to see Penelope there. I expected anger. Anger that I'd left my bed, anger that I'd come here. But she was too much of a professional.

"What happened?" I asked. "Is Veronica okay?"

My voice was so small.

"She went home," Penelope said, gently. "Already discharged." She reached out and took my elbow, lightly steering me back into the antechamber.

"Oh," I said.

I made myself picture her, happy. Happy, and beautiful, and *better*. I blinked rapidly against the tears that threatened, because in that empty room, all I'd been able to think was, *Something terrible happened here.*

Not, *At the end of this, you get to go home.*

She'd had a home to go home *to*. I was jealous. Veronica, I'm so sorry, but I was jealous.

My only saving grace is I didn't have long to be jealous, because Penelope was pulling my arm out straight, huffing out an irritated breath.

Beneath my skin, blood pooled dark and heavy, swollen and pendulous.

"Looks like the vein blew. Let's get you back to bed." She reached for the pump, fussing with it until the blood stopped flowing into my ruptured self.

What a waste, I thought. All that blood, painstakingly donated and dumped into the uncaring space between my cells.

They brought in an IV therapy nurse with an ultrasound machine. She used a warmer on the gel before plastering my skin with it, sliding the wand up and down, up and down, looking for a good prospect. But every time she began to advance the needle, my veins would close up, flattening as if cringing from the sharp metal.

She only got three attempts. After that, we had to find a different solution. The blood had already been disposed of; more than two hours out of refrigeration and it was no good to anyone.

Penelope kept a close eye on my arm, checking my fingertips, feeling for a pulse in my wrist. When I asked her why, she said, "There's a risk of what we call 'compartment syndrome.' Too much pressure from the hematoma and your circulation will be cut off to that group of muscles. We can fix it with surgery," she added, "but I don't think it'll get that bad."

"How did it happen?" I asked, gazing at the goose egg of turgid blood on my forearm. I wondered why she didn't just open me up, let it all spill out. It would have been faster, more certain, than letting my body absorb it all.

"Sometimes SWAIL can make the walls of your veins thin out," she said. "Although usually it's worst where we give the infusion."

At my look of horror, she patted my arm. "It'll reverse on its own with time," she said. "Just part of getting acclimated."

But with my peripheral veins inaccessible, they needed a new way to get the medication into me. "We can't just try again tomorrow?" I asked at shift change, Isobel standing next to Penelope as they discussed the surgery I was going to have in the early hours of the morning. The doctor had explained it to me when he'd stopped by a few hours before, but he'd been rushed, and I'd been feeling woozy again. I hadn't understood.

"A gap in the program," Isobel said, after a silent exchanged glance with Penelope, "isn't good for anybody. Your remaining cannula is only good for another half day, and we have no reason to think it'll be any easier to replace than this one."

"It's not uncommon to need a PICC or a port-a-cath," Penelope added. "Most patients in the trial get one before too long. It should be more comfortable for you, too."

I only realized later that Penelope still remembered my earlier hesitancy about the PICC. Or maybe it was Isobel.

Maybe Isobel already had some inkling that the port-a-cath was the better option.

Isobel brought me a laminated infosheet with my dinner, and I read it as she palpated the slowly reducing bulge of deep purple bruise. The skin was tender where it stretched, but otherwise I couldn't feel it. My arm was shockingly warm now that there was no chilled saline dripping into my veins. No pain medicine, either, except for the Tylenol I dutifully swallowed, with a promise of ibuprofen to come a few hours later.

The sheet was clearly borrowed from the oncology ward. It had helpful, colorful diagrams of a round silicone button over a small chamber, a catheter connecting that chamber into a deeper vein close to the heart. Once the button was surgically installed, my skin would heal over, and new medications would be injected each time they were needed. They could even draw blood from it, and there was much less risk of infiltration into the tissues surrounding it.

Of course, if anything went wrong with it, I'd be in a lot more danger.

"They'll probably use conscious sedation during the surgery," Isobel said. She looked a little more rested this time; maybe she'd taken a few days of PTO. Maybe she hadn't seen me out of my mind and disoriented for days on end.

I don't know how to feel about that. How I felt about it back then. If she'd seen me like that, surely she would have said something. Right?

"That's the kind where you're awake, but don't remember anything?" I asked.

"That, and they give you enough Valium to make you not care, either."

I prodded at the Jell-O cup on my tray. "I think I'd prefer going under completely. Sleep through it."

She didn't respond, but looked like there were words trapped under her tongue.

"Say it," I pushed, then immediately cringed and looked down at my spoon. Isobel was just doing her job; no matter how much my suffering had made me latch on to her the night of the painful infusion, no matter how personal our sparring had felt before that, she was just my nurse.

But she did say it. "General anesthesia isn't really like going to sleep. We just say that to make it less frightening."

I studied her face. "But you're going to frighten me."

"If you want me to."

With that kind of introduction, not knowing would be the worse option. I nodded.

"It's closer to inducing a coma. A controlled one, one we know how to manage, but it's not sleep. Nobody wakes up from a week sedated on a ventilator and feels refreshed. And there's a higher risk of something going wrong. If you don't have to go under, I wouldn't."

I ate my Jell-O. It slithered down my throat, slick and tasteless. On balance, which option would I prefer? Either way, I wouldn't remember. Either way, I'd be partially obliterated.

Maybe there was a third option. Maybe I could just stay awake.

No, I wanted that even less.

"Is there anybody you want us to update during the surgery?" Isobel asked, when the silence had stretched too long. The formal, clinical *us*; it would be Isobel calling. I tried to imagine her calling my mother. No, I couldn't do that to her.

But wouldn't it be nice, to have somebody waiting to hear how it went? Maybe... maybe...

"Parents? A partner?"

She must have noticed the lack of GET WELL SOON! balloons.

"No," I said, keeping my voice studiously light. "I'm, uh. I didn't tell anybody." A lie, but easier to explain. "Just in case this doesn't work, you know?"

I probably blushed. I'm a bad liar, and I'd just made myself sound humiliatingly depressing.

But it would've been worse to say, *Nobody cares because they're all tired of my bullshit. Of my not getting any better.* I hadn't even been lucky enough to have my father decide it *would* work and oh, happy day, his irritating little nightmare would finally be over!

Veronica had had her parents; she'd been better off than I was. But she'd also been so shyly happy about Adam visiting. Maybe she'd also gone through the same isolation at some point. The same withdrawal from life. Maybe Isobel had seen this before and knew the exact score.

I was so tired, trying to manage all of that. To predict it.

It didn't matter.

"I'll be here when it's over," Isobel said. "You should try to get some rest now."

She took my tray. She was most of the way to the door when I found the bravery to ask, "Isobel? Why are Dr. Santos's notes redacted?"

She froze in the doorway. "Requirements from the pharmaceutical company funding the trial," she said, finally, not looking at me. "Standard practice. But I don't agree with it."

And then she left, before I could push further.

I stared at my phone for a long time, wondering if I should call somebody. Let them know what was happening to me. Get an outside opinion.

Maybe, if I straight-out asked for somebody to care, they would do me a favor and show up.

· Chapter Fourteen ·

GRACEVIEW MEMORIAL

Room:	775	Phone	XXX-XXX-2775
Date:	August 20, 2023	\multicolumn{2}{c}{MON TUES WED THURS FRI SAT (SUN)}
Patient:	Margaret Culpepper	\multicolumn{2}{c}{PAIN SCALE}
Doctor:	Santos	\multicolumn{2}{c}{1 2 (3) 4 5 6 7 8 9 10}
Nurse:	Isobel R.	Pain medication last given:	2000
Charge Nurse:	Tristan P.	Next dose:	after surgery
\multicolumn{4}{c}{Today's Plan! *Port-a-cath installation.*}
Diet:	NPO	Fall Risk:	Low
Activity Level:	Normal	Our goal is to have you discharged on:	September 30, 2023
\multicolumn{4}{c}{*Prevent falling! Call for help getting out of bed.*}

I didn't call anybody.

I was asleep when Isobel came in to prep me for surgery. She wasn't alone; the same IV specialist as before came with her. They evaluated the SWAIL IV site and decided it was still usable. I had expected an anesthesiologist, but it was just them, murmuring over me as I clawed my way back up to awareness. I wanted to be present until the precise last moment.

Once they were satisfied, Isobel helped me change; my gown opened in the front now. There was paperwork, too. My signature was a mess, but recognizably mine.

"I'm going to lower the back of the bed," Isobel warned, and I nodded. I sat forward as she made the adjustments; I'd tried slowly going down with the bed before, but it was surprisingly awkward.

I was staring blankly at my whiteboard when I realized—
"Did you know Veronica?"

Isobel's expression went blank. "Yes," she said, after a moment's thought.

"Can you not talk about the other patients?" Maybe it was some kind of HIPAA violation, though Adam had certainly seemed free enough.

"It's unprofessional," she said, relaxing a little.

I almost stopped there. Didn't push. But I kept thinking about those redactions, about how terrible the timing had been: Veronica had her seizure, I lost time, and now there was nobody to compare notes with. "Penelope said she'd gone home."

Isobel hesitated before nodding. I know she did. But at the time, I just thought she was being overly cautious.

"I was wondering—I wanted to talk to her, yesterday. About all of this. Since she's through the other side and all. Is there any way you could—"

"No," she snapped. Then she shut her eyes and took a deep breath. When she looked at me again, her expression was just embarrassed. Not sad. "I'm sorry, that's just not the sort of information we can give out."

"Then can you call Adam? Mr. Marsh." The last time I'd seen him—well, there was the vague memory of after I'd birthed the blood clot, but really, it had been *before*. Before SWAIL had gotten going. Before that hazy gap in my memory. I should have asked for him first thing, but I'd been so distracted, trying to sort myself out.

Adam would fix things, though. Or at least give me perspective. Comfort. Mango yogurt, if my diet allowed for it.

Isobel did a piss-poor job of hiding her disapproval. But she said, "I'll see what I can do."

I didn't get a chance to ask what the problem was *this* time; Isobel got a page that we were good to go. She disengaged the brake on my bed. We passed through the antechamber, into the hall, and over to an elevator. The lurch of descent felt strange, lying down.

They held off on giving me any sedatives until we were in the procedure room. Isobel left me in the hands of the nurses who staffed the IR suite. When the physician arrived, there was a choreographed dance of fact-checking, making sure I was the right patient, that this was the right procedure, that they had the right meds.

"If it helps," said the nurse about to bolus propofol into my veins, "you can count down. Your call."

I counted. The lights were bright. There was a discussion

going on behind me about what music to play. My veins stung with the intrusion of the medication. By the time I got to *seven*, I knew something was happening. The world was growing dim, and I couldn't tell if I'd said the word or only thought it. *Don't fight it*, I told myself. Embrace it, even; it was meant to feel good, it wasn't like how I'd lost myself on the SWAIL medications. But it felt too similar, and I panicked. I fought it. I think I moaned Isobel's name. I know I tried to sit up.

Somebody held me down, a light touch that felt simultaneously like it weighed five hundred pounds. I shut my eyes as the world tried to spin away from me, and I thrashed. *Stop*, I told myself, *stop, don't fight!* But my body wouldn't listen. Nothing would listen, nobody would listen, and I didn't want to be here anymore—

And then the hands on me were gone.

My blood pounded in my ears, but the panic faded. They must have given me something else, something fast acting. I lay there, boneless, waiting to feel some touch, some pressure that confirmed they'd begun the procedure. Or to wake up back in my room, or in a recovery lounge. Except nothing happened and, finally, I opened my eyes.

I was alone.

The gurney was sitting in an otherwise empty procedure room. The lights overhead flickered, the bright sterility of the hospital replaced with shadow and the scent of mildew. The nurses and physician were gone. I couldn't hear anything through the doors, and nothing on the intercom, either.

The music had stopped, if it had ever started playing at all.

With too much effort, I made myself sit up. The sedation

made me hazy, detached, like I was hanging suspended just above my body. But the wrongness cut through the fog enough that I could swing my legs over the edge of the gurney. The tubing that snaked from my arm tangled on the rails, and I hissed as the cannula pulled free, medical tape tearing from my skin.

It barely bled, though. Just a little pinprick hole. Who knew I had so little blood in me?

I eased my feet onto the floor, expecting cold linoleum. But it was body temperature, and slightly soft, giving gently as it took my weight. I made my way to the main door and pushed it open, revealing the hallway I'd come from.

My gaze swept across the walls, looking for—

There. A red button. *CALL FOR HELP*. Something had happened to my care team. I lurched across the hallway to it, slapping it with my right hand twice, three times. Nothing changed, not where I stood, but surely a call light was flaring to life somewhere else. Somebody would come.

Nobody came.

The longer I stood clutching the casing of that button, the more I registered what was around me. Just like I hadn't noticed the leads stuck to my skin two nights ago, at first I didn't notice the subtle pulsing of the walls. They flexed and contracted in time with my own breathing. And that give beneath my feet, it flexed as well, up and down, up and down. I still felt paint beneath my hands, and the floor, though soft, was still vinyl in texture. But farther away, back toward the elevator I had come through, I wasn't so sure. And then there was the smell, iron in the air, faint but constant. Blood, and not mine.

I was walking before I could stop myself. Leaning forward, straining toward the dark stains I had mistaken at first for patterning on the floor.

But they *were* in a pattern. Like the way skin sometimes turns a mottled purple when far too cold. Organically regular, spattered and streaked. Somebody had to have been hurt. Some horrific disaster. Maybe that was why the hall was empty.

I struggled to understand. I couldn't organize everything I was seeing into a coherent whole. Blood under the surface—no, the floor—no—

I tore my gaze away and looked around me.

Every door was open.

In each room, the walls pulsed as if alive, and the oxygen hookups slid into the drywall skin like needles. Electrical wiring formed loose sutures, linens wound dressings.

I started to panic.

I ran.

At the end of the hall, the elevator car was pristine. I threw myself into it, then jammed the DOOR CLOSE button with my elbow, afraid to touch anything. I don't know why I didn't hit the button for the ground floor. Maybe there wasn't one. But I sent the elevator back to the ward. Back to my room.

No, that's not true. I do know.

I couldn't see it then, but I can now: I was dreaming. Or having some strange drug-induced hallucination, but there isn't much difference between the two. The mechanism only matters as far as it answers this question:

Was what I saw real?

(Was it true?)

Floor seven, west tower. It was worse here, whatever had

happened. The walls were undeniably living tissue, but slick and streaked pink and gray. My nose burned with the macerated smell of antiseptic, shit, and urine, alcohol and ammonia gouging my sinuses. I cowered in the elevator car, unwilling to touch anything, unwilling to disembark. But I could see somebody moving, down by one of the patient rooms. Clean lines, broad shoulders. *Adam.* I crossed the threshold before the elevator car could swallow me once more.

My feet sank into a layer of soft, golden fat that split beneath my toes. My stomach heaved, and I stumbled, hands outstretched to catch myself against the closest wall. That held firm, turgid like where the blood had pooled in my arm, but its surface wept. I staggered on through the hallway-become-body, diseased and suppurating.

This is inside me, I thought, or heard, or said. (I don't think I said it. I don't think I would have opened my mouth.)

At last I found a clear patch of floor, a path that Adam must have carved with his expensive shoes. Had it parted for him, this sea of flesh, or was he just willing to get a little dirty to uncover a way forward? I'm not sure which option my subconscious picked, or if it had to choose at all.

My hands and feet were sticky with fluid. I wanted nitrile gloves, or operating room booties. Something besides the gown I wore, now gaping open in the front. But there was nothing, nothing between me and the filth I'd stumbled through. I wiped it off as best I could, but I never stopped moving. I had to get to Adam, had to ask him to get me out of here. Stop the trial, wash me clean.

I reached the room he'd turned into. This door was closed. There was a red circle with a bar across it posted on the metal.

The whole of it was spotless, and the antechamber beyond; I could see in through a little window. But I was filthy, contagious, I couldn't go in. Surely the door would be locked against me.

I tried anyway, and it opened soundlessly.

Everything grew hushed. Even my own ragged breathing became a gentle murmur, far away. I shed my filthy gown and reached with trembling hands for the sink faucet. I soaped myself to the elbow, the shoulder. Everything moved too slowly, but I was careful. I wrapped myself in a paper gown and stepped into the inner chamber.

This room was as clean as the antechamber, but the air was heavy and humid. The lights were bright. There was nowhere to hide. Nowhere to shield Adam from me; he was simply gone.

But Veronica was there, in a bed that was also a mouth, its lolling tongue wrapping over her body like a blanket or a mortuary drape. Her flesh was ulcerated, the skin she'd been so delighted to see clear now chewed up and spat out by something worse than her rampant immune system. Little kisses that had turned poisonous and putrid.

I could see her cheekbones, yellowed and pitted. They looked like they would crumble at the slightest touch. And her chest did not move, though the thing that was her bed breathed around her.

Dead. Dead, and food for monsters.

I came to her bedside. I stared down at the mouth, at its gleaming gums and pearlescent teeth. Human teeth, but out of order, bicuspids at the front, incisors lining the back, the whole geometry of it wrong, shaped to accommodate Veronica's supine corpse.

I hit the nurse CALL button. I hit it again, and again, and *again*, but nothing changed. Nobody came to help. There was only me and the body, and I made myself reach into that maw. Veronica didn't deserve this. We didn't *deserve* this, this final betrayal of our bodies, and where were the nurses? The doctors? Adam?

We were alone. In death, we would always be alone. By the time my hands reached where she had been, she was already gone.

And the bed swallowed me whole.

· Chapter Fifteen ·

I woke up in my room. Not all at once, but with the slow stuttering gasps of awareness I was growing familiar with. Images, sensations, snippets of thought; all served to distance me from that nightmare, to blur the edges of it. I didn't sit upright in a cold sweat, or if I did, I don't remember it.

But I do remember Isobel changing my gown to a different sort, one that opened far enough down the front to give her access to the port beneath my skin but otherwise stayed firmly closed. I remember the sun shining in through my window. I remember plucking at the bandage on my chest, and a firm but gentle hand pulling mine away and holding on.

I drifted through shift change. I think I remember Isobel sitting in my room, wearing street clothes instead of scrubs, but that might have been a dream.

By the time I had full awareness again, she was gone.

The only thing that followed me from that dream was the image of Veronica, lifeless in her hospital bed. It hovered just behind my waking thoughts, flashing to the forefront when I hit the CALL button to ask for help getting to the bathroom.

Flashing again as I paused beside my bed, momentarily too afraid to climb back in.

Haunting me as I settled against the pillows.

My phone was on the bedside table, plugged in and fully

charged. My fingers were clumsy as I unlocked it. When I fumbled the code on the first attempt, I caught a glimpse of my reflection in the dark screen. Red patches decorated my face along my hairline, below my eyes, a psoriatic flare underway.

I remembered Veronica's skin, ulcerated and—no, clear and healthy—

This was pointless. Veronica had gone home. Penelope had said so, Isobel had all but confirmed it.

Except now that I really thought about it, hadn't Veronica said she had an entire month left of treatment? They'd been about to rebuild her immune system. I knew I'd lost a few days, but not weeks, not months.

I typed her name into my search engine. Veronica . . . had I ever *seen* her last name? Had it been on the screen in the antechamber? I couldn't just search *Veronica Graceview Memorial*; hospitals didn't keep public lists of current patients. But maybe she'd mentioned it herself on social media. Maybe—

The door to the antechamber opened, and I jumped, startled, and dropped my phone into my lap.

It was Adam. Just like I'd asked for.

"Good morning," he said. I hadn't realized how much I'd missed his voice. My whole body leaned toward him like a plant seeking sun, phone forgotten. He'd brought flowers again, though a more standard bouquet: sunflowers and lilies and pom-poms in shades of orange and pink and gold. Cheerful. He set them on the table by the window, along with an insulated bag from which he produced two containers of soup. They steamed when he took the plastic lids off.

"Can I help you up?" he asked, extending a hand. His nails were manicured. Mine were ragged and brittle. I didn't want to see my skin against his; the rough red spot just over the prominence of my wristbone, small now but bound to spread, looked bad enough without the comparison.

"I'm okay," I said, and carefully maneuvered my legs over the edge of the mattress. My chest ached a little; the drugs were all but out of my system, and that included the local anesthetic from the surgery. It was manageable, though. A four at worst.

I couldn't feel the linoleum through the warm socks I wore, their silicone grippers tugging at the floor as I shuffled over to the chair he pulled out for me.

"I heard you had surgery this morning," he said, polite as always.

My hand drifted to the dressing over my port. "Having some issues with the IVs."

"Some of the compounds we're utilizing are rough on the veins," he agreed, sitting down across from me.

"Penelope said that this happens sooner or later, during treatment."

"Usually later," he agreed. "But every patient is different."

I grimaced. "Does it happening this early mean it's going to get worse?"

"It always gets worse," he said, then lifted his chin a bit, gesturing toward my spoon. I hadn't touched it. The scent of the soup enveloped me, spiced beef broth, soft-cooked vegetables. But I wasn't hungry. The *flesh*-scent edged on the gratuitous. I thought I could smell iron, just below the surface.

I swallowed down bile and peered behind him at the whiteboard. We were back to *normal diet*. No way to beg off, then. I dipped my spoon below the murky surface and scooped out a piece of sweet potato. It broke apart in my mouth, delicious and nourishing. My disgust evaporated.

"So, how are you finding it here?" he asked when I'd polished off half the bowl. He'd taken only a few courteous bites of his own. The food, of course, was for my benefit—and he'd almost certainly checked on what I was allowed to eat before he . . .

Bought? Made?

Would he have made me soup himself?

I was getting distracted. "Strange," I answered him, after a moment's concerted thought. "Bad," I added.

His expression turned sadly empathetic. "I'm sorry to hear that. Is there anything I can do?"

Give me my full medical records. The memory of those blacked-out swaths of text hit me hard, and I put down my spoon, fighting off the urge to cover my face with my hands and retreat.

"Margaret."

Meg. I'd told Isobel to call me Meg. Why hadn't I told him? I liked him well enough, wanted him nearby, except . . .

Except maybe I'd picked up on something, some hint not to really trust him, even at my weakest.

I looked at him curiously. "Did you come to visit me, before? A few days ago, after—I passed a clot, apparently." I groped for the words. "Decidual cast?"

I remembered him being there, but only that: a sense of presence, of him observing. No recollection of him *staying*, or interacting with me.

But he shook his head and said, "No, the last week has been a bit busy, I'm afraid."

He was lying.

I looked down at my soup, thoughts racing in two different directions. Hurt, that he hadn't been there when I'd decided he'd cared enough to come. And confusion, because I knew. I *knew* he'd been there.

But if he'd come because he cared, he wouldn't lie about it.

And yet I could think of no other explanation. Voyeurism? Nobody wanted to watch somebody scream and thrash in a hospital bed, unaware of what was real and what wasn't. And that didn't seem like him, anyway.

Then again, I didn't actually know Adam Marsh.

"Margaret?"

"Sorry," I said, voice small. "The meds make me hazy."

One of his hands engulfed mine. "I understand," he said. "You don't need to apologize to me."

"I think you should go." In my nightmare, Adam had walked into Veronica's room, but he wasn't there when I followed. Just her, and the bed. The tongue. The teeth. I was shaking now, and when I stood, Adam stood, too. He took my elbow to steady me. His touch burned, my skin overreacting, nerves lighting up with pain. I jerked away, and for just a moment, I thought I saw anger in his eyes.

Then just frustration. The frustration of anybody forced to deal with an erratic, paranoid invalid. I hated myself. I hated him.

I just wanted to sleep.

I never wanted to sleep again.

"Do you want me to leave?" Adam said, no longer touching me, no longer helping as I shuffled back to my bed and crawled in, drawing the sheets over myself. No tubing attached me to a pole right now. A small indulgence, that freedom of movement, curtailed by my exhaustion and frailty.

I wanted many things, in that moment. Most of all, I wanted my brain to go quiet so that I could enjoy Adam's attention fully. Bask in somebody caring for me who wasn't being paid to.

(He was being paid to. There was just enough distance between me and his paycheck, though, that I could ignore it.)

But my brain wouldn't go quiet. I kept seeing those black boxes in my medical records. "For now," I said.

He packed up the bowls. I watched, wondering which direction I was making a mistake in. "When will you be back?" I asked, helpless to stop my weaker nature, when he was almost at the door.

He looked back at me, and his expression softened. "Soon," he said. "I'll never be far away. I care about what happens to you, Margaret."

I exhaled shakily. "Thank you," I said, and watched him leave.

Something hard pushed into my thigh. Gaze still on the door, I fished in the sheets and found my phone. When it unlocked, it showed the social media search I must have hit GO on when Adam came in.

And there was a hit at the top. I recognized the profile picture. Veronica, smiling, but it must have been before she had entered treatment. Her skin was worse than mine had ever been, rough and red and patchy across her nose. Her eyes were dull, but she was smiling. Happy, regardless of how she must have felt.

I clicked. I stared, wanting to see a post about how relieved she was to be home. Instead, the top post was a link to an event.

JOIN US IN CELEBRATING THE MEMORY OF OUR BELOVED VERONICA MCNEIL.

She was dead.

· Chapter Sixteen ·

"You lied to me."

Isobel didn't stop what she was doing, hanging the next SWAIL IV bag. "I try not to." Her hands moved over the tubing, taking inventory, planning. Barely paying attention to me.

I didn't want whatever was in that bag. "Not just you. Penelope, too. I know Veronica is dead."

Now her hands paused. "Meg..."

"I saw her funeral announcement. And even if I hadn't, I can do the math. She wasn't finished with the protocol. She was too far in to just stop."

Isobel turned to me, chest rising and falling as she took a few shaking breaths. "That's right," she said.

"I *asked* you. And you lied." It hurt so much more, coming from her. Everything hurt more from her. I hated her again in that moment, just like I had the night we'd first met. Why did everything have to be so painful? So difficult?

"Patient confidentiality, Meg," she said.

"The patient is *dead*."

"You knew the risks!" she snapped. "I told you to leave, and you decided to stay. So yes, I lied to you. What good would the truth have done? Scared you? Made you change your mind?"

"Should it?"

"I don't know what you want me to tell you." She keyed open the supply drawer below the computer and pulled out alcohol swabs, a packaged needle. "It's sad. It's a tragedy. She didn't deserve to die. But she did, because when you destroy your immune system, anything can get in." Isobel shook her head, leaning on the cabinet. "We can clean this hospital down to its studs and lock you away in a positive pressure room and never let anybody near you, but that only helps your odds. It doesn't fix the game in your favor."

My anger faded. It left in its wake the exhaustion that was growing so familiar, and I sagged against the pillow I'd brought from home. The pillow, I now realized, that harbored whatever bacteria lived in my house. Bacteria that could kill me, one day.

So that'd have to go, when the time came. And no more flowers from Adam.

Oh, god. The flowers. Had the flowers I'd gathered made Veronica sick?

But Penelope wouldn't have passed them along, not unless it was safe.

Right?

"Are there other patients in the trial? I just . . . I just want somebody to talk to. Somebody who can tell me what comes next." My voice cracked. "Not like you can. From the inside, from living it. That's all I wanted."

It hurt to talk, canker sores on the buccal flesh of my mouth rubbing against my teeth. *The mouth*, I thought again, the bed that was a mouth. I grimaced. Isobel's gaze focused in on my lips, and the frantic energy left her. She was once more the focused professional.

"You're in pain."

"It's fine," I said, not wanting her to care.

"I can do something about that, at least. You've got a standing order for a numbing gel, if you want it."

If you want it.

"Just tell me," I said, flinching as my molar caught one of the sores.

"No," she said. "No, there's nobody else on the ward like you. Everybody else is just using our empty bed space. Meg, do you want the gel?"

There were so few of us with Fayette-Gehret that I'm not sure why I was surprised. But there was so much money in this wing. So much effort on Adam's part. And there couldn't be profit in treating us; I couldn't be the only one who'd blown through all her savings and limped along on a rotating menu of credit card debt.

And there was the paranoia again. That insistent cynical voice pointing out every shadow I could jump at. Reminding me of the redacted portions of my medical records. What was in them? What couldn't I be allowed to see?

(Not just me; who else in the program had access? Who were those notes for?)

I wanted it to go away. I wanted to think about the other potential outcome—that I'd get my life back, if I just suffered a little more, a little worse.

The canker sores were from my old life, though. I didn't need to suffer those.

"Yes," I said, finally. "Fine, yes, I want it."

"I'll be right back," she said.

When I'd signed up, I'd tried to prepare myself for what this would be like. I'd scrolled the shopping lists and skimmed through posts about what a "long-term" hospital stay was like. Of the latter, I'd say that over half were from the perspective of friends and relatives and partners, focusing more on advocating for their loved ones and dealing with commute fatigue than on the experience of the patient in the bed. Two-thirds of the rest were about stays far shorter than mine, three or four days, repeated but quick inpatient visits. The last third were largely written by cancer patients, and even their stays were often shorter than mine was scheduled to be.

The people who stayed this long didn't generally get to write their own advice columns.

Still, they'd covered a lot of what I'd experienced already. The boredom. The strange rhythm of my days, the interruptions, the frustration of trying to get questions answered. The periodic indignities.

Most of them never touched on the deep emotional experience of it, though. The paranoia, if it was there. The potential for grief. The rage.

The way it was hard to determine, sometimes, if you were resting to regain your strength, or giving up and checking out until you could cope again.

Isobel returned, scrubbing her hands in the antechamber and donning a fresh pair of gloves as she entered the room. The little packet of gel and a packaged swab came out of her pocket and got wiped down with antiseptic. She scanned the gel, then my wristband, before finally tearing both open. I watched the whole dance, how precise it was, how practiced.

"Open your mouth," she said.

Exhausted, I complied. The hand not holding the swab steadied my jaw, and I focused on that point of contact as she dabbed the gel over my sore gums, the fake-mint flavor filling my sinuses as she worked.

"I used to work in the ICU," she said, voice soft. "During COVID. I lost so many patients, Meg. I can't—" Her voice caught there, and she swallowed, mastering herself. "I burned out. Badly. I took this job to try to recover, but I'm still working on that."

"Oh." It was muffled around the swab, and it made her withdraw.

"Don't lick it," she said. "Or it'll numb your tongue, too. I'll give you some water to spit with in a second."

I nodded, silent and focused on where my tongue resided in my mouth, and looked over her again, more closely than I had before. She was around my age, close enough that I hadn't registered it at all. Her scrubs were the standard pale blue, not like Penelope's occasional brighter sets, and she didn't wear any makeup. I thought I could see that damage now in the shadows under her eyes, in the defensively firm set of her shoulders, but that may have only been her personality animating her, or the distortions of the lens I was looking through.

And she was beautiful. I felt horrible for noticing it: the way her dark eyebrows, heavy and sharp, set off her honey-brown eyes, the shape of her lips, the line of her neck as she swapped out her gloves again and went back to prepping my infusion. She wasn't here to be beautiful. There had to be some scientific name for it, the psychological predictability of latching on to your caretaker.

Embarrassing is what it was. But if she noticed, she didn't hold it against me.

The pain in my mouth was gone, at least.

At the strike of some internal clock, she got me a little paper cup of water and a basin. "Swish and spit," she said. "It'll probably get on your tongue some, but better that then down your throat." I did as instructed, the spitting causing a momentary pinprick of pain—and then that, too, deadened down. I eased back against my pillow, and after another round of scanning, Isobel leaned over me, opening the collar of my gown to one side.

"What I meant to say," she murmured, "is that I'm sorry."

My day-shift nurse had already accessed the port-a-cath. I'd had to wear a mask while she scrubbed the skin down with antiseptic inside the boundaries of a sterile window drape. I'd tried to figure out the purpose of each step, but she moved quickly. I know she flushed the needle, which had a ninety-degree bend to it, and all the tubing, too, meticulous and steady. The needle bit when it went into my chest, but once in, I couldn't feel it at all. There was a small disc of something she slid between the needle and my skin. The top was blue. And then she covered the whole thing with Tegaderm and labeled it with date, time, and her initials.

I would've preferred it if Isobel had been the one to do it. Pathetic, but I tried to forgive myself. It was just so—intimate.

Isobel hooking up the drip wasn't quite as intense, but she was still close, hovering above me. "I'm... tender," she said. "Rough around the edges. Sometimes I say things—sometimes I'm not as professional as I should be. I can talk to Charge and have somebody else swap in as your main night nurse, if you'd like. I'm not sure I'm doing you much good." She gave me a pained smile.

"I had this fantasy," I confessed, speaking without any sort of planning, with barely any decision to tell at all. "That while I was here, it would be uncomfortable, sure, but it would be—simpler." *That I'd be cared for.* I didn't say that part, I knew how pathetic I'd sound. I knew she might not even understand what I meant, the difference I was trying to articulate. "But I'm always afraid. Or—not afraid, but nervous. Paranoid. There are so many pieces in motion and I can't see *any* of them."

"I understand," Isobel said, leaving the close space just above my chest and moving to the pump to program it. "It's hard, trusting other people who are only there to do their jobs."

"That's not what I meant," I said, and then I felt it, the new medication flowing into me, starting far deeper than it had before. I shivered. "I don't know what I mean. It's just . . ."

But the words wouldn't come.

"A hospital is an organism, too," Isobel said, after a moment. "The people in it keep it clean, keep it fed, keep it alive. And the health of the hospital is the health of its inhabitants."

Alive. Alive, like in my nightmare. Pulsing. Oozing.

(She knew. She knew, even then.)

Her jaw moved side to side, an unconscious nervous tic, her gaze focused past me to the window. The lights were on, but dimmed, and we could almost see the outside world. I wonder if she'd ever had a dream like mine before.

"Normally patients don't see much of that. They're here for a short time, or they've got other concerns, bigger concerns. But the longer you're here, the more you'll see. Unfortunate deaths, accidents, mistakes, people checked out to the point of malignancy. Maybe that's what you're responding to. You're plugged into an organism that's bigger than you, and as part of it, there are aspects of your health that are out of your control, that you can't even comprehend. That we either want to or have to shield you from."

Then she paused and looked back at me, gaze unwavering. "Or maybe I'm projecting my own issues on you. But—believe me when I promise I'm doing all I can for *you*. You are my patient. You are my responsibility. I can't say that what happened to Veronica won't happen to you, but I can promise to do everything in my power to stop it."

She looked like nothing so much as a medieval knight, taking a chivalric oath to fight back against an uncontrollable, darkening world. I should have laughed. Or maybe I should have broken down and told her what I'd dreamed of.

I did neither. I just leaned into it, the warmth of her regard, her fervor.

"Thank you," I said. And for a time, it was almost enough.

· Chapter Seventeen ·

I had another blood transfusion in the morning, this time successfully, and as another week passed, I regained some of my strength. The medication still shrouded me in fog for several hours a day, and my body developed new aches, new pains, new raw spots, but I was able to shower without assistance, and even read on occasion. I visited the lounge more days than not, though I had to wear a mask whenever I left my room now.

I never asked about Veronica, or my medical records. I didn't know where to begin. And as the days passed, they buried her.

Several evenings, before shift change, I stared at my phone and considered calling my mom. I got as far as selecting her name in my contacts list. But I felt like I was finding my footing. Adjusting in a way that I hadn't been able to before, in the chaos of those first days of med corrections and learning the rhythm of the ward, in the drama of my port insertion and Veronica's death. Now, the days were manageable. Isobel was there three nights in a row, then Louise for a night, then another floater, and soon Isobel was back. I could rely on that rhythm, and the rhythm made the paranoia recede.

I even began to feel . . .

Cared for.

And that was new. Intoxicating. Rationed out to me a bit at a time, in Isobel's assiduous attendance to little quality-of-life things: more numbing gel, making sure my robe got laundered and returned to me, setting me up with a custom blend of beverages from the patient nutrition stock.

I clung to every scrap and tried to ignore all the discomforts she couldn't fix.

"You should start taking longer walks," Penelope said one day. "Now that you're feeling a little better."

She said it while typing notes into the computer by the bedside. I looked up from where I'd been fussing with my phone, fresh out of a shower. "What?"

"More than just to the lounge, if you think you're up to it. We don't want you to decondition," she said. "Dr. Santos always recommends his patients take a walk at least once a day before lockdown, side effects allowing. Your dizziness is mostly gone, isn't it?"

It was. In its place was a persistent lack of appetite, and the last two nights I'd sweated through my sheets and blanket, but nobody seemed worried about that.

"Where would I go?"

"Anywhere in the hospital," she said, smiling.

I frowned, alarmed. "What if something happens?"

"Do you think something will?"

I licked my cracked lips; hospital air was dry, and no amount of ChapStick could stop my desiccation, it seemed. "No," I said, hesitantly. "But . . ."

"Just wear your mask, and take it slow. Your wristband will make sure you come back to us, if you fall or get disoriented."

"And I guess the gown's a giveaway."

"You don't have anything else on the docket today," she said. "Would it feel better to wear real clothing?"

I stared. "That's an option?" I asked.

"Sometimes."

A shock of fury, deep down; Isobel had never told me that. Nobody had, but of all of them, Isobel should have been first to volunteer it. But when I pushed back on that anger, I could see the logic: Most days, I was being poked and prodded at unpredictable intervals. Most days, I'd barely gotten myself to the toilet on my own more than once or twice. Most days, it wouldn't have made any sense. And at night, I was meant to rest.

And there was the inertia to think of, too.

(But didn't Isobel promise she was doing everything she could to protect me? Didn't losing strength fly in the face of that? But maybe, in her mind, my room was the safest option. Even a mask wasn't a guarantee. I was more than two weeks into SWAIL, and lockdown was no doubt coming up swiftly.)

"It'd feel better," I finally said, a little choked up. I put on as brave a face as I could manage, and even though Penelope saw straight through me, she didn't say anything. She just helped me maneuver out of my gown and back into the clothes I'd worn the day I was admitted. Jeans, a loose short-sleeved top, sandals. Maybe too cold for the hospital, but I didn't care. Even the pinch of my bra felt magical.

I gazed at myself in the mirror above the utility sink by the antechamber door. My skin was already clearing from its most recent psoriatic flare, faster than it ever had before. I remembered Veronica mentioning the same. My body was slowly ceasing its assault on itself.

I looked almost healthy. But there were still hints: I held myself gingerly, and my hands shook when I wasn't paying attention. The skin beneath my eyes looked thin and bruised. My scalp was visibly pink and a little bumpy from old plaques, even as my hair grew longer.

But most people wouldn't notice. Or, if they did, it wouldn't be conscious. I could blend in, if I wanted to.

"Just be back in time to tell food services what you want for dinner," Penelope said, handing me an N95, and then sent me on my way.

The elevator was only an elevator. No feelings of doom accompanied me into it. I had to shuffle aside to make room for a few people in scrubs, and a visitor (or a wandering or discharged patient, I suppose, but they looked plugged into the wider world), and it was so strange, being so close to other people. People who weren't there *for* me. People who looked right past me because I was just another passenger, not because I was lying awkwardly in a hospital bed.

When the elevator doors opened on the ground floor, the people in scrubs went one way, chattering about somebody's time-off request, and the visitor went another. I barely got up the nerve to disembark before the next round of passengers was boarding, and I slid out past the small queue.

The last two times I'd been here, after evening shift change, the visitors and outpatients had all cleared out. Any staff still working had been tucked up on their specific floors, the gift shop and cafeteria all shuttered for the night. But now, the lobby and the hallways leading to labs and pharmacies and the other tower, so much wider than the ward hallways above, were full. Conversations, muted but omnipresent, washed over me. People occupied the chairs by the planters, people sat out on a patio formed by the convolutions of the building, people flowed past me in all directions.

I walked as if in a dream once more. It was almost too much. Overstimulating. I'd gotten out of practice, dealing with humanity. God, there were just *so many people*.

The patient lounge on the ward wasn't always empty, but we were, all of us, rather ghostly. Quiet, inwardly focused. Not sociable, not . . . normal. Not just living.

And outside, the sun was shining. A bus rumbled past. People pulled into the drop-off arc, pulled away, came to and from the parking garage that squatted across the street.

The world spun on, more enticing than I'd ever found it before.

And the doors . . .

The doors were right there.

My phone was in my pocket. My wallet, too, and I realized with a small lurch that I hadn't thought about my wallet in weeks. There'd been no reason to. Whole aspects of my life before had been closed off, rooms shut up against the passage of time. What was I going to do with it, order a GET WELL SOON balloon for myself from the gift shop?

I could leave, though. Not even pause to check myself out. A week ago, I would've done it. When Veronica's death was fresh, when I was still so overwhelmed, I would have taken the chance.

But the Tegaderm pulled at my skin when I moved, reminding me of the port-a-cath sitting quiet on my chest. I couldn't leave with that still inside me; who could I go to, to remove it? Supposedly it would be stable for months, maybe even years, but there was still the risk of infection.

Infection.

That risk was everywhere. I scanned the lobby, eyeing an elderly woman hunched over in her wheelchair, a toddler with a racking cough, the throng in the open-air waiting zone for blood draws and other labs. Sniffles, coughs, muffled sounds of discomfort; I wasn't in the ER, but everybody around me was at the hospital for a reason. Outpatient procedure, visiting a sick relative, preparing for admission—

A cough erupted from my throat, coarse and unexpected. Not the light cough of a passing irritant, but deep and central. I covered my mouth reflexively, palm brushing over my mask, then pushed my hand against my sternum. My eyes watered faintly.

I was becoming a fucking hypochondriac.

It was just the slow shifting of my symptoms, I told myself. I knew how to handle my bowels, my skin, but SWAIL was slowly changing all of that. Yes, I was at risk, but the risk wasn't so elevated. I wasn't in lockdown yet.

Penelope wouldn't have let me out if it wasn't still safe, surely.

I was anonymous as I made myself do a circuit of the public areas on the ground floor. I found I grew winded quickly and had to walk slower than my natural gait. *Decondition*, Penelope had said, and I had. I was shocked when I had to sit down at another bank of planters and benches. Medication side effects I could understand, and the usual weaknesses of my body, but how had walking become so difficult, so quickly?

Then again, was it really so surprising? I hadn't walked farther than the lounge in the last two weeks. I'd barely showered at times. My ability to stay vertical was occasionally... dubious.

It made more sense now that bad luck could have killed Veronica even while she was on the way back up. She must have been weaker than I was.

Had she taken walks, before lockdown?

I should have gone to see her again, after my trip to the garden. I should have done a lot of things differently. Arguably, I should have walked out of the hospital that day instead of taking the coward's choice. But if somebody would have listened to my lungs, they probably would have found it was already too late.

· Chapter Eighteen ·

GRACEVIEW MEMORIAL

Room:	775	Phone	XXX-XXX-2775
Date:	August 29, 2023	\multicolumn{2}{l	}{MON (TUES) WED THURS FRI SAT SUN}
Patient:	Margaret Culpepper	\multicolumn{2}{c	}{PAIN SCALE}
Doctor:	Santos	\multicolumn{2}{c	}{1 (2) 3 4 5 6 7 8 9 10}
Nurse:	Shannon L.	Pain medication last given:	0800
Charge Nurse:	Tristan P.	Next dose:	1200
\multicolumn{4}{c	}{Today's Plan! SWAIL continues ☺ New testing!}
Diet:	Normal	Fall Risk:	Low
Activity Level:	Normal	Our goal is to have you discharged on:	September 30, 2023
\multicolumn{4}{c	}{Prevent falling! Call for help getting out of bed.}

I did eventually make my way back up to the seventh floor, in time to order dinner. I ate it, even though I wanted nothing more than to collapse into a hopefully dreamless sleep. With each bite, I thought about *being sick*. About all the different things those words could encompass. Most of the people in my life weren't quite sure how to categorize me. When I first started having problems, *sick* came easily to their lips. But now, with it so settled in, without the trappings of contagion or an easily parsed diagnosis of cancer, *was* I sick?

Was I making myself sick now?

Would I only be sick if I came down with some cold? If I developed pneumonia? What if I just got a UTI from not wanting to get up to pee on the days I was so exhausted I could barely chew?

Isobel wasn't on shift that night, and I couldn't open up to Louise. I tried to sleep. I woke up twice soaked in frigid sweat, but when Louise checked, I wasn't running a fever.

"I'll tell the doctor," she said. She didn't sound worried, so I tried not to be, either.

The doctor ordered a wider panel of labs.

"He's just being cautious," Louise assured me. My five a.m. blood draw was expanded by a few vials, with festive red and gold caps, and Louise took a swab of my nasal passage and my throat. I had to give a fresh urine sample.

I didn't cough during any of it, and maybe I forgot about it. Maybe I wrote it off. Maybe I was afraid to look directly at it. I didn't feel sick, just tired. My body was falling apart, but wasn't that the point? I suffered through the pokes and prods, gave what was needed, and forced myself to eat half the breakfast that I had ordered. Some distant memory of my grandmother saying, *You need to keep your strength up*, pushed me on, even though the oatmeal tasted and felt like glue.

"Well?" I asked when Shannon, my day-shift nurse who

was usually charge (at least according to my whiteboard), popped in with a small bag of neon-yellow fluid.

"Nothing conclusive," she said, hanging it beside the bag of saline they'd had running into me all morning. I'd already had to pee twice. I watched as she swapped the yellow stuff in its place.

"Banana bag," she said, when she caught me staring. "Favorite of emergency departments everywhere. Some of your levels are a bit uneven, which might be contributing to the fatigue. At best, it'll perk you up. At worst, you'll just get to enjoy some fluorescent pee." It was clearly trained patter. I wondered where she'd transferred from. If she was here recovering, like Isobel was.

"I'm going to leave this to run for a few hours," she said. "And by the time it runs out, hopefully we'll have more answers. Do you need anything?"

I shook my head. The pump resumed its clicking, and the line turned from clear to yellow. Shannon made a few final notes on the computer, and I settled into myself.

The banana bag didn't feel like much of anything going in. I eyed the TV remote that I rarely used, then grabbed my phone instead. I'd finished a book on the language of cults and moved on to a romance novel, but it wasn't grabbing me. I'd run through all of that one guy's videos, but I was hopeful for a new post.

There wasn't. When I reflexively opened up my social media, though, there was an alert asking if I wanted to RSVP to Veronica's memorial. I closed out of the app entirely, feeling vaguely ill.

Before I could overanalyze the low-grade nausea in my gut, I heard the door beyond the antechamber open, and Adam's voice, saying, "Knock knock. May I come in?"

He sounded tentative. I hadn't seen him since I'd sent him away a week ago, and I felt a momentary throb of shame. But then, he'd lied to me, too. He must have known Veronica had died. Perhaps it was best he'd stayed away. Perhaps I should have kept him away then, too.

Isobel was right, though. What would telling me have done? Could I hold corporate confidentiality against him?

And I had missed his company, as embarrassing as that was. The way Isobel made me feel, noticed and valued—he'd been the first to make me feel like that. I wanted them both, if I was honest with myself.

"Sure," I said. My voice was rough from lack of sleep, but I'd managed a shower between the second time I woke up drenched in sweat and now. My sheets no longer reeked of me. I set my phone aside.

Adam was in another of his suits, though his tie was loosened, his hair less neatly ordered. Casual Friday Adam, perhaps, though a glance at my whiteboard showed me it was Tuesday. He held another flower arrangement, this one a frothing collection of ferns, some golden on the underside with latent spores, topped with lobes of purple-blue hydrangeas. Veronica would have loved it. "By the bed?" he asked.

"The windowsill, maybe?"

I glanced over to see if there was space.

Veronica sat in one of the chairs.

She was dressed in her hospital gown, her long hair pulled

back from her face. It was marked by patches of red ulcers, raw and wet. Livid. Her chest rose and fell, every rib visible as they pressed against her emaciated frame.

Confused, I twisted back to face the door, but Adam was gone. There were no flowers, no fronds, no sign of him at all. Veronica, by contrast, remained exactly where she'd been when I looked again.

She gazed outside, at the mountain, at the green trees, and I found myself gazing with her. I hadn't noticed the view in days; had it always been so beautiful?

But why was I thinking about the view at all, with her corpse so close to me?

It's not real, I told myself. But it wasn't comforting. Not real, but I was perceiving it all the same: the iron bite in the air, the spots of rot along the window frame.

It didn't matter that Adam was gone. Likely, he'd never been there in the first place.

Was I alone? Had there been something else in that banana bag? But why not tell me first?

Veronica turned from the window, looking directly at me. One of her eyes was bloodshot. My heart ached, even as my skin crawled.

"I went looking for you," I said. "The other day. I'm—I'm sorry." Why was I so fast to apologize? Why, even when I was frightened, did I feel so responsible for her?

"It's not your fault," she said. And was I imagining it, or did her rasping voice linger on *your*?

No. I was imagining things. "Is that why you're here? To forgive me?"

Veronica shook her head and rose from her seat. Her legs

were so thin, they looked like the bones would snap if she took a single step.

"He brings you flowers, too?" Veronica asked. She was closer now. No steps taken at all, just there, then here beside me, close enough that I could smell the living rot of her. Her breath was sour-sweet, the fermenting apple scent of ketoacidosis.

Flowers.

The flowers were just beside us, bright and alive. But Adam had disappeared; how had they gotten there? I stared at them, at the golden discs of spores, at the gaps between the hydrangea petals.

Her fingers brushed over the blooms, and they wilted, browned, fell apart.

I followed the path of each petal, transfixed, teetering on the edge of—something. An incomplete thought, scratching at my gray matter. He brought me flowers. He brought us both flowers. But we were both his patients.

No, wrong word.

Projects. We were projects. He wasn't a doctor, a nurse, anything medical. He brought us flowers. He . . .

I looked up.

Veronica was no longer there. In her place was Adam, looming over my hospital bed. There was an alarm going off, and I didn't understand.

"What happened?" I asked, my voice cludgy and slurring.

"An absence seizure," Adam said. He clasped my hand. I was so weak, sagging against him, shaking.

"No," I said. "No, no, I— Veronica—"

Veronica had suffered absence seizures. Veronica had been here. She'd sat in the chair Adam usually chose. She'd been right there, and I couldn't stop hearing her words, over and over again.

I tugged at the fabric of his shirt; he'd shed his suit jacket at some point while I was lost in my own skull. In response, Adam drew me against him. It was wrong, it was too much.

He was my fucking pharma rep. (Not a doctor. Not a nurse. What had I been trying to figure out?)

I fought that added contact, scrabbling away. The banana bag IV was still plugged into my port. The tubing tugged, and the IV pole skittered on the floor.

"Shh," he murmured. "You're okay."

"Stop touching me!"

"Do you really want that?"

All I could think of was Veronica's bed, the tongue. How it had held her, swallowed her. What was happening to me? It was like I lived in two different realities: the rot of the hospital in my hallucinations and the pristine room that was the actual location of my care.

I started to cry.

I clung to him when he made a token move to give me space, curling up in the shelter of his body. I couldn't stand to be alone, not then. My boundaries crumbled.

There were other voices in the room. We weren't alone.

"Give us some space," Shannon said. "Sorry, Mr. Marsh, I'm going to need to kick you out. Margaret, look at me, please."

I shook my head. The alarms were still loud.

"I'll be back tomorrow," he promised. "It's okay. You'll be okay. Just breathe."

His cologne clung to me. It burned in my throat, but that

was almost welcome. His hands covered mine and made me release my death grip on his shirt.

"I want to go home," I whimpered.

"Not today," he said, so kindly it only made my heartbreak worse. But I let go of him, feeling small against my hospital bed. I stared at him as he fell back behind Shannon and two other people I didn't recognize. I watched him, even as a light shone into my eyes, even as my care team began taking inventory. I was here, in bed. He was there, disappearing into the antechamber, out into the hall. He was there, walking away.

They were calling something out over the PA system. I could hear my room number. *Priority page.*

The flowers he'd brought me sat beside my bed, just where Veronica had touched them.

I don't remember if they were still whole.

Chapter Nineteen

More tests.

I calmed down sometime during that first examination, but it remains a haze. They probably administered some kind of anxiety med. Nothing strong enough to drop me insensate to the mattress, but enough to take the edge off. To help me be compliant as they wheeled my bed from my room, into the elevator, down to imaging. I remember being slid into the CT machine, and then my hair being combed and shaved out of the way, leads sticking to my newly bared skin.

It was too late, though. Whatever I'd seen was long gone, and with it, any evidence of the seizure.

Nobody ever asked me what I saw. I suppose that isn't relevant to a diagnosis.

They added a yellow band to my wrist. "Increased fall risk," Shannon explained as she updated my whiteboard to match. "Until we know if you're likely to have another seizure."

"That might be the only one?"

"It might," she said, noncommittal, heavily implying that it was unlikely.

"When it happened to Veronica," I ventured, "she was already in the rebuild phase."

"Try not to worry about it," Shannon told me. That kind smile of hers looked more like pity in the late-afternoon light.

"I didn't even get a dose of SWAIL today," I continued, half desperate for a real answer, half wondering how she'd respond.

Her answer was the snap of her pulling off her gloves. "You should get some rest," she said, breezing past everything I'd said. "Use the CALL button if you need anything."

Beside me, the pump went *tick tick tick*, back on normal saline with a bolus of anti-seizure medication.

At least, that's what she'd told me.

I felt better when shift change came and Isobel was back.

"It can happen at any time during treatment," she said when I asked about the timing, without any evasion. "You'd have to ask a neurologist about the mechanism, but I imagine it's less about an immediate reaction to the medication and more about long-term changes. It's not just the presence or lack thereof of your immune system that does it."

I eyed the cooler waiting beside my bed. "'Long-term changes,'" I said. "As in, the seizures might just keep happening?"

"I couldn't tell you," she said, and I believed her. That didn't make me any more confident, but at least she wasn't lying to me.

"We don't have to start immediately," she added, when I didn't look away from the box holding my next round of potential torture. "Do you want to eat something first?"

I'd gotten a sandwich for dinner, but had only managed a

few bites of it. Shannon had cleared the tray away, and hadn't mentioned it at shift change, but either she'd told Isobel outside my room, or Isobel had gotten to know me too well.

"Not really," I said, leaning back in my bed.

"Could you?" she pressed.

I groaned. "Yeah, sure."

"I'll be right back."

She was gone for just a few minutes, minutes I spent staring at the ceiling and wondering why the hell I was doing this to myself.

Had it really been all that bad before? I hadn't been able to work, but maybe I hadn't tried enough. Maybe there were still lifestyle changes I could have made. Maybe . . . maybe . . .

Isobel was back before I could figure out that next maybe. She set two glass containers on the table by the window, then came to fetch me from the bed. That fucking yellow bracelet meant I wasn't supposed to get up by myself, even with her right there in the room, even though I was feeling fine.

But her hands were warm and strong. I almost leaned into her, then remembered how pathetically clingy I'd been with Adam and stopped myself.

"I was expecting a cup of broth," I said, as I got a better look at the very familiar dishes.

"Mr. Marsh left these in our fridge for you," she said, easing me into the chair.

"I guess Shannon forgot about them?"

"Something like that."

I mulled that over as I popped the lids off the containers. The lids were different colors, but the contents were identical; he must have left his own portion along with mine. Tonight's offering was the most elaborate yet. Salad with duck breast, cooked medium rare and sliced thin, all drizzled with some sort of citrus sauce. A few wedges of clementine, what looked like pomegranate arils. It smelled heavenly, but my stomach still barely stirred. I definitely couldn't eat both.

"Have you had dinner?" I asked.

Isobel was hovering at my elbow. I expected a quick affirmative, or a deflection. Instead, she shrugged. "Energy drink and a meal bar," she said. "Breakfast of champions."

I'd never given much thought to how working night shift might skew the rhythm of her day. But I'd been there, too, sleep cycle all out of whack, my day starting as the sun was beginning to set. I pushed one of the dishes across the little table.

"Here's a morning snack, then," I said, then added, "Please?"

I expected her to say no. And she did hesitate. Boundaries between patient and nurse, maybe. Even I felt awkward, once the words were out of my mouth. But after a moment, she sat down and reached for one of the plastic forks she'd brought in. "If you insist," she said.

And then relaxed, the lines of her face easing, her eyes luminous in the lowered lights of my room in the evening.

"First dinner date in a while?" I asked, then mentally kicked myself.

She laughed. "First time eating real food in a while that's not from the cafeteria. Penelope's mentioned your lunches with Mr. Marsh before. I figured he must be bringing something good."

I considered this. "I had the impression you didn't like

him," I said, eventually, though I couldn't place my finger on any one instance.

"I think he shouldn't be hovering in my unit," Isobel said, mixing up her salad. I followed suit. "It makes some of the nurses uneasy. And there's always the question of who's really in charge, him or Dr. Santos. But he's a nice enough man." She popped a bite of duck into her mouth, and I tried not to watch the way her lips and jaw moved as she chewed. The way her throat shifted as she swallowed. "He seems to make you more comfortable. Veronica, too."

I blushed and ducked my head. "It's . . . nice to have somebody on the outside who cares."

"I wouldn't say he's on the outside, exactly. But I know what you're trying to say." She speared a clementine wedge. "You don't have to answer me, but have you given any thought to telling people you're here? Family, friends. Coworkers."

I was chewing on a small forkful of salad, an aril crunching between my teeth. The canker sores had almost all healed up, and the acidic dressing stung only lightly. I barely felt it as I swallowed, blood rushing in my ears. I still didn't want her to know how thoroughly I'd been abandoned, but she'd already figured it out, hadn't she? She'd seen right through my excuse.

And the weight of keeping up appearances was so heavy. The scales tipped, and for once, it was easier to lay myself bare.

"I don't think anybody would come," I said.

Isobel frowned. "Nobody?"

"I alienated a lot of people, when I got sick," I said. It was easier to look at my salad than at her. "The ones that were willing to put up with a nebulous *something's wrong*, I eventually turned on." Not directly, not about being sick, but about other things. One canceled plan at the last minute? They were disrespecting my time, no matter the reason. Talking about a promotion at work or a lucky break with a hobby? They were dominating the conversation, leaving no room for me. I'd lost Jess that way, and Rory, and Michael. If I'd gotten over myself just a little, maybe they would've stayed.

"I hated everything that was happening to me, and I guess I decided they were part of it," I added, wincing. I hadn't thought about it this clearly in months. Maybe a year, since the last break. And then what about the rest? The friends who hadn't gotten sick and tired of me being sick and tired, the ones who had the stamina to go the distance?

They'd pitied me.

Or I'd thought they'd pitied me. Believing me meant seeing how pathetic I was, and who could respect me after that?

Really, all I'd wanted was to be better. I could see that now. I didn't want anybody to see me vulnerable.

And that was still true. It was just easier when I didn't know my nurses. When my doctor came by only rarely and half the time when I was sleeping. Now, with Isobel listening to me, no longer eating, I felt the beginnings of that fury rising up again.

No. Not this time. I wasn't going down that road willingly. I took a deep breath. I made myself eat more of the salad, even though my stomach felt as if it were packed with ashes. And Isobel let me, getting up only to fetch my tumbler of water from my bedside tray.

"It used to be," she said a little while later, "that immunocompromised patients couldn't have things like fresh fruit.

Raw produce of any kind, really. Mostly an issue in oncology wards and with AIDS patients."

I relaxed as she spoke. The subject change was entirely obvious and wholly appreciated.

"We've gotten better at finding a balance of what's palatable versus what's low infection risk. You're going to be on what's called a neutropenic diet."

I snorted into my salad. She lifted a brow, and I almost laughed for real.

"It means 'associated with a deficiency of neutrophils,' which are a type of white blood cell. Get your mind out of the gutter." She said it with such gravitas, too. "Your food's just going to be cooked and processed and pasteurized. No runny eggs, no blue cheese, no *unwashed* produce. Less fun, but not terrible."

"And is Adam going to stop bringing food?" I asked, sobering. I did appreciate the meals, even when I couldn't enjoy them.

"He can bring it, but I won't be giving it to you. Same with the flowers, unfortunately."

The flowers.

I twisted in my seat to look for them. In the half-light, they were more shape than color. *He brings you flowers, too*, my brain's misfiring neurons had said. Or, no, it had been a question, hadn't it? Like Veronica was realizing something?

I shook it off. A seizure wasn't a vision. It was only my brain acting out a hodgepodge of ideas from my memories. I'd been paranoid from the moment I checked myself into the hospital. No wonder that my brain chemistry was trying to make it worse.

Turning back to Isobel, I asked, "Those flowers I got from the garden. I told Penelope to give them to Veronica. They never made it, did they?"

"No," she said. "But we told her. She appreciated it."

We were quiet after that, a few heartbeats of remembrance. I tried not to think of the apparition of her beside my bed.

"Will I be alone?" I asked, eventually. "When the lockdown happens."

"No. I'll have to limit my time in here, and wear PPE to be safe, but I'll be available. We'll use the video chat system linked to the antechamber."

I wet my lips. "That system didn't work, though. With Veronica."

"It's not perfect. We're not gods." Her tone had sharpened, but she caught herself, shaking her head. "Sometimes there's something you're already carrying. Lower your defenses, it rears up. Shingles is pretty common. Have you had chicken pox?"

I subconsciously scratched my arm. "Not sure," I said.

"I can check your records," she offered. But I shook my head and made myself eat another bite of my dinner. I chewed mechanically.

Things were only going to get worse here. I'd known that. I'd even adjusted to that. But the seizure was new, and maybe permanent. There was no guarantee it wouldn't happen again. Even ignoring the looming specter of Veronica's death, pushing forward with this wouldn't just be unpleasant; it might change me for the rest of my life.

And for what?

Maybe it was the quiet in the wake of the day's drama that

did it. That made leaving seem like a possibility again. Not something considered in the heat of the moment, but quietly, thoughtfully.

"How long would it take," I asked, after I'd swallowed, "to get better again? If I discontinued treatment tomorrow? How long would I be vulnerable for?"

Isobel's container was empty now, and she sat back, chewing and thinking. The golden glow of streetlights below my room lit her from beneath, gilding the line of her chin. "Not too long, I don't think. At a certain point, your body will become incapable of creating the white blood cells and other building blocks it needs to mount a defense, which is when we flip to rebuilding. But you're not there yet, so you shouldn't need help for it to bounce back." She looked me over, gaze dropping to my port, to my otherwise clear skin. "With the disclaimer that I'm not a doctor, and I'm certainly not *your* doctor, I'd say you should be okay if you wore a mask and stayed away from people as much as possible for, say, three to four weeks?"

"And when the GI issues and psoriasis flare back up, I'll know I'm recovered?"

"Something like that. I'd give it another week to be safe, but that's just me."

"*Would* it be safe? With just a mask?" It seemed impossible, but cancer patients went home every day, didn't they? And I'd gone the whole pandemic without getting sick, not just dodging COVID but the flu and the common cold, too, for over two years. Working freelance remotely had its benefits.

I didn't have an apartment to go home to, of course. But . . . I could always call my mom. Or even somebody else, local bridges I could rebuild. And long-term stay motels weren't that expensive, were they?

"You could do it," Isobel said.

I could.

And I would.

· Chapter Twenty ·

Isobel started the discharge process.

"It's going to take a while," she warned me. "Medically and administratively. You'll probably need another Neuro consult to develop an outpatient management plan in case your seizures continue, and there's going to be paperwork to discontinue SWAIL. Don't be surprised if Mr. Marsh tries to convince you to stay."

"There aren't many test subjects available," I said, with a grim little laugh. Inside, though, I wasn't so amused. Was there any truth to that? That his kindness was an act he'd drop when I was no longer a source of data?

"Margaret," he said a few hours later, shortly after shift change, "I just want you to be sure. If you stop now, everything you've gone through will have been for nothing. You're almost to the halfway point. If I—if SWAIL can make you better . . ." He trailed off, frowning.

His concern *looked* genuine. I wanted to believe it, even while I also wanted him to be helping me on my way.

"I'm sure," I said. "I'm sorry, I didn't fully understand the risks. Now I do."

He covered my hand with his, without hesitating, without checking to see if I minded. I remembered crying against him. Clinging to him. It was so tempting, to do that again, but I made myself stay put. "I should never have introduced you to Veronica," he said, after a moment. "What happened to her was a tragedy. But it's not common. I can get you the numbers."

"Based off how many patients?" I asked. "Somehow I think your sample size isn't useful just yet."

A muscle in his jaw twitched. I'd hit something tender with that.

Discharge took most of the day. I had to wait for the neurologist, then for Dr. Santos, then for another quick round of tests. Adam came and went, too. There were multiple rounds of paperwork and Penelope walking me through patient education.

"Do you have somebody available to drive you home?" she asked.

"No," I said, "but I'll just call a car. It's fine." I didn't mention my lack of apartment, and when I had to put down an address, I put down my mom's, even though it was half the country away.

"I can connect you with a social worker," she said. "It's standard."

"I'd rather not." I just wanted to be gone.

Between visits, I stared at my phone, mentally drafting a text to my mom. I wouldn't be going to her place, but I needed to tell her. I needed to tell a lot of people.

By lunch, I was waiting on the removal of my port. The incision wasn't fully healed yet, which should have made it quick, but the interventional radiology suite they needed to do it wasn't going to be available for another half hour. I'd finally texted my mother. *I'm all done*, I'd said. *Didn't work. I gave them your address so you might get some mail.*

She was going to insist on flying out, and I was going to have to argue her down again. But maybe it would be worth it, to have her here. I was going to need *some* help, if only to go to apartment showings with a functional immune system in my stead. Except I'd need to spend all my time and limited energy soothing her, catering to her, reassuring her that she was doing the right thing.

I wasn't willing to go that far.

I was scrolling through my contacts list, considering for the fifth time who was most likely to let me hole up in their guest room after months without contact, when I coughed.

It was a small thing, and I cleared my throat, shaking it off. There was Liam, I reasoned; I'd met him through a local book club I'd tried attending, and though I'd stopped going after two sessions, we'd kept in touch enough for him to flirt with me by text, for me to tell him I wasn't interested, and for him to recover admirably and move on to occasional exchanges about interesting Reddit posts. We weren't close, but that was good. I hadn't blown up on him, or retreated from him.

Katie was another option; I'd just ghosted her. But I knew she'd bought a house, so she'd probably have the space.

It'd be a big ask, either way. But I'd checked my bank account, and the longer I could put off paying for a motel room, the better. I'd be getting paid a small fraction of what I'd counted on for getting this far in SWAIL, and it would take a week or more to process.

It would have been easier to stay a little longer. I'd almost changed my mind, but—

Another cough interrupted my train of thought.

And then another.

What started as a small, weak cough grew and grew until I was convulsing with the force of it. Fine one minute, and hunched over in bed the next. I squeezed my eyes shut and breathed through it, diaphragm spasming, until, at last, it passed.

When I opened my eyes again, I saw blood.

Blood spattered on the white sheet over my legs. Soaking into the fabric, beading on the screen of my phone. My lips felt slick, and when I reached up with one trembling hand to touch them, my fingers came away wet and red.

I stared at them. My ribs twitched with another nascent round of coughing. I thought of a hundred classic novels and movies, fainting heroines, blood on handkerchiefs.

Unseeing, I groped for the nurse CALL button. I hit it, the summoning bleep filling my head, fighting against the thumping of my pulse.

"Hello, nurses' station. What do you need?"

"I—I think—"

Don't tell them. I could hide this. I just had to make it through my port removal. I was going *home*. But the blood was so red, and before I could apologize, before I could say anything at all, I descended into another coughing fit.

"I'll be right there."

No, no, *no*, this couldn't be happening. Coughing turned to sobbing, my flesh convulsing, hunching in. My chest burned. My eyes burned. The door to my room opened, and

Shannon was there, and Penelope. They eased me against the bed, quickly taking inventory. Penelope went and grabbed a mask.

"She's got a fever," Shannon said. I heard it as if through a tunnel, staring up at the ceiling as they worked, as the cold metal of a stethoscope pressed to my twitching chest. I sucked down a slow, deep breath, fighting back the tears and another threatened coughing fit.

Whatever Penelope heard had her pulling back and exchanging a long, silent glance with Shannon.

But I knew. Healthy people didn't cough up blood.

"I want to go home," I said, voice soft.

Penelope just looked sad.

Eventually, after blood work and a chest X-ray, they left me alone again. The coughing had subsided, the tears had run dry, and I sat there, scrubbing at my phone screen, trying to get the last faint streaks of blood off the glass.

My mom had responded to my text, finally. *What???? Call me.* But I couldn't do it.

The TV screen in my room turned on. Adam looked out at me from it, grim. "Hello, Margaret." He hadn't bothered coming into the room. The door to the antechamber was firmly shut. "Your discharge has been put on hold," he told me. "I'm so sorry."

"What's happening?" I asked. I already knew, but I needed to hear it. I needed to take the blow from somebody outside myself.

"They're going to have to run some more tests," Adam said, "but your symptoms are consistent with tuberculosis."

I shut my eyes. Took a deep breath and resisted the urge to cough again.

"I want to talk to Dr. Santos."

"He's not available right now, but he'll be by later. Margaret—"

"I want to go *home*."

Adam shook his head. "You need treatment. In your current state, this could be deadly."

He was right, but I didn't hear him. I was stopping SWAIL. My "current state" was temporary. Everything was going to go back to normal. I'd take antibiotics, maybe come back for a few outpatient follow-ups. People didn't die from tuberculosis anymore. Did they?

(They did when they had wrecked immune systems. But mine wasn't supposed to be that bad yet. I wasn't on lockdown.)

"Let us take care of you," Adam said. The field of view through the camera in the antechamber was strange. He seemed to loom, leaning in, and I thought I saw desperation in his eyes. But was that for me or his research project?

None of this was fair.

"I've barely left my room!" I protested.

"You could have already been carrying it," he said, but I knew that wasn't true. They must have screened me for it when I was admitted. Part of all those skin scrapings and blood draws.

"No," I said. "No, no, it's something else."

He shrugged. "Then you caught it here. It's possible. You've been out of the ward a few times, right? Hospitals are unavoidably breeding grounds for certain illnesses. No amount of cleaning can get them out. Sometimes our precautions just aren't enough. It's unfortunate, but—"

"*Fuck* your unfortunate!" All my rage was in those words. I vibrated in my bed, my chest heaving, bloodstains on my sheets. But I was so weak that my words were creaking, halfway to breaking already. "I want to go home, Adam. I'm done."

Adam reached out, as if he could still touch me through the screen.

I flinched.

"Margaret," he said, so gently, "I am sorry. I am. But if the test comes back positive, you're going to have to stay."

Chapter Twenty-One

The tests took time.

Time to develop. To grow. To be observed. To just make their way through the obstacle course of the hospital, from phlebotomist to lab tech to pathology and back up the chain again. They cultured my blood and wanted to take my spit, too, but I couldn't produce anything. I tried, and my body fought, refusing to cooperate.

Maybe that was the more honest reaction. Or maybe it was reflex, now that my nurse was in full PPE, as if she feared that I was somehow deadlier than the hospital that had infected me.

After, I was left alone. Adam was gone. Penelope was keeping her distance, now that I wasn't coughing anymore. I scrolled on my phone, reading through the CDC's webpage about tuberculosis, and then the WHO's, and Mayo Clinic's, and the full Wikipedia page. I clung to small details, like how fast my symptom onset had happened—*far* too fast—but then again, I wasn't a standard patient.

I could go home, though. That's what everything said. Adam had been wrong. As long as I was more or less stable, I could still go home. They just needed to figure out what, exactly, I was dealing with, and then they'd update my discharge instructions and send me on my way.

Because I wasn't that sick yet.

I didn't think I was that sick yet.

From there, I read up on the infections that bred in hospitals. Adam had been right; organisms like MRSA and *C. diff* and tuberculosis haunted hospitals. Had for as long as sick people were cared for in buildings dedicated to that purpose. Some doctors in the 1800s had advocated for the burning down and rebuilding of hospitals every decade to keep the spread in check. Cleaning and sterilization had won the day instead.

But "environmental services" could only do so much.

Bedside shift report still happened, but at a distance. Isobel and Penelope stood side by side on the video feed from the antechamber, and I couldn't bear to watch. I stared up at the ceiling instead.

"Margaret, how is your pain?"

"Fine. I feel fine." I didn't, and they knew it. We all knew it. I was on antibiotics, but until they saw exactly what strain they were dealing with, it was possible they were doing next to nothing. My joints had already started to hurt. I clutched a wad of tissues for my intermittent coughing fits. My dramatic predischarge one had been the worst, and a part of me held out hope that this was all a misunderstanding. That I just had, I don't know, a small ulcer in my windpipe. That the blood was incidental. That happened sometimes, didn't it?

But I'd already been shown my chest X-rays. They were visibly wrong, even to my eyes.

"Tylenol PRN," Penelope said, and I tuned them back out, until it was just me and Isobel.

I managed not to cry until then.

I rolled onto my side, trying to gain some modicum of privacy in my bed. My bed, that I wasn't supposed to get out of without help now. My pillow from home, my extra blanket—were they what had gotten me sick? Something had betrayed me, but I didn't know what.

They didn't smell like home anymore, though. They just smelled like the hospital. Like this room.

"Meg," Isobel said, her voice sounding . . . strangled.

I drew my knees up to my chest. "This isn't happening," I mumbled.

She made a little noise of concern, and I had to look then. I blinked through the scrim of tears at her face on the screen. Penelope had left her side, but there was no way of knowing if she was still close by.

"There's a dose of the SWAIL medication for tonight," she said.

I shook my head. "I'm being discharged."

She glanced away from me, as if she needed a moment to collect herself. "I understand that. But Dr. Santos doesn't want a gap in care, in case—"

"I'm being discharged," I repeated. "There's not going to be a gap. It's just going to end." I swallowed against the urge to cough again. Not when Isobel could hear.

"I'll record your refusal," Isobel said. "Do you want something to help you sleep tonight? Cough suppressant?"

My jaw fell slack. "You'll record my— Isobel, I thought you . . ."

What? *Were on my side?* But now I was sick. Allegedly, or allegedly badly enough that Adam thought I was going to stay. Maybe that changed things. Maybe I *was* being foolish.

No. I rejected the idea out of hand. I knew what I wanted: to be done, to be home, to recover on my own time.

"I thought you understood," I said, and rolled onto my back, staring at the ceiling. A cough rattled through me. I kept my mouth shut, but it hurt. When I could speak again, I said, "But yes. To the cough suppressant."

The cough suppressant was the type with codeine. It worked, beautifully, but it also dragged me down into dreamless sleep about thirty minutes after I took it. Isobel had lingered for a minute or two after administering it, as if she wanted to say something, but I was alone when I fell asleep.

I woke up to a dark room. Every light out, save for the few blinking indicators that couldn't be obscured. There was some illumination from the hallway lights, but it had to filter through the small windows in two doors to get here. Moonlight provided the rest.

I listened for the *click click click* of an IV pump, waving my fingers above my body, searching for IV tubing.

Nothing. She hadn't started anything while I slept. No saline drip, no sneaky administration of SWAIL while I was out cold. My skin flushed with hot shame; had I really thought she would?

No. But I'd been afraid she might have no other choice.

The clock in my room was analog, and too shrouded in shadow to make out. I fumbled for my phone on the bedside tray but found only a now-warm can of ginger ale and a packet of crackers, offerings left for me while I slept. A paper handout about tuberculosis that had been perfectly adequate while simultaneously being too simplistic to satisfy me.

I twisted onto my other side, shutting my eyes for a moment against the flare of pain that brought. I was stiff and aching, and still so tired, but I didn't think I could get back to sleep. Not yet, anyway. I groped for my phone without seeing, then gave up and opened my eyes.

It didn't help.

And I wasn't alone.

There was a shadow by the bathroom door. Person-sized and unmoving, too far away from any light source for me to make out the features.

I struggled to sit up. "Isobel?" I asked. It was too early to be my morning blood draws. She was the only person I could imagine being in here with me, except—

Well, except for Veronica.

Either way, the shadow by the bathroom door didn't respond.

"Who's there?" I demanded in a shaking whisper.

The baggy outline of coveralls. And beside him, the silhouette of a cart? Black on black, something large and low to the ground, crowned with protrusions. A broom, a mop. A bucket. A custodian. But not the women who had come and gone so far during my stay, whom I'd begun to recognize.

It was the man I'd met the day I'd been admitted. Or at least the shape of him.

But as I squinted in the gloom, his outline slowly registered as wrong. The lines of his cart weren't as straight as they should have been. All of him seemed misshapen, warped, like swollen and pitted flesh. Like something collapsing in on itself for all the rot inside.

And he still hadn't answered my question. Hadn't said a single word.

I fumbled, at last, for the nurse CALL button. Because I wasn't dreaming, and I wasn't hallucinating, and my room was supposed to be on lockdown, and he was *wrong*.

But before I could hit the button, he turned and left.

He left by the door. Hallucinations didn't need to use a door. The terrified paralysis loosened for just a moment, and I scrambled out of the bed, tangling in the sheets enough that I nearly fell. If I'd had to contend with IV tubing, I would have. My socks squeaked against the flooring as I threw myself after him. I could hear his voice in my head from that first day, saying, *If there's nothing keeping you out, try going in.* The antechamber door opened for me, and so did the main one, out into the hall.

But when I slid to a halt in the hallway, looking around wildly for the custodian, he was nowhere. There was only Isobel and the charge nurse for tonight, staring at me from the station. And then Isobel was up and moving toward me, and I waved her off, staggering toward the nearest room. Maybe he'd gone to the next.

"Meg!" Isobel barked. I'd reached the door, but it was shut tight. And the next. At the third, she reached me, grabbing me from behind, her arms winding around me and crushing me back against her chest. I cried out, thrashing.

"Meg, what are you *doing*?" she hissed in my ear.

"I saw him!" I cried, voice stronger now than it had been

in my room. It filled the hall. "I saw him, he was in my room, where did he go?"

Isobel cursed under her breath. "Saw who?" she asked, and she was trying so hard to be gentle, but she didn't have the emotional stamina. She was exhausted, and frustrated, and frightened.

And all of that passed into me, making me tremble, try to jerk away. "A-a man. Somebody from environmental services. But something was wrong with him, he was sick, he was—"

Contaminated.

Contaminated, like Veronica, like I'd dreamed of the hospital being, even before I'd known about what incubated here. This whole place seethed and writhed. Alive and sick, getting sicker, spreading, spreading—

"Meg, I need you to go back to bed," Isobel said.

"No!" I shrieked. "No, I need to go *home*. I'm going home. You can't stop me, you can't," and I was crying then, because when I said "can't," I didn't mean physically. I meant that she couldn't want me to stay, could she? I was terrified, and betrayed, and so far beyond exhaustion that it had looped back around into mania, a full-blown panic. I thrashed in her arms, and she almost lost her grip. But I was weak from too many days spent in bed, my muscles quietly atrophying. *Deconditioning.*

"Don't you see it?" I begged, sobbing now. "It's everywhere! I'm not safe here, I can't be safe here, it's only going to get worse! You have to help me leave. You have to get me out. Isobel, please!"

I felt a needle prick in my right thigh. Charge, who'd come

up behind us in the panic. "Four milligrams lorazepam," she said.

"Should be enough," Isobel confirmed.

I bucked, panicking.

"Shhh," Isobel said. She shifted her hold on me, better pinning my arms. "Give that a minute to work, you'll feel better. And then we can talk in the morning."

"No," I sobbed. "No, no, don't do this." My breath hitched into a shower of coughs.

Isobel didn't flinch away, but then, I wasn't facing her, was I? "You're in distress," she said. "Let me take care of you."

Charge was hovering nearby. I stared at her, imploring, as I shook. But she still had the syringe.

"Let me leave," I whispered.

And then the world grew hazy, and I stopped fighting.

· Chapter Twenty-Two ·

Except that isn't what happened.

Later that morning, when I thought I was coming down off the drugs I remember in brilliant detail being injected into my leg, Isobel came by the room. She didn't look disheveled, but I figured she'd had time to pull herself back together. And the PPE she was wearing hid so much of her.

"They didn't send you home after that?" I think I mumbled.

She settled into a chair close to the bed but out of reach. I wasn't in restraints. "What do you remember about last night, Meg?" she asked.

"I'm sorry," I said. I could remember the panic still, clearly, but I wasn't high on adrenaline anymore. So disorienting, to go from out of my mind with terror to being woozy in my bed. All that was left was a certain level of paranoia, defensiveness. My gaze flitted around the room.

"For what?"

My lips were chapped. "I could have—I could have hurt somebody. Gotten somebody sick. But I saw something, in my room."

"Is that why you came out?"

I nodded. "But I didn't mean to freak out. You didn't have to restrain me." Through the drugged haze, a prickle of irritation rose, then swelled into the memory of fury. I'd been erratic, sure. Almost raving. But she'd been so quick to grab me.

Isobel shook her head. "I didn't restrain you."

I looked down at my arms, sure I'd see bruising where she'd held me so tightly. Maybe I would see the pinprick of the lorazepam shot if I pulled the blanket off my legs, but—

But there was nothing.

"Here," Isobel said. She reached over and set my phone on my bedside tray. "Go to your records app. My notes should be accessible by now."

Wary, I took my phone and navigated to the right place. Isobel's name was on the newest addition. I opened it, expecting it to be partially or entirely redacted like Dr. Santos's progress notes often were.

Progress Note by Nurse Isobel R, RN at 08/31/23 0747

I looked at the clock. It was almost nine in the morning. I'd slept through my blood draw and, apparently, shift change.

"Shouldn't you be home?" I asked.

"Keep reading," Isobel said. "Please. I want you to know what I saw."

> *At 0330 patient left room unassisted and without communicating with this RN. Pt did not acknowledge nursing staff's multiple verbal requests to return to room and attempted to leave ward at main door. Ambulating with even, steady gait. Door remained*

locked. Pt did not appear to notice that door was closed, and walked into it repeatedly.

0335: After consult with charge RN Shannon L., decision was made to allow pt to leave the ward with escort to avoid potential injury. RN notified security of pt's elopement and followed at a safe distance, communicating to pt repeatedly that pt should return to bed and sleep.

Verbal attempts to orient pt to time and place received no response. No signs of physical or psychological distress observed for the duration of patient's time off unit. Flat affect.

0337: Pt began making statements that did not correspond to this RN's questions. "Why are we here? This isn't where we belong. But it's out here, too, isn't it?" Pt touched a wall. Eyes appeared unfocused, but general demeanor expressed interest. Pt continued: "Is it always like this?"

RN attempted to engage pt on subject of hospital decor. Received no acknowledgment.

Pt continued to elevator bank but did not attempt to call a car. Pt said, "Do they know?" and did not provide clarification when asked who "they" were. Pt appeared to be responding to internal stimuli.

0339: Pt said, "I'm getting sick. I can feel it growing in my lungs. My stomach. Like there won't be any room left for me, soon. Did it happen like that for you, too?"

Pt did not clarify who she believed she was speaking to. However, pt previously expressed distress upon learning of a fellow patient's death, and has subsequently mentioned this patient in association with an *observed absence seizure. This RN has notified Dr. Santos of indication for mental health consult.*

0342: Pt's affect changed despite no action taken by RN. Pt looked down at her body, facial expression suggesting confusion. Mild lassitude in facial muscles. Rigid posture. RN attempted to get pt's attention again and was successful. Pt left the elevator bank and approached RN.

RN requested that pt accompany her back to pt's room. Pt responded, "A strange host, a strange bed to languish in. Why?" Pt's voice and intonation were markedly different than baseline, disjointed and in a strange rhythm. No slurring. Pt's eyes could not maintain focus.

Informed pt that pt is known to this RN, and that pt's room has not changed since admission. Repeated request that pt return to room. Pt approached RN, and asked, "Can we live inside you?"

Pt reached out with left hand for RN's hand. RN did not avoid contact, in an attempt to better judge symptoms. Before physical contact was made, however, pt collapsed to floor. RN was able to assist and guide to floor. Pt found to be unconscious with patent airway and pulse palpable, strong, regular, appropriate rate and rhythm. Pt's eyes were closed. No visible injuries. See Post-Fall Note.

0345: Security assisted in transporting pt back to room. Examination showed vital signs within acceptable limits. See flow sheet documentation. Pt normotensive, axillary temp 99.8 F, regular heart rate and rhythm. Pt appeared to be sleeping.

0358: Dr. Santos paged. Dr. Santos ordered 2 mg IV lorazepam q2 hours PRN in case of agitation. Symptoms discussed as consistent with sleepwalking episode, despite no prev mhx. Possible recurrent absence seizure, based on potential repeat reference to recently deceased patient. Discussed neuro and medication eval to avoid future occurrences.
Will continue to monitor.
Staff directly involved: this RN; security officers Jenkins and Vu; charge RN Shannon L. (consulted); Dr. Santos (notified). No other patients, staff, or visitors present.

I felt numb. Strange, displaced, watching myself from outside my body. It wasn't just seeing myself from Isobel's perspective, though that was disorienting enough.

It was the total disconnect of what she'd experienced, and what I knew had happened.

"That's not what I remember," I said.

"But you do remember something."

My cheeks heated. I didn't want to tell her, suddenly; the whole thing seemed shameful, if it hadn't actually happened. Maybe Isobel was lying to me, but I don't think so. She had no reason to. She was sitting by my bedside when she should have been heading home to sleep, and she looked so worried.

"Must have been a nightmare," I said, weakly.

"Tell me about it?"

I shook my head. She didn't press.

I thumbed at my phone, scrolling back to how she'd just—

followed me as I wandered, out of my mind, through the seventh-floor halls.

"Why didn't you stop me?" I asked.

Isobel shrugged. "It would've been dangerous. For both of us."

My head hurt. I rubbed at my temple. "I remember you grabbing me from behind, pinning my arms. I remember you stopping me."

"That would have impacted your ability to breathe. You could have clocked me in the nose. It only happens like that in TV shows, Meg." She sounded almost amused.

I didn't laugh.

"I don't know how to feel about—this. Any of it." Afraid. I was afraid. Not gibbering with fear, but the cognitive dissonance of it all left me twitchy and ready to run. What I remembered of that night didn't feel like a dream. The details were too vivid, too persistent. It wasn't fading away, and it still hasn't. "Why—why tell me? Show me this? You didn't know what I went—what I thought I went through—"

She hadn't known I'd be distressed.

Isobel stretched her legs out in front of her, brow creased. "I wanted to make sure you were okay," she said, after a moment. "And I wanted to know if you . . . Well, if you remember who you thought you were talking to."

Veronica. She'd said as much in her notes, or as close as I guess HIPAA allowed for.

"There at the end—I don't know. It didn't really feel like you were sleepwalking." She fussed with her PPE, and I saw a peek of her jeans, in between her booties and the gown. She was in street clothes. Fully ready to clock out, or already had, but she was here, with me.

It was a lifeline. Just enough human care. Something beyond the impossibility of what I was going through.

"I remember," I said, slowly, "that I was certain I'd been contaminated. That the hospital wasn't safe. But that's just—because of getting sick. Right?"

She considered, then nodded. "Most likely," she said. "I'm off for the next few days. But I'll be thinking of you. Okay? Don't be afraid to sleep. Try to stick to awake in daylight, asleep at night. It'll help keep you oriented. And just—"

I looked at her, wide-eyed.

"Just let the medicine do its work. I'll see you in a few days."

And then she was gone.

Chapter Twenty-Three

GRACEVIEW MEMORIAL

Room:	775	Phone	XXX-XXX-2775
Date:	August 31, 2023	\multicolumn{2}{l	}{MON TUES WED (THURS) FRI SAT SUN}
Patient:	Margaret Culpepper	\multicolumn{2}{l	}{PAIN SCALE}
Doctor:	Santos	\multicolumn{2}{l	}{1 (2) 3 4 5 6 7 8 9 10}
Nurse:	Penelope W.	Pain medication last given:	1230
Charge Nurse:	Tristan P.	Next dose:	1630
\multicolumn{4}{c	}{Today's Plan! *Begin treatment for TB*}
Diet:	Normal	Fall Risk:	Medium
Activity Level:	Limited	Our goal is to have you discharged on:	October 27, 2023
\multicolumn{4}{c	}{Prevent falling! Call for help getting out of bed.}

The diagnosis came with the lunch that I didn't eat. *Mycobacterium tuberculosis.* They started me on a different IV drip. It felt like nothing going in.

Adam came to see me a few hours after that. My head was foggy. I didn't know if that was the emotional whiplash of the previous night, the TB, SWAIL, or something else. So many things wrong with me. Under attack from so many directions.

He came into the room this time, properly gowned and masked. He sat a fair distance away.

There were no flowers, and the bouquet by my bed had disappeared sometime in the night.

"Good morning, Margaret," he said.

I was sitting up already, mattress raised. "I want to go home," I told him, clearly enunciating each word. "But Dr. Santos hasn't been by. Can you get ahold of him for me?"

Adam looked pained. "I can, but he's not going to discharge you," he said. "I'm sorry. The hospital is going to keep you here until you are no longer infectious."

I stared. "What?" I asked, voice wavering. "How?"

"Graceview has decided you are not currently capable of making your own medical decisions."

I pushed at the bed, trying to sit forward. Wanting to get up. "Nobody talked to me about that," I protested. "Nobody checked in with me. I haven't been—evaluated?" I was struggling for the words, but Isobel's notes had recommended at least a psychiatric exam that I knew hadn't happened.

Right?

And Adam confirmed it. "Nobody needed to. If the hospital has reason to believe you can't or won't follow treatment instructions and are at risk of infecting others due to your current medical state, they can hold you until your condition improves."

I shook my head, sharply enough that my vision hazed for a moment. "My condition would *improve* if I was off SWAIL."

"We have no indication that's true." Adam laid his hands on his knees. They looked wrong, in all that nitrile. I wanted to rip them off him. "With your history of seizures—"

"There's been *one*, and we don't even have proof that's what it was—"

"And your erratic behavior last night, on top of your compromised immune system—"

"You did that to me—"

"Margaret, *stop!*" he shouted, getting to his feet.

He'd never raised his voice before. It thundered from him full force, and I jerked back as if burned. His chest rose and fell as he struggled to regain his composure, moving his shoulders with it, and then he was smoothing his hair back and closing his eyes. Breathe in, breathe out. I unconsciously mimicked him.

"You have two choices right now," he said, eventually, voice at a reasonable volume and tone once more. The mask, back in place. He was looking at me again, holding intense eye contact. I couldn't pull away. "One, you *can* discontinue SWAIL like you've asked to, and you stay while they treat you for the tuberculosis. Your mental state is evaluated on a regular basis until you're deemed able to make rational decisions. And then you can decide to leave.

"Or you can take option two: you trust us. Dr. Santos manages your tuberculosis in tandem with completing SWAIL. At the end you walk out of here healthy. Completely healthy."

"You can't promise that," I said. "Is it— It can't be safe, continuing SWAIL. Not with an active infection." It made no sense. And Adam, I reminded myself, *was not a doctor.* Never had been. "I should be having this conversation with my doctor."

Adam sat back down. "Dr. Santos is busy," he said, bland, like he was commenting on the weather.

I crossed my arms, my thumb idly brushing over the rising edge of my port, carefully keeping distance from the IV tubing that snaked to it. "I can wait."

It was the wrong answer in a series of wrong answers. Adam's expression grew withdrawn, remote. I felt that withdrawal acutely, a gathering chill.

"I am trying," he said at last, "to help you."

"Then tell me something useful," I snapped back.

His brows drew down. Then he sighed and sat back, crossing his legs. "Very well. How expensive do you think your tuberculosis care will be?"

"I did my reading. The state will cover it."

"Basic treatment, yes, to ensure you're no longer infectious. But long-term effects? Other opportunistic infections?"

I flinched. My old bare-bones insurance plan had only gotten me access to my rheumatologist and offset pharmacy costs. And I hadn't had even that since the new year.

I hadn't cared, because SWAIL was fully paid.

Tuberculosis wasn't SWAIL.

"I can't do anything about the cost," Adam said, gently. "Not if you're a private patient."

I grimaced. "But if I resume SWAIL..."

"Then your adjacent medical treatment is all covered," he said.

"That's disgusting," I said, nauseated. I drew my knees up

to my chest, wincing at how sore I was, how sluggish. "You're holding me hostage."

"Margaret."

"You don't want your trial to end because I'm rare, so you're entrapping me with medical fees."

"I am doing no such thing. I am explaining your options to you. You can make your own choices. But from where I'm standing, resuming SWAIL is the best one available. Financially, and for your health, too."

"Veronica is dead!"

He looked away. "Yes," he said, after a moment's ringing silence. "She is. And we know why, and Dr. Santos is going to use that knowledge to protect you."

That unstoppered the tears still inside of me, and I sagged back, pressing my forehead down against my knees. *Click click click* went the pump.

He was right, was the worst part. I *was* sick, even if tuberculosis made no sense, even if this was all happening way too fast. I was seeing things. I was dirt poor, and I hadn't found a place to stay anyway, and now I'd be putting anybody who helped me at risk. Maybe if I'd had my own private hole to slink back to . . . but I didn't. I had this hospital, and this trust fail, and no other options. I knew exactly how thin my bank account was.

And it wasn't like anybody here *wanted* me to die.

"We caught the tuberculosis early," Adam was saying. "Maybe not as early as possible, but certainly early enough that they should be able to make you quite comfortable. This is a setback, but it doesn't have to be the end."

"I'm scared," I whispered.

I don't know if Adam heard me. I do know that he got up from his seat and came over to my bed, sitting on the very edge of the mattress. He held out his hand as if to rub my back, but waited for me to acknowledge him.

Even after everything, it was tempting. The warmth of him, the solidity. And a small, cruel part of me wanted to get him sick, too. He was offering, wasn't he? But his mask was still in place, and he didn't seem afraid.

I didn't move, and eventually, he let his arm fall.

"I'll do it," I said. "I'll resume SWAIL."

Because what other choice did I really have?

· Chapter Twenty-Four ·

That day's SWAIL bag was pink.

I hated it. I trembled as Penelope hung the bag and sent it *click click click* into my port. It ran concurrently with my other meds, the port keeping them from interfering with one another—at least, I assumed so.

Penelope remained in the room for the entire duration of the day's treatment. She spent it at the computer, and she seemed busy enough, but I understood: I wasn't trusted alone with this. The antibiotics, sure, why not, but not SWAIL.

They were probably right. I was so angry, so afraid, that if left alone to stew, I likely would've taken the needle out myself.

As it was, I pulled up an audiobook on the rewilding of a former farm in England, and I half listened as I hyperfocused on every tiny physical sensation inside my skin. The movement of my stomach. The slight itching where medical tape kept the line in place. The twitching of my toes that increased whenever I tried not to move a single muscle. The coughs that periodically shook everything up, and the faint taste of blood in my mouth when they were productive.

I'd almost bored myself into a doze when the pump alarmed. I blinked, rapidly, trying to reorient. Penelope was by my side, disconnecting the IV tubing, capping my port access. "All done for the day," she said. "More antibiotics in a bit, but first we're headed to imaging, to see how things are going in your lungs."

"Yippee," I muttered.

"Do you want to use the restroom first?"

I did. She stayed with me the whole time, at hand in case I fell. I felt old and frail, and I tried my best to ignore the whole thing.

After, she helped me back into my bed and lifted the side rail again. "I'm going to step out and get a few things sorted, make sure they're ready for you. But I'll be back soon."

And then I was alone again.

That, I think, was the first time that my isolation felt *good*. The first time it relieved me and loosened something inside of my skull, letting me breathe. Of course, breathing led to a coughing fit, but even that felt right. Purgative. In its aftermath, I reclined against my pillow, not to rest but to enjoy the feeling of a moment's privacy.

My phone buzzed from where it sat in my sheets. When I unearthed it, my mother's number glowed on the screen, and after staring at it, dumbfounded, for three rings, I reached to hit ANSWER CALL.

The screen went dark before I did, but my mind was racing. Maybe my mother could help. Maybe she could get power of attorney, or something. Make my decisions for me instead of letting the hospital.

It wasn't my first choice, but I was navigating to the missed calls screen to call her back when Penelope appeared in the doorway.

"It's time," she said.

I set my phone onto the bedside tray, and she helped me out of the bed and into a waiting wheelchair. It felt strange, to sit up with my legs bent at the knee instead of stretched out or curled up awkwardly.

"After imaging, you'll be taken to an OR for a bronchoscopy and lung biopsy," she said, and I must have gone pale, because she added, "You'll be sedated."

Sedated, like I'd been the first time I'd hallucinated. *A dream, it was a dream.* Dreams were normal. They weren't absence seizures. They weren't disorientation in the middle of the night that left me wandering and talking to invisible people, remembering that I was screaming and fighting my nurses. But I still shook my head. "No. I don't want to be sedated, and I don't want the biopsy. The tests came back positive, right? Conclusive?"

"We need to be sure it's only tuberculosis," Penelope said. She toed the brake off on the chair, and we were ready to move. "Sometimes it's comorbid. Other infections can spring up."

My stomach soured. "Oh," I said.

"It's okay," she reassured me. "We're doing this early to make sure we catch everything. Here, you'll need to wear this mask out in the hall."

"I feel like a petri dish." One scored and streaked with a riot of colors, each one some fresh contamination. I took the mask from her and slipped the elastics over my ears, molding the nose wire to my face. It didn't feel like enough protection, for her or for me. Anxious, I scratched at my wrist. Penelope watched but didn't comment. "I don't— Will I be able to talk? After?" Or was this a way to shut me up for a while?

Paranoid, paranoid, and I couldn't tell if it was warranted or not.

That first loss of time, when SWAIL was just getting

started—in hindsight, the timing seemed calculated. Veronica was declining, and I was too out of it to know.

"Your throat might be sore," she said, as she wheeled me through the antechamber. "But it's minimally invasive."

Unless they find something terrible. More terrible than the blood I was coughing up. I hunched in on myself, a child afraid of the dark. As long as they didn't do the tests, they'd never know, and they'd never have more ammunition against me, other ways to keep me in their care. I was a prisoner, and Penelope still treated me like I was just a patient. I wanted to cry.

I wanted to call my mom.

But it was too late.

I remember getting x-rayed. Then somewhere between that dimmed room and the OR, the sedation kicked in and erased everything that came before it, including the moment the drugs entered my port. One moment, I was in the hallway. The next, I was back in my room. My mask was off, and I think my gown was different.

No visitors. No adventures in a rotting dreamscape. Or, at least, none that I can relate now. I woke groggy and disoriented, my throat aching. My IV was out, the pump off, the room quiet. It was still light out, though, so I hadn't lost much time.

I stayed where I was, too tired to become frantic. I turned my head from the wall that contained the antechamber and the bathroom and gazed, longingly, out at the mountains.

Veronica hadn't been able to see those mountains. She'd only had the garden, and the other wing of the hospital.

Slowly, my attention moved inward to the table where Adam and Isobel had taken turns eating with me—now a thing of the past. And from there, to my bedside tray, and I remembered, foggily, that I needed to call my mother.

But my phone wasn't on the tray.

My lips were parched and cracked from whatever they'd done to me to get at my lungs, my throat sore, my body still uncoordinated from the drugs. But I fumbled down the railing on the far side of my bed from the door, and I got first one leg, then the second, over the edge. No tubing connected me to the pump, so I was free to slide down, my knees buckling and dropping me to an undignified crouch.

This was so much harder than I remembered. Than it should have been. It took immense effort to stand and to remain upright. I swayed, pitched, caught myself.

Environmental services had obviously come through, the room's antiseptic smell once more prominent, rough on my irritated throat. They must have tidied up. If my phone wasn't in my bag, I'd just get my laptop and—

And that wasn't there, either.

I had my suitcase cracked open and spread out. There was nowhere else for it to be. But I still grabbed my backpack again and checked anyway. Not there, either. Even the power cord was gone, and when I looked at the outlet I usually charged my phone at, that cord was gone, too. Disbelieving, I went to the dresser.

Nothing. Nothing, nothing, nothing.

"Margaret?" came Penelope's muffled voice. She was still on the other side of the antechamber door, suiting up. "I need you to get back in your bed, please. Or if you're not sure you can do that, I need you to sit down where you are. I don't want you falling."

I didn't get back in bed, or sit down. I moved to a bank of cabinets. I couldn't imagine why anybody would have put my things over here, firmly in the land of the nurses, but—

The antechamber door opened. Penelope crossed the space in a few hurried strides. "Margaret," she said, more firmly this time. "Come on. Back to bed."

"My phone," I said, shaking my head. "My phone and my laptop are missing."

"I'll look for them," she assured me.

"No, you don't understand, where could they have gone?"

"I need you in your bed, please. Let me worry about that."

She wasn't worried. I knew that with gut-wrenching certainty. She wasn't worried, because she knew where they'd gone, because *she'd* been the one to take me out of my room. For tests, yes, because two things could be true at once. But also so somebody could come and sever my connection with the outside world.

Penelope touched my upper arm, and I yelped, jerking away from her as if burned. I moved back toward my bed, but only because I was looking for the phone I used to call in my food orders to the cafeteria.

It was exactly where it was supposed to be.

I stared at it, heaving for breath. Before long, I was doubled over, coughing. Blood pattered onto the floor, and I clutched my head. Why take my phone and laptop but leave the room phone? It made no sense. Except—except they could monitor that phone, surely. Control it. Cut it off if they needed to. Yes, that was it, that was—

"Margaret," Penelope said, firm and slow and steady. "Deep breaths. It's going to be okay."

I flinched and spun, expecting to see the glint of a needle in her hand. But her hands were open, palms toward me. I looked from them to her masked face. For a moment, I saw Isobel, confused and horrified.

No. That hadn't been real. That had never happened. I was acting crazy. I had to get control over myself, because they could use this against me, too. Proof that I couldn't make my own decisions.

"Where could they have gone?" I repeated, once I could sound, at least to myself, like I wasn't ranting and raving.

"Probably taken to be disinfected, and somebody forgot to return them."

"They could've done that here. They could have told me."

"Yes, they could have. Sometimes wires get crossed. Can you get back in bed for me, Margaret? I'm afraid of you falling."

I almost said that I was fine—but she was right. I felt unsteady, physically weak. I held out a trembling hand, and she took me by the elbow, assisting me the last few steps to the bed. I let her guide me onto the mattress. I sat still and rigid, hoping I looked authoritative, fearing I looked unhinged.

It would be easy for them to dismiss me if I shouted. If I panicked. I had to be calm.

"It could also be," Penelope ventured, once my rails were back up, "that they were stolen."

I frowned. Stolen? Yes, that was possible. But that sounded like the paranoid ramblings of a disoriented patient. Like an elderly woman, complaining that her necklace had been lifted by thieves, when really it had been her daughter removing it at admission for safekeeping. But it was more mundane than a conspiracy against me, more plausible, and more plausible, too, than some attempt at cleaning gone awry.

But was it a trap? Was there any right move here? Was I supposed to concede that maybe I hadn't had my laptop and phone at all?

"It happens," Penelope said. "It'd be the first time I've heard of it happening on this floor, but not the first time in the hospital."

"Wouldn't somebody have seen something?"

"Maybe. I'll ask security."

I nodded, shakily. *Stolen.* Had I seen my wallet? I couldn't remember where it was. I'd had it, walking around the hospital. It might still be in my pants pocket. It might be gone.

Penelope lingered, cleaning up the blood with her bootie-covered shoe and a washcloth that was tossed into the biohazard hamper in the bathroom, making sure I was comfortable. Then she left, but only long enough to fetch the newest round of medications. I stared past her as she hooked everything up, as she took my vitals, as she fetched the TV remote for me.

"I am so sorry this happened," she said, when there was nothing left to do. "You should feel safe here. Do you think you can rest?"

I almost laughed.

What else was there left for me to do?

· Chapter Twenty-Five ·

Things got worse after that.

They never did find my phone, or my laptop. They did confirm my wallet had been taken, too. Without a phone, I didn't have an easy way to cancel all my credit cards, but they were already close to maxed anyway. I'd lost access to my tool restoration videos, but the television got HGTV, which, while a pale imitation, was fine enough. I couldn't check my medical records anymore, but with how redacted they were, did it really matter?

I could have probably asked somebody to search for my mother's contact information, but the more time passed, the less I believed she could help. I gave up; it was easier not to think about any of it, especially as my symptoms grew more pronounced.

I spiked a fever that evening, despite the antibiotics I was on. My lymph nodes grew swollen and tender. By the end of the week, even my bones hurt, and I'd begun losing time again—though this time in the more common way of a full-blown infection, seemingly always simultaneously exhausted and restless, half-asleep and half-awake. My ribs ached from coughing that was only held partially in check by the strong antitussives I was prescribed.

And through it all, SWAIL continued. I don't know how much of my misery was from the tuberculosis, or the accompanying nascent fungal infection my lung biopsy revealed, or the side effects of the medications, or the destruction of my immune system.

I was sick in a way I'd never been before.

They'd been right to keep me. I admitted it to myself three days after the diagnosis, shivering in an ever-widening pool of my own sweat. They'd switched me to using a bedside commode instead of a toilet. I couldn't even stand to take a shower; my nurse that day stayed in the bathroom as I sat in a plastic chair, determined not to have her sponge me down, determined to not lose even more strength. But my vision was so tunneled that I couldn't find the shampoo.

In my dreams, my room decayed around me. I could see through the walls, through the floor, to other patients just like me. Some perched on the precipice of death, some suffering back toward life, some lying motionless, all consciousness extinguished but their bodies continuing on with the push-pull of machinery.

When I woke, I wondered if that could be an option for me: sedate me down into a coma and work on my body while I didn't have to inhabit it. I didn't want to go back to that rotting place, but I was trapped in my own frail body and there, at least, I no longer hurt.

Sometimes I had visitors, but only when I slept. The image of my mother, fretting about the state of my room, acting like the boils on the wall were just cobwebs. Not real, that one, because I was certain she would have stayed. Dr. Santos, and maybe that one could have been real; he was there and gone so fast, and when we spoke, we spoke of nonsense. Dreams of phlebotomists that I could only tell were dreams because they took all my blood from me, leaving me a dry husk, and I broke apart as a cold wind from the mountain beyond my window blew through.

If Adam visited me, in dreams or otherwise, I don't remember it. But I did want him. For all the rage in me, I wanted him there. I longed to steal him from my memories, the warm, sweet man who'd made everything feel easy.

Isobel was there more nights than not. Or it seemed that way, at least. Nights melted together, or split apart, and it was too difficult to keep track, let alone compare them to what I thought I understood about shift schedules. But my memories—my real memories, not the fragmented, fractured pieces that I can't distinguish from dreams—from that time are of her. Not Louise, or Shannon, or any other floating night nurse. Days, whoever was behind the mask blurred. But nights, nights I waited for every glimpse of Isobel, even when I was too exhausted to speak.

She read to me one night, over the video feed from the antechamber. I remember that. I'd been fitted with a nasal cannula that day, and I'd regained some feeling in my fingertips, but otherwise was too exhausted to do more than lie there and listen. It was something technical, and I only slowly realized that it was a manual I'd helped write. I couldn't imagine how she'd found it, and might have written it off as unreal, but she left it on my tray. It was still there in the morning, bought used for four dollars, out of date by three editions now.

When I was lucky, I bobbed on the surface of my consciousness, dipping in and out with ease. When I wasn't, each transition was terrifying. I checked the whiteboard every time I stirred. It became my lifeline.

"You forgot to update it," I managed one day, when Penelope had left Isobel's name up on the board. "Update it. Please update it."

"Of course," she said, and I was gone again before she had it erased.

That night, Isobel was back. I managed to hold on through antechamber shift report. They thought the aspergillosis might have been eradicated. My lungs were recovering; they'd be trialing me on room air again in the morning.

"Margaret is continuing to tolerate SWAIL well," Penelope said, and I laughed. It sounded more like helpless sputtering, and Isobel's head jerked up. I waved off her attention, hand pressed to my chest.

"I'm fine," I wheezed.

I listened to the rest of the litany and fell asleep to Isobel entering the room to write her name on the whiteboard.

"Easy does it."

I woke up to Isobel maneuvering me onto my side. Her hands were warm through the nitrile as she moved my gown out of the way and pressed the bell of her stethoscope against my skin. She'd warmed that, too, no cold shock of air-temperature metal, and I nearly fell asleep again.

But I didn't want to sleep. I listened to her as she listened to me. I considered shifting, making some soft noise that would make her have to start over again, prolonging the contact. But I held still instead, in the little bubble formed by the dim working light she had on, not enough to rouse me on its own.

The bell glided down to the other side of my spine, and I

shivered. What could she hear? How bad was the congestion? They'd caught the infection before it should have done that much damage, but I'd still needed the oxygen.

I was like dry grass in a parched field, and the lightning strike had come. I was ablaze.

"There we go," murmured Isobel, easing me onto my back. I stared up at her, drinking in what I could see in the half-light. There were dark circles under her eyes, like she hadn't slept, the skin thin and delicate. And her hands, usually so steady and sure, trembled faintly when she let go of her stethoscope.

"You look tired," I said, after it was obvious that she knew I was awake.

I couldn't see her smile beneath her mask, but the skin around her eyes crinkled. "Always," she said. "Skipped my usual Doubleshot today in the rush to get here."

"Couldn't wait to take my temperature?"

She patted my shoulder, and I sighed, abandoning the half-conscious attempt at flirtation.

"I worry about you," she confirmed, drawing her stool up beside my bed. "Some would say too much. It's healthier to emotionally clock out when shift's over."

"But you transferred to a ward aimed at long-term treatment," I said. I groped at my chest, feeling gently for the IV tubing I knew was there. I'd been plugged in for days now, and earlier that day, I'd been set up with an external catheter, to spare me even the effort of using the comode. With so much volume in, there was too much volume out for me to manage on my own.

I'd been reduced to a series of tubes and bags, alerts on a

monitor, and the occasional mouthful of pudding. And bouts of coughing. The coughing still woke me from time to time. It was so much easier to detach from this bed during the day, to drift, but when Isobel was there, I tried to stay present, no matter the humiliation.

"You'd be surprised," Isobel said, and I struggled to remember what she was responding to. "I usually don't get to know my patients this well."

That drew me into myself, like iron filings following a magnet. "Before me," I said, taking careful breaths to fend off a coughing bout that would send her skittering out of the room, "how many were there?"

"How many patients?"

"SWAIL patients," I specified. There had been Veronica, yes, but before that . . . I'd never thought to ask before.

She considered. "Five . . . no, six, but one discontinued treatment. Five, from start to finish."

Five. Both more and fewer than I'd expected. "And how many of them died?"

"Are we counting Veronica?"

I nodded.

"Then two."

Two. Two dead patients out of six. A one in three chance of . . .

"That's so many," I whispered.

She nodded. "It's so many." A one in three chance of dying, and that hadn't been called out more strongly in the intake documents? Fuck, but I wish she'd told me that sooner. That second night, when she was trying to talk me into leaving.

"Why . . ." I gasped, then coughed, and it took a few minutes to stop. She waited through it. "Why did nobody tell me? And don't say"—wheeze—"you didn't want to scare me."

Isobel looked down at her hands. "They died of different things," she said. "Not SWAIL itself."

"Bad luck, thirty-three percent of the time?"

"There's no reason SWAIL should be that risky," she said, shaking her head. "It's—our failing. Something we're getting wrong."

"They should stop the trial."

"Maybe. I don't know." She wasn't looking at me anymore. She was staring off into the distance, unseeing. "I don't . . . Nobody else has as bad of a record as I do. The other locations in the trial, they've had maybe one death between them."

I frowned. "Don't blame yourself." I had to fight for each word. "What about Penelope?" She was on the same ward. Had the same patients.

"Veronica died at night," Isobel said, and dropped her head into her hands. She braced her elbows on the bed railing. "So did Oscar, the other patient I lost. Always at night. On my shift. Tells you something, doesn't it?"

I should have felt afraid then. Angry, maybe, demanding to know why she hadn't just quit. If she was so convinced she was the link between the deaths of her patients, how could she allow herself to stay? But through the haze of my illness, I remembered what she'd told me about her career. About her time in the ICU, about losing so many patients during the height of COVID. I knew why she was so ready to blame herself. And I knew, too, why she couldn't leave.

She was determined to fix this. And none of it was her fault.

At least, I hoped it wasn't.

"You're a good nurse," I said, reaching out and taking one of her hands. She twitched away from me, but not from fear of contamination. It was the breaching of another boundary, this one between patient and nurse, but I wouldn't let her go. "A good nurse," I repeated, "and a good friend."

I half expected her to shrug me off with some comment about how we weren't friends. But instead, she just stared at me. And then she gripped my hand in turn, tight, too tight. I let her, because the ache in my joints made it real. Real, real, real.

No matter what they tried to tell me later.

· Chapter Twenty-Six ·

GRACEVIEW MEMORIAL

Room:	775	Phone	XXX-XXX-2775
Date:	September 5, 2023	\<MON (TUES) WED THURS FRI SAT SUN\>	
Patient:	Margaret Culpepper	**PAIN SCALE** 1 2 3 4 5 (6) 7 8 9 10	
Doctor:	Santos		
Nurse:	~~~~~~	Pain medication last given:	0200
Charge Nurse:	Kathleen P.	Next dose:	0600
Today's Plan! *Continue treatment for TB*			
Diet:	Normal	Fall Risk:	Medium
Activity Level:	Limited	Our goal is to have you discharged on:	December 31, 2057
Prevent tuberculosis! Never leave your room again!			

There's so much that I'm missing, from that week, from what came next.

I've built what happened to me into a narrative, because a

narrative is the only thing that can persist in the tidal flow of my reality. A progression of events, a recitation of how I felt, even as it all grows distant and gnarled and knotted. Some of it I think I remember with full clarity; other parts I know I've reconstructed, inferred, deduced. Faked. Invented wholesale.

And some of it I must therefore be misremembering. Some of it I must have dreamed and thought I woke, or saw but thought I dreamed. Like the shadowy figure in my room; like Isobel restraining me. I know it happened once, and logic dictates it must have happened more than once.

I have never been so aware of the impermanence of memory. Of identity.

How much have I lost? How much can I really understand now, with so much that underlies it gone? How much of me remains? Was the girl who walked into Graceview the same girl who is trying to pull the pieces together even now? Or has she been eroded? Replaced and rebuilt, a ship of Theseus in a hospital bed.

Am I my consciousness? Or am I my body, with its record of interventions and injuries and illnesses, this thing I've divorced myself from so fully out of necessity? The thing in the bed. Is that me?

Is it?

I did eventually sleep that night, but I woke again well before dawn. I heard rustling in the antechamber, the herald of somebody come to visit me. Not Isobel, because I could recognize the sounds of her gowning up now, so I figured it was the phlebotomist, come for another round of labs. I almost went back to sleep. With the port in place, they took their blood from the tap; there was barely any sensation to it at all. Handy, because now that I was well and truly sick, they came every four hours, sometimes more often.

Drip, drip, drip. All the moisture in me originated from the saline bags that ran nearly round the clock, draining out of me again almost as quickly.

I'm not sure what kept me from drifting off again. Maybe some ancillary disorientation, making me struggle to define my environment before I would trust it enough to drop off again. I looked around the darkened room at the familiar furniture, sketched out by the glow of the pump, the faint sodium light from the parking lot outside my window.

My whiteboard. Date, diet, fall risk, nurse—

Isobel's name wasn't there.

I stared, trying to get it to make sense. I remembered watching Isobel write her name. And while the days and nights ran together, I could have sworn I still felt her hand around mine. My bones held the imprint of her grip. But her name was gone, and in its place was just a smear of gray-black, like somebody had erased it with the side of their hand.

The antechamber door opened. Heart pounding in my ears, I turned to face my visitor.

Adam had added to his PPE. My nurses at that point didn't wear face shields, just masks. I wondered if something had changed with me, or if he'd gotten a little more paranoid all on his own. He was still wearing the standard-issue paper gown and gloves, though. He hadn't graduated to the full body suits I remembered seeing in coverage of the Ebola outbreaks of 2014, but something about being able to see my faint reflection in the curve of plastic covering his face made me feel ashamed. Small, shrunken, but noxious.

And it was too early in the day. He shouldn't have been there. He should have been in bed, at home, far away. Not coming to sit in the chair by the window, his usual haunt.

Haunt. *Haunting.* He shouldn't have been here, so chances were good that he *wasn't*. That this was a dream, or a hallucination.

But it felt real. The *click click click* of my pump. The heavy hurt of breathing, now familiar but still terrible. The ever-present faint pressure of my PureWick external catheter.

"You're awake," he said. He sounded pleased, not surprised.

"Why are you here?" I asked.

"I worry about you," he said.

(Isobel said.)

(They both said?)

"It's early." My voice slurred. But I was aware of it, which was probably a good sign that I was more in control of myself than usual these days. "Or very late."

"Yes," he agreed. "How are you feeling?"

I shook my head, trying to get everything to connect. "You shouldn't be here. Why?" I pressed again, because him worrying didn't explain the hour, didn't explain what he would have done if I hadn't woken up.

I didn't dare look away from him, but I kept thinking about the smear on the whiteboard.

"Where's Isobel?"

"I don't know," he said, confused. "Wherever she is when she's not on shift. Home, I imagine."

My fingers curled to fists in my sheets. "She's on shift."

"I'm pretty sure she's not. I didn't see her at the nurses' station when I checked in." I couldn't read his expression in the dim light, through mask and face shield, but I think he must have smiled. "And I brought donuts. Everybody comes out of the woodwork for donuts."

I looked away, finally, momentarily overwhelmed by the thought that with everybody clustered around his offering, nobody would be paying attention to me. I was vulnerable. But to what? I couldn't think of anything that made sense.

And I wanted one of those donuts. The impulse was so incongruous and pathetic that I almost screamed.

"Meg?" Adam asked.

I'd never told him my nickname.

Stomach dropping, I turned back to him. But my head swam, and the light was different. Brighter, haloing him, dawn coming up behind him.

And Adam was no longer wearing his PPE.

Not the face shield, not the gloves, not the gown. He was dressed down, even, not in the suit I was familiar with, but in slacks and a Henley zip-up sweater. Comfortable and comforting. The fabric looked so soft.

Everything was slipping away from me. Out of my control, out of my understanding. I was dreaming. Or I was seizing. Or I was sedated and hallucinating. One of those, or all of those.

"I hope you don't mind, but I tried to get in contact with your family," Adam said.

"No. No, stop." I shut my eyes. But I opened them again just as quickly, because alone in the shell of my body, I was too unmoored. I needed to be able to see, even if what I was seeing wasn't real.

He pulled his chair to just beside my bed. "I spoke to your mother," he said. "I let her know you're doing well. So you don't need to worry."

No mention of asking my mother to help manage my care, of course, but I'd never asked. And did I notice the omission then? I can't remember. I do remember flinching at the thought of her. "I told her I was being discharged," I said. "She tried to call me. She'll want me to come home."

Adam's brows rose in surprise. "She didn't say anything about that," he murmured. "I can call her back. What would you like me to tell her?"

I stared at him. Did I want Adam to be talking to her? Could I have stopped him? He might have been lying about getting in contact with her. Of course he was lying; he wasn't really there.

"Nothing," I said. "She—she's going through a lot herself."

Nothing, I thought, *because she might come to check on me and I don't want you waiting for her.*

And then the last scraps of my sensible mind: *There is no conspiracy, you're sick, he's trying to help.*

"I'm sorry to hear that," Adam said. He looked over the wreck of me, the nest of tubing, all gleaming in the dawn light. This close, his face was shadowed. I couldn't read his expression.

Then he turned from me. He went to the whiteboard, frowning at the smear where Isobel's name had been. Carefully, he wrote *SHANNON* in its place. The board behind it turned white and clear, properly cleaned up. More evidence that he wasn't real. That none of this was real.

Then he erased the circle around the 6 on the pain scale from earlier that night, and I watched as he adjusted it to a *2*.

"I'm still in pain," I said, confused. I tried to tell myself it didn't matter, but my certainty slipped away from me. He'd done this before. I'd watched him do this before. But the board didn't determine treatment. It was just for my convenience.

So why change it?

"You won't be soon," he soothed, then came back to my side. For a moment, I could see the outline of his face shield, the bulky drape of his gown, but when I squinted, I just saw the cashmere sweater, the line of his jaw.

My head hurt.

He reached up and ran his fingers along the tubing from my dwindling saline bag, down, down, down to my chest. Like he was checking for kinks or bubbles, the same motion the nurses did, but lingering. Slow. As if savoring. Not hesitating, he wasn't unsure at all.

Then he took a syringe from his pocket.

"What are you doing?" I asked, disbelieving.

"Taking care of you," he said, inspecting it before removing the cap. He didn't scan it, or my wristband, took none of the steps that the nurses did, just hooked the syringe into one of the open lumens.

It wouldn't even leave a mark.

"Stop! Adam, don't!" I reached for him, but it was too late. He said nothing, depressing the plunger in one smooth and easy motion, the same way Isobel did, Penelope did, like he had the training. But he didn't. He wasn't supposed to be here. He wasn't supposed to be doing any of this.

I grabbed his wrist, but it was too late. The substance, whatever it was, was already inside me.

"Shhh," he murmured. His free hand touched my sweat-slick forehead. Not measuring my temperature, but soothing, stroking my hair. I flinched, and my cheek met his palm. Like every time before, the skin-to-skin contact was like a drug, so uncommon, so needed. It short-circuited me.

Or maybe that was whatever medication he'd injected into my port. The world was growing fuzzy. I struggled to stay in it, to observe whatever he was doing to me. When he pulled away, I let him, my own hand falling limp onto the mattress. I stared down at my body as he took that hand in his. As he wrapped soft restraints around my wrists, tethering me to the bed rail. The PPE was back. His hands squeaked faintly as he worked.

I kicked at my blankets as he reached for my ankles, and only then did I try to shout.

But I couldn't. I could only cough, and thrash, and hope somebody would see my heart rate spiking. Would think to check on me.

He covered my face with a cloth, like I was a bird to be quieted.

A tug at the cannula entering my port. I couldn't tell if he was injecting or drawing. In the warm moist dark of the space beneath the cloth, I hyperventilated. I kept kicking, because he'd abandoned restraining my legs, focusing instead on doing what he'd come to do, which was—

Was—

What?

And why would he do it with no PPE?

Then I remembered that this wasn't real. Just like Veronica in the bed, just like my dreams of my mother. I was just sick.

Just sick.

I closed my eyes, and let the world fall away.

Just before shift change, I came back to myself. The phlebotomist was leaving; I could hear the rattle of the cart in the antechamber. The sun was full bright now, cutting through the fog that wreathed me. The dream clung, though, sticky on my skin, in my eyes. I struggled to raise the back of my bed, so that I could see.

Everything looked like it should have, as far as my addled brain could tell. My cannula was clean. My drip of saline was almost done. Somebody had emptied the bag connected to my PureWick.

On the whiteboard, the smear was gone, cleaned up, the space now occupied by a clearly written *SHANNON*. And there was a pain level of *2* circled.

The Adam that had changed the board hadn't been real, but somebody had been here, somebody had changed it. A nurse? Had I spoken with a nurse, dreaming it was Adam the whole time? I pictured myself, babbling nonsensically in my bed. Them, giving me pain medication.

It made sense.

It all made sense.

But then what had happened to Isobel? I remembered speaking to her. I knew I hadn't lost a day. I half expected her to walk in the door, but it was Shannon, just like the board said. Adam hadn't been here, not really.

Was the same true about Isobel?

Chapter Twenty-Seven

They trialed me on room air, and I passed.

A strange, stressful anticlimax; the respiratory therapist turned off the flow of oxygen, which had been at its lowest level for a day by then, and removed the cannula from my nose, and then we sat. We both watched the monitor, waiting for my saturation to fall. I waited to feel lightheaded, or the stirrings of faint distress.

Nothing happened.

So the respiratory therapist left, and Lauren, my newest day-shift nurse, took over, looking in on me every twenty minutes or so, making awkward small talk when she did. At first, I thought it was out of some feeling of social obligation; then I realized she was just assessing my mental status. Alert? Oriented? Starting to sound short of breath or confused?

But no. I was getting better. I had a few bouts of coughing, but nothing I couldn't recover from. I felt . . . fine.

Almost fine enough to write off the events of that morning, but not quite.

Every time she entered the room, I tensed. The mask, the gown, every time they resurrected the memory of Adam by my bedside. Sometimes, I could feel the restraints on my wrists again, though when I peeked, always when Lauren was gone or not looking, my skin was unmarked.

Just another nightmare to shrug off. But it clung and clung.

Between Lauren's visits, I eyed the room phone. My conversation with Adam may not have happened, but I kept thinking about my mother. More than anything, I wanted some anchor to the outside world. Something that wasn't five minutes of home renovation content to three minutes of commercials, something that wasn't the rhythm of hospital life.

Except I didn't remember her number. She'd dropped the landline I'd memorized as a kid years ago, and she'd always been programmed into my phone, even if we didn't always speak. With a sinking paralysis, I realized I couldn't call her. Or anybody else, for that matter. The few numbers I still knew were uselessly antiquated. I barely even had food services committed to memory.

That realization made my skin crawl, my bones itch. Exactly the kind of agitation I needed to avoid.

Soft sounds came from the antechamber, Lauren donning her PPE. Again, my pulse jumped, and this time, I couldn't manage it. I wouldn't be able to hold it together if she came in. I'd been shown how to turn on the camera and microphone to address whoever was in the antechamber, and I fumbled it on for the first time, clumsy but effective.

"I'm okay," I told Lauren, who was frozen, startled, gown not yet pulled down over her scrubs. "You don't have to come in again." My voice came out breathy, rushed, but then, I had a respiratory disease.

Her gaze flitted back and forth, no doubt looking at my

vitals on the other screen, assessing my color, my alertness. "I do," she said, after a moment. "It's best practice." She didn't sound convinced, though, and she didn't continue putting on her PPE. She didn't want to be in here, any more than I wanted her to be.

That made me relax a little. Less reactive, more determined. "Really, I feel fine. How much longer is on the timer?"

"Fifteen minutes." She looked away, out to the main hall. No chance she was coming in here. "I suppose," she said, finally, "that I can just watch from in here."

Not as good as being left completely alone, but better. Safer. There wasn't anything she could do to me from out there.

"You're doing well," she added, awkwardly, and I wondered what, exactly, Shannon had told her about my history. At bedside shift report, the conversation had been more or less neutral: I had tuberculosis, I was undergoing SWAIL, I was a fall risk but used my call light appropriately. But out in the hall, Shannon might have told her about my periods of instability. Certainly about the seizures.

Something was making her uncertain around me. Maybe what she'd been told, or maybe just newness to the ward. That last was an assumption, but I hadn't ever seen her before, hadn't heard her name before.

Still...

I hadn't asked Shannon about Isobel, too afraid of how she might react, what she might think, if I really had imagined Isobel being there, or lost track of so much time. But Lauren and I didn't have that history, and didn't know how close Isobel and I had gotten. It felt safe.

"Was Isobel on shift for part of last night?" I asked.

Lauren looked at me blankly. "Who?"

My appetite was nonexistent. The medication had decimated it, and my silent panic erased the last scraps. I knew I had to eat, knew my body was burning like a furnace to fight off the infection, could feel how weak I was getting. But every spoonful of Jell-O broke against my gums into slick fragments, catching in my throat, making me gag.

The only way I got it all down was the fear of being fed by tube instead. My skin crawled when the tubing to my external catheter brushed against my thigh, and my hand itched to tear the cannula out of my port, my port out of my flesh. I couldn't stand it much longer, not feeling like this, even with the small respite of losing the oxygen line.

I knew, rationally, that Lauren was probably just new, like I'd guessed. That she didn't know night shift yet. And yet her lack of recognition, her nervousness, it all primed my paranoia back to full pressure.

And all that pressure had nowhere to go.

I couldn't even pace, still confined to my bed, the PureWick and alarm both tethering me down. I could only sit there and eat my Jell-O and wait for Lauren to finish up hanging that day's SWAIL infusion. When she was gone, I couldn't even scream, because I didn't want to bring her running back.

Instead, I pushed myself hard against my sheets. They stunk of me. Of my medications, my sickness, my immobility. But that stench also meant I was real, that I was present, that my existence had consequences. I turned my head to the window, staring out at that same mountain view, out at weather that was slowly starting to change. Today there were rain clouds, the first of the season, a break in summer's long clear days and nights.

Time was passing. I was almost halfway through now, by my count.

I was real. The world was real.

My infusion hurt a little, not as bad as some, but enough that it kept me awake. The manual Isobel had brought me was still there, very much real, and I made myself read a chapter. Two. I could still remember working on this one, could remember the phone calls with one of the subject matter experts I was translating the knowledge of into a series of clear, comprehensible steps.

Beneath the rustling of the pages I turned, I could hear a rasping breathing.

I'm not sure how long it took before I realized it wasn't my own.

I set the book down, careful to not make a sound. I opened my mouth, quieting my own exhales. But there it was, in and out, in and out, almost in time with the IV pump but not quite.

I bit my lip to feel the pain, but I couldn't tell if it felt right, or if I was drifting again.

"Stop," I whispered. "Stop, go away, I don't—I don't want this."

"You're getting sicker," Veronica said.

She wasn't anywhere I could see, so I followed the sound of her voice. Of her breathing. Carefully, I arranged the tubes and leads connected to me, and I shifted onto my side. Then farther, leaning against the raised railing of the bed, reaching with trembling fingers until I could find the latch and lower it.

And then I looked over the edge.

Veronica crouched beneath my bed.

Her hair had grown more tangled since that last time I'd seen her, and her lips were red with blood. There wasn't enough room for her, and her spine pressed against the underside of the bed frame. Beneath her was a murky, tacky-looking substance, gluing her to the floor, clinging to her bare legs. Her head was twisted unnaturally so that she could meet my gaze.

"The seizures," I said, slowly.

"To start with," she agreed. "And then the rest."

The rest.

"Can't you see it?" Veronica asked. "Can't you hear it coming?"

Her skeletal ribs rose and fell, and the sound of her breathing grew louder. Where before it had rasped, now it roared, her mouth opening wide. I could feel it, the pulse and suck of oxygen, and I clapped my hands over my ears, shutting my eyes against it.

And then, just as swiftly as it had arrived, it was gone, replaced with the sounds of my room that were so familiar now I barely heard them. I opened my eyes, finding myself still curled at the edge of the mattress.

Veronica was gone. But the mess was not. A thin biofilm coated the floor where she'd been, the pinky-peach of something living. From me? Or from SWAIL, dripping from a bag, taking root? My gorge rose, and I forced myself upright, clawing for the nurse CALL button.

How long had it been there? How much had it spread? Why had nobody noticed it?

Lauren's voice came out of the attached speaker a moment later. "Yes?" she asked, voice tight with annoyance.

"Can you call environmental services?" I asked, my voice so small, so tight in my desperate attempt to sound reasonable. "I think there's something growing in here."

They put me in another bed, in another room, while they bleached the floor and scrubbed everything else down. Not Veronica's; hers was already assigned to a new patient. I couldn't guess whether it was for SWAIL or not. The only way I could have known, I guess, was if I'd seen Adam haunting that doorway.

But he wasn't anywhere in the building, at least according to Lauren, who hovered nearby the entire time I was in the spare room, doing a piss-poor job of hiding her distaste. I don't know what she thought I'd do. Make a run for it?

"Are they going to culture it?" I asked, voice muffled by the mask I had to wear.

She jumped, as if she'd forgotten I could speak. "What? No. Why would they?"

"In case it gets me sick, too," I said.

"It's just a spill," she said.

But I noticed that she changed her gloves again soon after, and I heard her scrubbing for longer than usual once I was back in my room, trying not to cough from the lingering fumes. She knew something, or feared something. Me, or the room, or . . . whatever was making me sick.

What was it Isobel had said, the night I decided to leave?

A hospital is an organism, too. The people in it keep it clean, keep it fed, keep it alive.

And I'd known exactly what she was talking about. She'd continued on as if she meant it metaphorically, hospital-as-ecosystem, but no, it was an organism. A rotting organism. A sentient, watching organism.

It wasn't just my tuberculosis, or the distress and personality change occasioned by a prolonged hospital stay. What I was seeing was *real*. It was dangerous.

And I needed to talk to Isobel.

Chapter Twenty-Eight

But Isobel wasn't on shift that night.

And she wasn't on shift the next night, either. Or the next. Or the next.

Of course, that assumes I could trust my perception of time, but the tuberculosis seemed to be on the back foot, beaten down enough that my periods of lucidity were growing longer. Veronica didn't visit again, or Adam, real or not. I slept for long periods, but when I woke, I was miserable but coherent at least half of the time. Even when I wasn't, it was a sort of muzziness, and not the full-on disorientation and lack of memory that had come before. They discontinued the external catheter when they were satisfied I could handle the bedside commode again, and a few days later, the occasional walk to and from the bathroom.

Lauren took every opportunity not to enter my room, and I encouraged it. But as the days passed, I wondered if Penelope, too, was gone. If there had been some sea change while I slept. Louise took nights, or Shannon, and I didn't ask either.

And then Penelope was back. One morning, I roused for bedside report, and I recognized her eyes, cheerful and focused, above her mask. I'd never been so relieved to see her. It was like some link to the real world had been restored, even though she was no different from the other nurses. One more piece of normalcy, perhaps, was the better way to think of it.

I waited to ask until she returned with my breakfast and the newest SWAIL infusion. I let her hang the bag, this one cloudy like milk. I'd never seen that style before.

She caught me looking. "Priming," she said. "You're almost bottomed out. Soon we start climbing back up." The fine lines by her eyes crinkled as she smiled. "It's a long bottom, but things will only get better."

That should have made me happy, hearing that. But instead, I thought of that scum on the floor.

They were going to grow something in me. My new immune system, yes, but *how*?

I took a steadying breath. That panic could wait.

"Do you know when Isobel will be back?" I asked, prodding at my croissant like I might actually eat it, not looking directly at her. *Casual, act casual.*

"She left the unit," Penelope said, just as lightly.

My stomach dropped. "No," I blurted, head up, staring at her now in disbelief. "No, she wouldn't have done that." She wouldn't have left *me*. The only way she would be gone is if something had happened to her. "Is she okay?"

I didn't have an active bag of saline at the moment; she had to lean in close to flush my cannula and hook me up to the IV drip. She was so steady. For half a second, I wanted to rip the mask off her face, to see her expression.

"She's fine," Penelope said, and I had no idea if she was lying. "Or will be. She just needs some time. She's gone through a lot, you know."

"I know," I said without thinking.

The Graceview Patient

COVID. The ICU. Burnout. Maybe—maybe she'd just hit a wall. But she wouldn't have quit, I knew that in my gut. Not until I was through the program, or gone home. Fired, then, maybe, or put on leave. Maybe she had a drinking problem. Or, what, narcotics? But she'd always been alert, on top of things, just—just tired. Just angry.

Could it have been me? I'm sure there were rules about getting too enmeshed with a patient, but we'd only talked. Had dinner once.

Unless there was something I was forgetting.

Penelope had straightened up but was looking at me strangely. And the only thing I could think of was running out into the main hall, yelling about having seen something in my room, begging to go home. But that hadn't been real.

She'd been afraid of something, though, the next morning. What I'd said had spooked her. What had it been?

Can we live inside you?

"I'm going to get this running, okay?" Penelope asked, and I nodded, staring blankly at my croissant.

We both knew I wasn't going to eat it.

The new bag burned.

It was like everything from that moment forward was designed to stoke my obsession with Isobel's disappearance to a fever pitch. I hadn't had a bag this painful just going in since the night Isobel had tried the heat pack trick. Penelope didn't offer it, but I also refused to call her back in. Not until I'd sorted through my feelings.

There were almost too many to manage.

Shame and longing and fear and anger. Exhaustion, always, and something very like heartbreak. Past any question of if it had been my fault, or if Isobel had chosen to go, past all of that, there was the abandonment. Betrayal. I'd told her that I had no one, she'd said she worried about me, and now... nothing. I had nothing.

I couldn't take it anymore. Sitting in bed, obsessing, worrying—no. No, I couldn't keep doing this. The PureWick was off. I wasn't dizzy. I was a little weak, sure, but I was only going to get weaker if I stayed like this. And I could feel my skin growing tender, sore spots on the backs of my thighs.

I looked at the yellow band around my wrist, next to my ID band, and I looked at *moderate fall risk* on the whiteboard, and I flipped them both off and moved to ease myself out of bed. I had the trick of lowering the rails now; I'd watched closely enough the last several times I was helped down. It was harder from the patient side, but not impossible. I pinched my finger, and the thing rattled going down, but there was no sign anybody heard.

And when I swung my legs out over the edge of the mattress, then eased my feet down to the floor, there was no wail of an alarm.

I stood slowly, carefully, hyperaware that my knees might choose this moment to go out. But my body held, and there was enough length in my IV tubing to maneuver myself and the pole around safely. I stood, on my own, for the first time in over a week. I nearly wept. It was so easy to lose pieces of myself from negligence, from distraction, from illness. But I could stand. And I could walk, step by slow step.

There wasn't much of anywhere for me to go, of course.

The window, the bathroom, the door to the antechamber. I don't know why I went to the antechamber, out of the three. Maybe just to see if I could do it. Maybe to see how different it was, now that I was truly locked down. But the inner door opened.

I hesitated.

I wasn't meant to be in this part of the room, especially not unmasked. It was dangerous. But surely not that much more dangerous than my room itself. Maybe by the door to the hallway, but not here, where everybody who came in to attend to my care had already scrubbed in.

I leaned in, peering around.

And I heard two people talking just outside the other door, and in the background, a faint, high-pitched whine that I couldn't place.

"—heard that that's why they're keeping her on the ward, it's just logistics. No other open beds in negative pressure–compliant rooms." Lauren. I'd figured she'd be off shift today, if Penelope was here.

"But *that* room? That is some cursed shit," another voice replied. I didn't recognize it. "Too many deaths in there. Too much weird going on up here. She should be in a critical care bed; it'd be better all around. They've rigged up isolation rooms before, they can do it again."

"Thank you for the vote of confidence," Lauren said, half muttering, enough that I wasn't certain that's what she said. The whine had cut out.

"She needs to be somewhere else, *assigned* to somebody else. We're better at our jobs when we don't get too close to the patient. If you think—"

Penelope's voice, steady and sharp, broke through them: "She's up," and whether the conversation ended there or not, I don't know, because I was already stumbling back out of the antechamber, pulse jackhammering. She probably meant whomever they'd been talking about, whatever patient they had in a room that could be any room. Except the only room I knew about that'd had a death in it recently was Veronica's. Room 772. Isobel had said there'd been only a few deaths before her, so there couldn't be multiple rooms like that, right?

And who would the nurses here already be close to, that they wouldn't want to risk failing her?

The door opened. I hadn't gotten back to the bed, but that didn't matter. I'd been wrong, clearly. There was some kind of alarm on the bed, or even just a noticeable change in my vitals. She knew I'd gotten up. So I just made it to the bathroom instead, leaning heavily on the frame.

"Margaret," Penelope called in from the antechamber. I could hear her gowning up. "You're not meant to be out of bed."

"Sorry," I said, and my shortness of breath wasn't an act. "I just—wanted to stretch my legs—"

"And you can use your call light to ask for help with that. We don't want you getting hurt."

I thought about pointing out the tender patches on my legs. "I'm going to use the bathroom," I said.

And even though I heard her say, "Wait for me, please," I still wheeled the IV pole in with me and shut the bathroom door.

I did manage to piss on command. And I kept my staring at my reflection to a minimum as I washed my hands because, as anticipated, Penelope opened the door just as I shut the water off.

(I looked horrible. But my skin was so beautifully clear.)

"I need you to get back in bed now," she said, and her eyes looked as friendly as they had at bedside report, but I could hear a quiet fury in her voice, under the gentleness.

I let her lead me back, meek, and not asking about how she'd known. I could take a guess. There were limited options: something in the bed that could tell, maybe based on weight, if I was there; some kind of motion sensor; or just a constant camera feed to the nurses' station.

Probably not the last, if only because it wasn't automated enough.

I didn't notice her resetting anything as she helped me onto the bed, then checked me over for any signs of injury. She noticed the marks on my legs all on her own and tutted over them. "Try shifting onto your side when you can," she said.

I wondered if that set off any false alarms.

She double-checked the SWAIL IV, then pulled a syringe from her pocket.

"I should have warned you," she said, thumbing off the cap. "Sometimes today's bag can cause some discomfort. Agitation, even. This should help stave off any pain or anxiety, but it might make you feel a little fuzzy."

I'm sure, even now, that she wouldn't have just given it to me without asking, without waiting for a response. But I'm equally sure that I said, *"Wait—"* and that she pushed the plunger down anyway.

So which was it?

· Chapter Twenty-Nine ·

That lost me another day. The bolus of whatever she'd given me wore off before shift change, but it left me hungover. Or maybe that was SWAIL. Something wasn't playing nice with my brain, giving me waves of what felt like shivers in my nerves, sparks of sensitivity that short-circuited any thoughts more complex than irritation at the same ad playing for the eighth time during one episode of whatever was on HGTV.

But in hindsight, Penelope did me a favor. Or, perhaps, herself a disservice. By the time I was able to be pissed and curious again, she was off shift, and Louise was on.

I didn't make the same mistake twice. I didn't ask Louise a single thing about Isobel. What I did do was ask for help going to the chairs by the window to eat my dinner. I made a show of actually eating it for once, and Louise took the opportunity (and the requirements of keeping eyes on me, no doubt) to change my bedding. It was a lot more awkward to do, now that she had to wear all that PPE, and it slowed things down. Exaggerated them. I pretended to be absorbed by whatever was on TV, eating slow spoonful after slow spoonful of flavorless "risotto" that I don't think had any cheese in it at all.

There was a thin blue mat under the mattress, right where my hips would be. It looked like it connected to a little box at the foot of the bed, tucked in and discreet. It would be hard to reach, but not impossible. I didn't look for long, instead focusing on smothering my excitement. This was the best option available, the one I had the best chance of figuring out a way around. I ate my risotto and tried to look as bland as it tasted.

Even force of will couldn't get me through another lime Jell-O, though. I left that and the last few spoonfuls of glop untouched.

Louise was still notably approving when she came to fetch me. We did a few turns around the room together. Because Penelope mentioned my wandering? Or just because of experience, knowing I'd benefit from the activity? Maybe even just to wear me out, because after that, she had me shower, and by the time I was dried off and in my fresh bed, I was exhausted.

It was maybe nine. I could feel the sucking tar pit of anger at my own frailty waiting to drag me back down, and balancing that draw against needing to look normal was almost impossible.

I was so glad when Louise left.

There'd be other visits through the night; they were drawing labs every four to six hours, and they'd last taken some just before shift change. And Louise was not Lauren; she'd be coming by for rounds every hour. Two at the outside, if I was lucky and she felt I was stable, and her workload was high. I'd wait, then, until the next batch of labs. Wait, rest, and experiment.

Penelope had recommended I lie on my side. So I did, testing the limits of where I could be on the mattress before Louise checked in with me. I never heard the alarm go off, but she appeared twice, the first time when I scooted too far up the bed, and the second when I'd gone searching for the box. By the time she came in on the second, I was in another experimental "pressure relieving" pose. I apologized both times; I had what I needed.

I knew she'd come when the alarm went off. I knew I could reach the box without triggering it, as long as I was willing to work blind.

And I knew there was a toggle, and if I pushed it to my left, it'd flip from BED to OFF.

I settled in to wait.

I fell asleep.

I didn't stir when they took labs, or when Louise rounded next. I slept right through, unaware. I don't know what meds I was given that night, or if my vitals changed. All I know is that when I woke, it was just before dawn.

"Get up," Veronica said.

And my eyes were open.

She wasn't there, but her voice lingered, almost palpable. She'd spoken right into my ear, clear and sharp, and I was sitting up without having consciously willed it. Like I'd been summoned. Like she was trying to save me, a ghost warning of a house fire, of some impending disaster. Disoriented, I stared at the whiteboard, then the clock, barely visible.

It was 4:48.

There was no sign of how recently Louise or anybody else had been there. It could have been just a few minutes prior, or hours ago. I had no way of knowing when they'd be back. And none of it mattered, because I wasn't going to get another chance tonight.

Either I was going to be able to sneak out of bed or I wasn't, and I'd find out pretty quickly which was the case.

Veronica's voice still echoing in my eardrums, I checked my chest. I wasn't connected to a drip. The pump was silent and dark. I drew my legs up, inch by inch. I'd practiced this, after Louise had responded to the second false alarm, before I'd dropped off. It hadn't called her back then.

I only hoped I was remembering this right.

I curled up pointed toward the foot of the bed, my hips still over the mat, my arm stretched out beneath me to the edge of the mattress. I groped along the molded plastic of the frame. My gaze stayed fixed on the antechamber door, ready to move at the slightest sign of somebody's approach. My shoulder protested, pushed to the limit of its ability to extend, but it wasn't enough, not enough, where was the *fucking* box? My vision was going dark around the edges as I bent and strained.

And then I felt it, the slightly different texture of plastic from a different manufacturer and the little nub. *Left or right?* I pushed left, before I could overthink it.

Nothing happened.

No feedback. I had to trust. And it was so hard, to trust myself, that I almost shoved the nub back to the position it had been in. But instead, I pushed myself upright. I shifted in bed, rolling sensation back into my aching shoulder. My skin buzzed with overexertion and tension. Carefully, I rolled onto my side and tipped my pelvis up. Off the mat.

And still Louise didn't appear.

I gave it two minutes. That was all I could bear before the anxiety got to be too much to withstand. Two minutes, no Louise, so I pressed forward.

I stood up and listened.

Nothing. No voices in the hall, no opening of the outer door. Not even the faint whine I'd heard before Penelope had come to fetch me, which I now realized was the bed alarm. I'd done it. But that didn't mean I had time, or that she wouldn't notice that she wasn't getting any signal at all from the bed. I had to move quickly.

I didn't take the extra minute to find my robe or my slippers. I was barefoot from the shower; I'd been too tired after to contort myself enough to get my socks back on. I tried not to think about the bare skin of my feet against the floor, the floor where that film had grown. I just moved. Antechamber, mask up. No need to do anything else, because a paper gown wasn't going to make me any less noticeable in the hall. Just enough for my protection, and then a moment to peer out into the hall, looking for the nurses' station. The angle was tough, but doable, and—

And it was empty.

Had Veronica known?

I should have been more afraid. I can see that, in hindsight. The voice of a dead woman had woken me up, and in the moment, I just—accepted it. Did I think it was a dream? Or was I just so tired that the fear slipped away from me?

But now I know better. It was Veronica. She woke me because it was time. Because there *was* no other time. She wanted me to see what came next.

How? *How?*

I left my room on wobbly newborn fawn legs that might have given out beneath me at any moment. Down the hall, in one direction, because I had just one shot at this, and I knew what room Lauren and the other nurse had been talking about.

Room 772. Veronica's room. A new patient's room, but already closed up tight, with that red bar image posted, *no entry, infectious.* Just like mine. And they didn't lock the door, just like mine.

I didn't give myself time to think. I trusted my gut and got into the antechamber before anybody came back into the hall.

I almost collapsed once the door was closed. Adrenaline could only take me so far, and beneath it, I was a shaking, half-broken wreck of a person. A coughing fit threatened to overtake me, and I pressed the heel of my hand against my sternum. I didn't have *time* for a coughing fit. Didn't have time to be frail.

If I could just keep it together, I could peek into this room. See what was there to be seen, what was so upsetting to that unnamed nurse, then get back to my room. Nobody would ever know. I'd have stolen back that small piece of my independence.

I already knew who I was going to see.

I wouldn't have tried that hard to get out of my room if I hadn't known. But I'd barely let myself think it, barely acknowledged it, until I was pushing open the antechamber door into the hospital room.

Because it was Isobel unconscious in the hospital bed that had once consumed Veronica, pale and shining with sweat, lips a brilliant red below a nasal cannula. She wore the same hospital-issue gown I did, and she looked so small in it. Her hair was in a rough braid over her shoulder, and I could see it was already matting from being rubbed against the pillow.

There were restraints around her wrists and ankles.

Her skin was chafed and red beneath them. She'd been struggling.

I took her hand, pulse hammering in my ears. I didn't understand. Seeing her like that—it cracked me open wide in a way my own infirmity hadn't.

Isobel moaned, eyelids fluttering.

"Come on, come on," I murmured, and let go of her hand to touch her cheek. "Isobel, come on, wake up."

When she looked at me, I don't know what she saw. Her eyes were unfocused, pupils huge and dark. She frowned, brow creased sharply, and she tried to reach for me in turn. When the restraints stopped her, she let out a piteous shriek and thrashed.

"Shh, shh," I whispered, glancing at the dark screen of the computer beside her. "You're going to set off an alarm if you keep doing that. Please, Isobel, it's me, Meg. It's me."

She subsided, the rage and fear in her face replaced by disbelief, desperation. "Meg?" she repeated. Her voice was slurred.

"I'm here. We're both here. What the fuck are you doing in here?"

I don't know why I asked. It was obvious. She was sick, very sick, at least as sick as I'd been. But I'd taken weeks to get that bad. How long had she been missing? Had it even been seven days?

"Did I get you sick?"

She shook her head, then squeezed her eyes shut, tears oozing out. "You couldn't. You couldn't get me sick, not with what you have." She sucked in an uneven breath. "Shouldn't have been able to," she amended, quieter, voice brittle and breaking.

"The tuberculosis?"

She laughed. "Tuberculosis takes months to show symptoms," she said. "And we'd have to report it to the state. But it's convenient. For explaining what's happening to you. For keeping you hospitalized."

I shook my head, uncomprehending. "Isobel?"

"Don't you see? It's something else entirely. Something we don't understand." She groped for my hand, and I gave it to her. "And it's getting smarter. Getting hungrier."

Veronica, in this bed. Veronica, beneath mine. The walls of the hospital pulsing, *pulsing* . . .

"Something was growing in my room," I said, slowly. "On the floor. Like a sheet of pink flesh. They didn't tell me what it was."

"Everything is growing," Isobel whispered with a humorless grin. "And the more it grows, the more it eats, the more it rots its host out. I can see it now." The grin faded. "Hear it," she mumbled. "It's getting louder."

"Louder?"

"It's so loud."

Isobel's grip went from tight to excruciating, and I flinched away reflexively. But I saw it, the moment the fire overtook her brain, the moment her gaze went from fevered to focused somewhere else. Her seizure wasn't the strange inaction of Veronica's, or mine. After a long moment's rigid tightening, it turned violent, archetypal, her body jerking against the bed, against me, against the world.

I had no idea what I was supposed to do. I fell onto the

bed with her, and there was the sense memory of that nightmare, of the bed swallowing me. I fought her even as her body fought itself. There was blood. I think she bit her lip, or maybe her tongue, but I couldn't make sense of anything I was seeing.

"Isobel!" I screamed.

The door behind me burst open, hard enough that I heard it hit the wall. "Margaret!" Louise barked, and she wasn't alone. The room was suddenly full of people. All masked, all prepared to separate us. I spotted two security officers. "Margaret, I need you to get off the bed, or we will need to move you."

Gloved hands pried Isobel's hands off me. Outside the PA system came to life. *"Priority page. Code blue. Adult. West tower. Seventh floor. Room seven-seven-two."*

I should have just gone quietly. But I could feel the divots Isobel had dug into my forearms, and I thought . . . I don't know. I thought she needed me there. *Knew* she needed me there.

Distantly, I registered the overhead voice, dispassionately calling, *"Priority page. Code gray. Adult. West tower. Seventh floor. Room seven-seven-two."* A different color. Still for Isobel? Or was it for me?

"No!" I screamed, fighting against somebody's grasp as I watched Shannon calmly pushing something into Isobel's line. "No, what are you doing?"

"Helping her," Shannon said, flatly. "Louise—"

"On it. Mark, hold her arms away from her chest, please. Easy does it."

They were so much stronger than I was. I didn't stand a

chance. Louise fitted a syringe into my own line, and I stared through my tears into her impassive face.

"She needs me," I said.

"I think you've done enough damage," she said, curtly, and then darkness overtook me.

· Chapter Thirty ·

"You can't keep going wandering," Adam said.

I didn't look at him. Looking at him was too much of a trial. Looking at him made me desperate to ask him every question that burned in the soured pit of my stomach. What was wrong with Isobel? What were they hiding from me? What had really killed Veronica? Did I actually have tuberculosis?

What was going to happen to me next?

He seemed happy enough to answer that last one. I was fairly certain he was real. He was keeping his distance, in a reasonable configuration of PPE, and he just looked tired.

Fuck him. He didn't know what tired felt like. Whatever Louise had given to me to sedate me this time, the hangover was worse than ever. Or maybe that was just the price I had to pay for daring to walk down a hall.

"You're very sick," Adam continued. "Your judgment is impaired. Do you understand that, Margaret?"

"Get out," I said.

"No."

I glanced at him. He was always so perfect. Beautifully calculated to put me at ease. Put everybody at ease. But I still remembered what Isobel had said, about tuberculosis. About it being convenient. And here I was, without my phone, without access to my medical records or even Wikipedia to check the simplest of facts.

"I'm withdrawing from treatment," I said.

It was the only card I had left, as far as I could tell. Adam wanted me compliant. He'd made such a compelling argument. But now Isobel was sick, too, and I didn't trust Adam as far as I could throw a plastic fork—which felt like it might only be half a foot now.

"It's too late for that," he said.

"I don't believe you."

"The medical hold—"

"That's only for the tuberculosis," I said, cutting him off. "And only applies until I'm getting better and can follow instructions. And I am getting better. Right?"

"Margaret."

"And if you remove SWAIL from the equation, I won't be so *impaired*."

"I don't understand what has you so frightened," he said.

I started laughing.

But the words wouldn't come out. Not about Veronica, not about Isobel. He couldn't have them, couldn't have *either* of them, and I didn't believe for a second that he was asking in good faith. He knew. Some of it, all of it, it didn't matter the extent, just that he was in on it.

"I want to be transferred to a different ward. A different hospital. I don't care. I am not staying here."

"A different hospital won't be equipped to care for you. And that's even assuming they have open beds. Please, you need to trust us."

I shook my head. "Dr. Santos—"

"Dr. Santos told you exactly what I'm telling you now," he said, softly.

I stared.

The silence stretched as I racked my brain. But there was nothing there.

The worry lines on his forehead deepened. "You don't remember."

"That didn't happen," I said.

"Yes, it did. This morning, during rounds. He warned me, when I said I was going to visit you—"

I clapped my hands over my ears. "Fuck you! You're lying!"

The screen came to life showing Lauren in the antechamber. "Is there a problem?" she asked.

She asked *him*.

"I want him out of my room," I said before he could answer. "And I want you to tell Dr. Santos I'm withdrawing from the trial."

I could see wheels turning behind her eyes. "Yes, of course," she said. "Mr. Marsh?"

He was already up, hands presented in apology. He moved into the antechamber and shut the door, but I could hear him stripping off the gown and gloves and mask, heard the kick as the sink turned on. Lauren had come into the room in his place and was swiping into her computer.

"You'll tell him?" I said, relief washing over me. "You'll tell the doctor?"

Lauren hesitated.

My heart sank.

"What?" I asked.

"You told him yourself, just this morning, Ms. Culpepper,"

Lauren said, so gently. "And he explained why that's not advisable."

I hadn't. I knew I hadn't. Or maybe it was more accurate to say that the me in that bed, at that moment, hadn't talked to the doctor. The outcome was the same. But if Lauren said it had happened, and if Adam said it had happened—

I wanted to scream.

"I understand that," I said instead, slowly, carefully. "And I still want to withdraw." I'd play by their fucking rules if I had to. "Inadvisable doesn't mean—"

"It's not an option, and he's prepared to ask a judge for a court order to that effect. We would be releasing you with no immune system, not in a state to care for yourself, with no permanent address and no responsible party to take you in." Lauren pulled a stool over and sat down. Not too close, never too close, but closer than she usually came. "I know you don't want to hear this."

"You can't keep me as a prisoner," I said.

"As a ward," she said. "And we can. We will, if we have to."

"I still want to stop treatment," I said, the world crumbling away beneath me. "I can still choose that. Can't I? No more SWAIL. Keep me here, but no more experimental drugs. I can just—wait. Wait until my body fixes itself."

"Oh, honey." She was younger than me, I was sure of it, but she said it with all the sincerity of a grandmother. "There's almost nothing left for it to fix."

My treatment plan changed after that.

They added a regular dose of a benzodiazepine. They didn't trust me not to somehow spit the pill out, so it came in the form of a bolus directly into my line, like clockwork. I half expected that to come with somebody sitting by my bedside night and day to make sure I stayed put, but I think my infection status made that unfeasible.

My nurses came by more frequently. Labs kept being drawn, over and over again. Despite the anxiety meds keeping me drowsy, the constant interruptions kept me up all day, all night. Was that by design, or just life in the hospital?

I tried to ask about Isobel, when I was too drugged up to remember that I didn't trust any of the answers they were bound to give me. Penelope wouldn't answer. Louise told me I needed to focus on myself, and that they were giving her the best of care. Lauren's response told me the most; she looked so uncomfortable as she tried to redirect me.

"It's my fault," I sobbed, unable to help myself. "She's sick because of me. She's going to die because of me."

"We're not going to let that happen," Lauren said, but she didn't say I wasn't responsible.

She'd known, I realized eventually. From the beginning, she'd known Isobel was sick, and she'd known I was the reason. That's why she'd jumped at the chance to stay out of my room. Why she was so hesitant to talk to me, to touch me. She was afraid.

I was monstrous. They were turning me into a monster, and hating me for it.

And through it all, the IV pump kept clicking away, SWAIL flowing into me. SWAIL, and antibiotics, and steroids, and other things I couldn't keep track of. *Drip drip drip*, diluting my blood, they were going to give me a PureWick again soon if they hadn't already. I had to reach down and check, physically, because I was so afraid I wouldn't be able to tell.

But it wasn't there. My nurse came and helped me onto the commode. I swayed, an unsteady tower of meat and bone.

(There wasn't much meat left. I was nearly as skeletal as Veronica had been.)

And then the bed again, and lab draws, and nurse check-ins, and *click click click click*.

Once, I got out of bed and made it as far as the whiteboard. In a desperate rage, I erased my nurse's name and wrote Isobel's in its place.

The next time I looked, it was gone. Fixed, or never written. I still don't know.

Would it have mattered, if I'd written out a plea for help instead?

Days passed, and they tried to make me sleep at night, wake during the day, but I fought it. It wasn't conscious. It was just my body, reacting and rejecting, manifesting my disorder.

I couldn't do it. I couldn't take any more of it. That's the only explanation I can give for what I did. I'd been there for so long, and seen the nurses set up my infusion pump multiple times a day. I'd listened to it going off when it ran dry. I'd soaked it all up, and here's the most important part:

I did not care what I did to myself, as long as it was something different. As long as something changed.

So it didn't matter that I had no idea what I was doing. It didn't matter that the pump's controls were stiff and unintuitive. It didn't matter that my fingertips were numb and clumsy. What mattered, in that dark and distorted place I'd reached within myself, was that I pressed those buttons, that the flow increased, that everything poured into me, and I laid myself out on the bed and let it sweep me away.

And then I could hear it, too. What Isobel had heard. What Veronica had heard.

I could hear the roar.

· Chapter Thirty-One ·

Have you ever been in an ocean cave? The kind on the shoreline that floods with the surf, then empties as the tide pulls back? So much stone, reflecting and amplifying the crash of the waves, the rush of water, breaking it apart and recombining it until it is deafening. Your skull turned into its own resonance chamber, a microcosm of the cave itself, the swell of breath, the sucking pull of an exhale.

If you're lucky, there's an upper exit, or somewhere safe to stand when the tide comes in.

The roar was everywhere. It was in every breath, every heartbeat. It was incomprehensibly loud, but it didn't hurt. It just blotted out everything that wasn't it.

On and on, it broke over me as I lay curled on my side in the hospital bed. My eyes were open to bare slits and no farther. My eyelids shivered with the thrum. I listened with every nerve in my body, vibrating along with it like a struck harp string. No variation on inhale, exhale. No change with the *thump-thump-thump-thump* of my heart, which I could only distantly feel and hear not at all.

And there, inside the roar, a distant note. The overlapping murmur of conversations. A brief fragment of Isobel's voice, saying *couldn't shouldn't couldn't shouldn't*, until that, too, was part of the maelstrom.

It wasn't the overwhelming crush of being sick. Of medication, of palliative care, of the dislodging of my consciousness from my meat. Medication was the method of action, yes, the pump dumping everything into me faster, faster, but this was something outside of me, too. Something I could feel. Something I could no longer ignore.

Listen, Veronica's voice whispered.

My body twitched.

A door was opening. Inflow, outflow. I could hear the rattle of cart wheels. The cart would stay in the antechamber, too difficult to disinfect, too dangerous, but the creature pushing it would come in.

Another door. A shape, approaching the bed.

LISTEN, Veronica demanded. And the roar receded. It didn't leave, no, but the tide went out, and I could hear what the technician was saying.

"Can you move onto your back, Ms. Culpepper?"

The name felt so strange against my skin. But I complied, spilling from my side onto the mattress. The room was still dark, the sun not yet risen. But he'd turned on one of the smaller lights in order to work, so I could see him. He wore a paper mask and a face shield on top of it, and he was double-gloved. I thought I saw his hands shake as he began to fill vials with my blood. He took it from my lower arm, not bothering with the port. Not a nurse, not my nurse. Somebody else.

Intruder.

He was a thief. A grasping, clawing little thief. The thought came from somewhere that wasn't me, and it rang behind my eyes.

A thief, but did he know what he was stealing?

He knew enough to be afraid. Like Lauren. And there was Isobel's voice again, *Tuberculosis takes months to show symptoms.* Everybody had to know that this wasn't natural, whatever I had.

My head lolled to the side. "Do you run the tests?" I rasped. "Or do you just take the samples?"

It was so hard, keeping track of who did what here. So many faces I only saw once, maybe twice. Had I seen him before? Was he the same man who had told me about my decidual cast?

Pathology had told him all about that one. Gossip spread like mycelium.

He startled a little, but kept his hands moving. "Just take the samples," he said.

"The nurses have been doing those lately." Part of being in isolation, part of managing my instability. Minimize exposure for me. No—*to* me.

There had to be a reason he'd been sent in. He was studying me. Interpreting something he'd need special knowledge for. Maybe the pathologist hadn't been gossiping.

Maybe he was lying about who he was. What his job was.

I thought of Adam, taking samples or medicating me without a trace. *Not real*, I'd thought, but maybe... maybe...

One of my hands flexed against the sheet, feeling out how much strength I had in me. I couldn't remember the last time I'd eaten, and the roar had settled in beneath my skin, keeping me at a distance from the edges of my body.

This man knew what he was looking for.

This man would have answers.

"Did you hear about what they found growing on the floor?" I asked.

One vial left. He hesitated before twisting it onto the connection for it. "No," he said. "No, nobody mentioned anything like that."

His skin had gone white beneath all that PPE.

But the gowns were just paper. His tore easily even under my weak hands as I rose from the bed in one smooth surge. "Jesus fuck!" he gasped, not loud enough that anybody would be able to hear, as I wrapped myself around him, ripping, rending, and then my weight overbalanced him, and we crashed onto the floor. I felt the jerk beneath my skin of my port being tugged by the IV tubing, and the needle in my arm slipped sideways.

He could hurt me badly. But he didn't, stunned and horrified. Trembling, I took hold of his face shield and peeled it off him. The whites of his eyes were so blinding.

"I know I don't have tuberculosis," I said. "Tell me what's happening to me, and I'll let you go."

His eyes darted around, frantic, to the CALL button (out of reach) and the doorway (shut, he'd have to yell very loudly, and he seemed too frozen to do that). My bed alarm would summon somebody quickly, but how quickly?

I dropped my hand to his. He was warm through the nitrile.

"Please," I said.

When I pulled his hand, he released the vial before it could do more damage to my arm. He let me have it. The needle slid free. Blood spattered onto him, and his heart beat so fast beneath my touch.

"It—it doesn't have a name."

Liar. But it didn't matter. I didn't need a name. "What is it?" I asked. "What does it *do*?"

I pulled the vial of my blood out of the needle, discarding the little butterfly. The cap was stiff, unyielding, but he stared at it.

He shook his head.

"We don't know. We—we can't culture it. At first—at first we thought it wasn't even pathogenic, thought it might be some chemical or procedural side effect. Like cancer from radium, before we knew what radiation does. But it spreads like an infection. And we—we keep seeing traces of it. Everywhere."

"Everywhere?"

"Everywhere, it's unavoidable. Like MRSA. You know what MRSA is?"

I nodded.

"But those traces, they don't make people sick. People weren't getting sick, we were just getting strange results on certain tests. Until . . . until they started these trials. Then people started dying."

Above us both was a mostly empty bag of SWAIL. Drip-dripping away, too fast. I didn't spare it a glance, even if he did.

"And now I have it."

He nodded.

"And Veronica. The other trial patient."

Another nod.

"It's—it's like a flip of a coin," he said. "Either the infection kills you, or they fix you fast enough. Just like any opportunistic infection. You need to let them fix you, okay? You need to cooperate. We're doing everything we can. I *promise*."

Everything they could, including taking samples from me. It clicked, then. They couldn't culture it in a lab—but they could in my body. I was the petri dish. I was the experiment.

"Jesus, god," he was babbling, "just—just put that down, let me go. Okay? Let me go. It's okay, you're scared, I get that, just..."

I sat back on my heels, grip loosening. The murmuring inside my bones had grown fractured, questioning, probing. Distracting. For just a moment, I wasn't strong.

He saw that weakness and began to fight.

He tried to get up, snatching at my hand. The vial went skittering across the floor. But I didn't need it. My mouth was raw, and the skin of my cheek split at the slightest pressure. Blood dripped from my mouth, onto him, and he sobbed as it soaked into his paper mask, as it oozed past to the skin beneath.

"Help! Nurse! *Staff!*" he shouted, but shouting opened his mouth, and I saw the change in him the moment my blood touched his lips. His voice broke, and he retched. I didn't care. I was rage and fury and strength, and I tore the mask from his face and bent down. I kissed him, smearing him with my blood, my saliva.

And then I sat up, triumphant, vicious and vindicated. There were no running footsteps, no doors slamming open

The Graceview Patient

this time. "Tell me," I said, voice slurred from the little cuts. "Tell me what happens next."

He said nothing.

But something was wrong with his face. The skin was swelling, turning puffy around his eyes, shiny across his cheeks. Too much fluid in him. It threatened to evert his eyelids, the rims growing wider, redder.

"Please don't," he whispered. "Please don't do this to me."

Beneath my hands, the skin of his arms grew loose. It separated from the muscle and fat. I felt it give way, and that, combined with his desperate plea, broke through to me. I let go. He collapsed, and I did, too, but away from him, in the shadow of my bed.

Nothing grew there but me.

Beneath me, the floor rose. Up, up by degrees, then down again, then shuddering with the force of a cough, a cough that ripped through my lungs, too. He jerked at the sharp crack of it, and where his skin was exposed, it was reddening, splitting, ulcerating. It moved so fast I could barely comprehend it, almost didn't understand the golden sheen of plasma slicking his broken-down flesh.

But the shriek that filled the air was not from him.

It wasn't mine, either. It was the roar, crashing down onto us both, the low dark weight of it, but through it came a piercing note. Screaming, inhuman screaming, and it reduced the world down to a bright and shining point.

I didn't want this.

I didn't want to be a part of this. Consumed by it. I was supposed to fight. To flee. But the shriek was everywhere, and then my voice was lifting, joining it, and the bright, shining point detonated and—

And I woke up to the technician packing up his things and leaving, blood vials sealed and ordered on his cart.

In the ringing silence, I leaned over the edge of my bed and vomited.

Chapter Thirty-Two

Louise found me like that, the infusion pump alarming as I sobbed and retched. She addressed each piece in its turn. First the pump, which she silenced, inspected, and then shut off. Then me, easing me back onto the mattress. She hit the CALL button while bent over me, ensuring I couldn't get up, and when somebody answered, she rattled off a quick, clipped list of what she needed.

"You're going to be okay," she said as we waited for reinforcements. Her gaze was on the monitors, watching my vitals. "Do you think you're going to be sick again?"

There was nothing left in me. I shook my head, then regretted it.

Another nurse arrived, along with the security officer from the other night in Isobel's room. He stood sentinel as Louise pushed a few syringes' worth of medication into my line and the other nurse hung a fresh bag of saline. They drew more blood for labs, speaking softly over me. And I let it all happen, waiting for the soft rush of a sedative to carry me off, the way it had so many times before.

But it didn't come. The second nurse left, and the officer made to sit in the chair by the window.

"I think we're okay," Louise said, and he stopped, all but hovering. "Margaret, how do you feel about a shower?"

I didn't want to move. But I felt stained. Fouled. Like I'd been the one having contagion-rich blood forced into my mouth. I hadn't done it, of course I hadn't done it, but I still had the memory of it.

I nodded. "Sounds . . . good." My mouth ached. My cheek was bitten open, that much was true.

"Wonderful. Mark, can you have environmental services swing by while we're taking care of that?"

After a long, wordless conversation between their gazes that I didn't even try to untangle, Mark left, and Louise paused the saline drip and detached me from the bag. She helped me from the bed and into the bathroom. There was a small seat built into the wall across from the sink that folded up and out of the way. She dropped it down and sat me there.

"Is it true?" I mumbled with my swollen lips. But if Louise heard me, she didn't acknowledge it.

Is it true? That I was infected with some mystery super organism? That everybody knew what I had, and was hiding it from me? That I was being used as a culturing medium? I stared at my reflection. At how gaunt I'd become, how beaten down. The whites of my eyes were a ruddy pink now, courtesy of the damage I'd done to myself, flooding my veins with SWAIL. My hair, shaggy and uneven, was clumped with sweat. I looked monstrous.

I *felt* monstrous.

And then, in the mirror, for just a moment, I saw Isobel in place of Louise. Isobel checking the water temperature. Isobel coming back to me and easing the gown off my shoulders. "Not monstrous," she said. "Just desperate."

I let out a weak, helpless sob. When I blinked, it was just Louise again.

"In we go," she said, guiding me into the spray and onto the seat in the shower.

She took her time. There were still some of my toiletries from home, which I hadn't used in weeks out of fear of some skin reaction. Louise didn't share that fear, I guess. Or maybe she judged the importance of using those familiar scents as worth the risk. And if I closed my eyes, I could imagine it was Isobel taking care of me, healthy and whole, not hurt by me. Not contaminated.

I was used to having help in the shower by that point, but this was different. It was kind in a way I didn't understand. Not just dutiful, not just thoughtful, but genuinely caring. Even once the water was off, Louise clipped my brittle nails as gently as possible. Dressed me with the softest of touches.

Concierge service, I thought, not understanding why she was doing it.

"There we are," Louise said when I was back in bed. They'd finished cleaning while we'd been in the bathroom; the floor was spotless, and they'd remade my bed, too. Fresh overlaundered sheets rasped over my bare legs, and I whimpered a little, then swallowed the noise. "How are you feeling?"

"Bad," I mumbled.

"Understandably," she agreed. She produced a comb from her scrubs pocket and untangled the unruly, patchy clumps of my hair. Just like with the shower, I was afraid to lean into it, but I was so desperate for comfort that I didn't resist. "You did a number on yourself, messing with the pump."

The pump, which was now encased within a lockbox, I saw. It extended up high enough to close over whatever bags were hung, too. No access.

I grimaced, then tried to wipe the expression off my face. "What?" I asked.

She continued as if I hadn't protested. "You're a very clever girl," she said, carefully teasing apart a knot with only the slightest tug on my scalp. "Which can either make you a wonderful patient, or a terrible one. No—don't act as if you don't understand me. I already know you're listening. And if you aren't, I'll say it again when you're lucid."

I'd made a poor attempt at feigning the drifting away I'd been forced into these last days. Clearly, there were elements of the experience I wasn't aware of.

Still, I didn't have to acknowledge her.

"Your brain is not your ally right now," Louise said, when it became clear I wasn't going to say anything. "The medications you're on can cause paranoia, confusion, erratic thoughts. And it's easy enough for me to list them, but experiencing them must be terrifying. I understand that. What our brain says is real is what *is* real, at least right this second. But you need to trust us. You need to let it wash over you. You can't let it make you hurt yourself like this."

I shut my eyes tight.

Louise stopped combing my hair and instead took my hand in hers. "I know everything in you wants to be *doing*," she said. "We talk about fighting illness. Beating cancer, that sort of thing. But this is what that actually looks like: you having the strength to trust your care team. You enduring. I want to see you on the other side of this, Margaret. And right now that's not where you're heading."

Was that meant to be a threat?

"This stunt of yours, whatever you meant it to do, it could have killed you. Do you understand me?"

I didn't move.

"Is that what you wanted?"

I cringed. "Of course not," I said. I hadn't wanted to die, no. It had been so much more complicated than that. And yet I couldn't articulate it. No matter how much I wanted to beg for answers, for the truth, I just couldn't do it. And unlike in my nightmare, I couldn't frighten the answers out of Louise, either.

I didn't *want* to frighten her. Or hurt her. Or hurt anybody. I just wanted this all to be over.

Louise squeezed my hand again. "This is your last chance, Margaret. The next time you do something like that—leaving your room without help, messing with your medication, any of that—we're going to take more serious steps to ensure your safety. That might mean restraints. A sitter. It's going to make the rest of your time here a lot more difficult. I don't want that, and I don't think you do, either."

"Just send me home," I said, finally, miserably. "I don't want to be here. Send me home."

"You know we can't do that. You don't have a living situation set up. You don't have a support network."

I think that was the first time I truly believed it. That I couldn't go home. That it wasn't safe for them to let me go. Maybe because I knew, at least in theory, what I was capable of. Maybe one day it wouldn't be a nightmare, and I'd infect somebody else just because I could.

Or maybe there'd just be another accident. Another Isobel.

I didn't know how it had gotten that bad. How I'd passed the point of no return, clearly so long ago that the idea of stopping now was laughable. But I had, and now Louise was right: If I wanted to come out the other side, I had to let go of control. Not give up, no, but go along.

That was the fight, wasn't it?

"I know," I said, finally. "I'm sorry."

"Don't be sorry," Louise said, and stood. "Just be here, with us. And get some rest. Do you want something to help you sleep?"

"No," I said. "I'm tired enough."

"I'm sure." She patted my hand. "Think about what I said. Remember it. Okay?"

"Okay," I said. I managed a weak smile for her.

And saw, just over Louise's shoulder, Isobel.

Another hallucination, of course, but a vivid one. She watched Louise tuck me in, then unlock the box and set my pump back at work. Click, click, and the box was closed, the key tucked into Louise's pocket along with that comb. Isobel's arms crossed over her chest as she looked on, evaluating. Weighing, judging. She stayed there, unmoving, until Louise had gone, leaving my lights dim. If I was having another seizure, either she didn't notice, or my mind constructed a separate narrative, playing out a different reality than the one Louise was handling.

"Isobel?" I whispered when we were alone.

She moved, finally, unfolding and coming to my bedside.

She looked exactly as she always had and wore full PPE. There were a few small differences, as if time had passed, a slight change to the set of her hair, but she wasn't flushed and visibly ill like she had been.

It was good to see her like that.

"She's right," Isobel said after a moment. "About this being your last chance."

When Veronica had haunted me, there had been a... a *staged* quality to it. A performative bent, the pause and rhythm of it. Isobel, by contrast, sounded so very real. And so very like herself.

"I'm surprised I'm not already strapped down," I said. And I would have been, if I'd really attacked that technician.

"They will, the next time they give you your infusion," she said. "Guaranteed. They're not going to risk it."

"Risk it," I repeated.

"You're so close to the inflection point," she said. "Where they switch to regrowing. They need you there, safely. No detours."

"So that I get better."

Isobel said nothing.

Ah.

My brain was playing tricks on me again.

I turned my face to the pillow. "Go away," I said. "I'm sorry, go away." Tears welled in my eyes. They burned more than usual. Everything was irritated, raw. Maybe my tears had become caustic, too.

"Meg," Isobel said, firmly. "You can't let this go any further. You're going to die if it goes *any* further. Do you understand me?"

I clapped my hands over my ears and curled up tight. "Go away!" I couldn't take this, couldn't handle the push-pull of reality, of hallucination, of my fears and desperation and hope all acted out like it was some shadow play. "Please, please, I can't do this."

"You have to," Isobel said. "For your own sake. For *mine*."

"There's nothing I can do!" I shouted.

"Oh yes, there is. Just one little thing, and then I'm going to get you out," Isobel said, and smiled.

· Chapter Thirty-Three ·

Please believe me: I never meant to hurt her.

"Is it going to be painful?" I asked. Isobel's hand, gloved like it should have been, rested lightly on my chest, her fingertips against the soft rise of my port.

"Yes. Probably very." She eyed it a moment longer, then nodded to herself and went to the supply cabinet beneath the computer station. She keyed in a code, one I didn't think I'd caught in all my weeks in that room. The nurses were very good at entering it swiftly and discreetly.

The drawer opened.

I know the drawer opened. Whether the Isobel I saw was real (impossible) or not (the only actual option), the drawer still opened. Louise wouldn't have left it open, and I don't think I could have opened it myself. But I know it opened, because that's where the scalpel came from.

Isobel set it on my tray table, the sterile packaging whispering against the plastic.

I was too frightened to touch it.

"Your hands are the only other option," she said. "I don't recommend it."

I looked down at them. My nails were clipped short, thanks

to Louise, and they were weak. My fingertips were an unsettling purple-gray, not quite black, but getting there. I couldn't feel anything past the last knuckle.

"There's still time to fix that," Isobel said, gently.

"But I have to take out my port first."

"Yes."

I took the scalpel. I peeled it out of its packaging, hands shaking furiously. I could hear Louise, telling me to just endure. That what I was seeing, hearing, feeling—it wasn't helping. That I couldn't trust myself, shouldn't.

And maybe that was true for the average person courting death; maybe even for me. But that scalpel was real and solid in my hands, and I hadn't left my bed. I hadn't known the code. I looked up at Isobel, shivering.

"What are you?" I asked.

Isobel considered. "I'm your nurse," she said, after a moment. "I'm your friend."

"You're a hallucination."

"To some extent." She didn't look at the scalpel. "I'm also dying in room seven-seven-two. We're connected. You've heard *it* now, too, right?"

I nodded, slowly. The roar. The roar that was just an overdose of SWAIL, but maybe not. I could hear it now, if I focused. It pulsed beneath us. Around us.

"And we can hear each other. Just like you've heard Veronica."

"Veronica is dead." Dead and long gone by now.

"She is," Isobel agreed. "Which means there isn't much she can do. But I can."

I looked down at the scalpel. "If we take my port out," I said, "they'll come in and sedate me."

"Yes. Then they'll take you to place a new one. And I'll wake you up when there's a chance. You just have to be ready to run." Wake me up, like Veronica had, in order for me to go and find Isobel. In order for me to start to understand.

It made sense, or was starting to. Maybe, in her own room, Isobel was staring into the distance, mid-seizure. Maybe her mind had gone walking. Maybe . . . maybe . . .

Maybe this was real.

"And then?" I asked, thumb pressing into the molding of the scalpel's grip, trying to feel the furrows and instead only feeling the blunt resistance. "Where do I go?"

"Home."

I winced. "Isobel . . ." There was no home to return to. Had she forgotten? Or had she not known? I couldn't remember now if we'd talked about my options again after that night we shared dinner. And that night, I'd been confident.

"Or somewhere safe, if not home. But you can't let them give you that next dose. You can't take that risk." She folded her hand around mine, around the scalpel. "Don't let them," she murmured.

You'll die if they go any farther.

"Okay," I said. "Okay, tell me what to do."

She didn't smile. I think if she'd smiled, I might not have trusted her so much. But she was solemn, focused. She took her hand away and traced one finger along the bottom edge of the port. "Take the dressing off, then cut here. The port is just under the skin and fat, above the muscle. Easy to insert, easy to remove. If you go in through the old incision, it'll be a fast job to patch you back up. A new cut buys you time."

The scalpel felt too light in my hand. I tried to imagine cutting myself open, and my muscles contracted, as if trying to pull me away from the threat. This wasn't like messing with the pump. That had been abstracted. Removed. This was . . . not.

"Can you do it?" I asked.

She shook her head. "No, Meg."

"You opened the drawer," I said. "You got the scalpel."

She didn't reply.

"I'm sick," I said. "I'm sick, and I'm alone, and you're not real."

"But I opened the drawer," she countered. "I got the scalpel. You're holding it right now."

I was trapped somewhere in between the learned helplessness of sickness and the desperate need of the human mind to fight, to *do*. Superstitious outbursts, any tiny way of making a mark, of pantomiming influence. And the exhausted certainty that none of it really mattered.

But then again, I had nothing to lose. If Isobel was actually there, if she was real, this would work. She would know what to do, she'd save me, and I'd be free. Or, more likely, I was hallucinating again—and cutting my port out would force them to restrain me, and I wouldn't have the choice to fight anymore.

Louise had been wrong to give me one last chance. If she was right, I couldn't be reasoned with.

I peeled up the dressing. My skin beneath it was tender but intact, and the needle came out easily enough.

"I'm sorry," I said, to her, to myself, and swept the edge of the scalpel along the bottom curve of the port before I could talk myself out of it again.

At first, there was no pain. I was certain I hadn't pressed hard enough. But then I felt the hot wash of blood down my breast, and the bright line of agony where I'd parted the flesh.

"Again," Isobel said. "Carefully, you haven't exposed it yet but you're close. Quickly, or they'll be able to fix it in room."

But I'd dropped the scalpel. It was somewhere in the sheets, and I was hyperventilating, panicking over what I'd done.

"Quickly!" she said. "They're coming!"

Had I screamed? I didn't think I had. But the pump was alarming, not working properly now that it wasn't pushing fluids into my chest.

My hands were the only other option.

I hooked my numb fingertips into the wound.

Then I screamed.

I could feel the port through a thin sheet of tissue. I hunched over, digging my fingers in deeper, clawing and scratching. A little more, a little more—there were voices in the antechamber now, and Isobel was gone, but it didn't matter, I could feel it, I could—

The flesh gave way, and I touched silicone. I tugged. I howled as it ripped free of where it had settled into my body, and the catheter threaded into my vein slithered and caught. There was so much blood. I closed my eyes against it, because if I couldn't see it, it wasn't happening.

But it hurt. It hurt. It hurt so fucking much. What was I doing?

What had I done?

My certainty faltered. I clutched at my flesh, not to keep it together but to keep myself together, to keep a hold on reality. The reality that my body was weak. That my mind was weaker. That Isobel was gone, and I had pulled my port half out of my chest, and Louise was rushing in with that same security officer from before.

This time, she didn't need to sedate me.

I passed out all on my own.

· Chapter Thirty-Four ·

I was vaguely aware of being wheeled through the hallway. The pain was far away. The terror, too. Nobody was holding my hand, and people talked over me. I couldn't understand the words.

Around me, the walls pulsed with breath. My breath, slow and steady, medicated down now. There was gauze on my chest, somebody's hand on top of it until the bleeding stopped. Then nothing. The wheels of the gurney, *squeak squeak glide*. A mask over my nose and mouth. Paper, not plastic. Nothing to help me breathe.

I waited for everybody to disappear, the way they had in my nightmare, when the port was first placed. But there were too many. The impression of bodies walking past, hurrying past, straggling past. So many bodies. So many reservoirs for infection, hosts and hostages.

Just sleep, I told myself. I imagined cradling my own body in my arms. I'd lost weight; I'd be just a bag of skin, a jumble of bones, all bound up in sinews too attenuated to allow me to move. If I slept, it would be over. Nothing left but to wait, and wait, and wait.

And go mad.

More than I already was, anyway.

Graceview was so expansive in its institutional copy-paste

aesthetic. Beneath the linoleum, it was an old, old building. Bones I couldn't see, but felt. *Thunk thunk thunk*, the wheels of the gurney clicking over them. And in between the bones, so many dead. Flu and tuberculosis and sepsis and trauma and so many other things, so many bodies that had given out, so many microbes feasting and replicating and spreading.

And my own little passenger, in my lungs and blood and skin, growing, growing.

The bed stopped moving.

"Get up," Isobel's voice said in my ear.

I opened my eyes.

I wasn't alone. I was in a room, but not my room. There were other beds, other patients. Nurses, circulating. More people than I had seen since I'd taken my last stroll through the main floor of the hospital, caught in glimpses through gaps in the curtains hung around my bed. The sight was momentarily stunning, disorienting in a way entirely separate from the drugs buzzing in my skull.

Louise wasn't there. The security officer was, but he was talking softly on his phone. My bed was closest to the door. Some kind of waiting room, before they took me into the OR? There was still gauze taped to my chest. No replacement port, not yet. They'd managed to get a fresh IV into my arm.

For all the bodies, there were no eyes on me. The curtains were a pitiful attempt at privacy, but they were enough. The cannula in my arm wasn't hooked to anything, just taped down to my skin. I wasn't restrained.

I got up. I left the gurney, and the room, and nobody noticed. There was no shouting, no running feet. The door I went through wasn't locked and opened not onto a main

The Graceview Patient

hallway, but a service corridor of some kind. There were signs and fluorescent lights, but there were no nurses' stations, and no doors to patient rooms.

Isobel wasn't there.

I faltered, finding myself alone. There was no voice in my ear, no shadow at the end of the hall beckoning me forward. But there was a path, of sorts. The linoleum beneath my feet, cracked and oozing plasma. I followed the line, head still foggy from whatever they'd given me, whatever hadn't been enough to keep me asleep.

Whatever Isobel had cut through to get to me?

She'd done it, whatever *it* was. Just like she'd promised, she'd gotten me out. Now I had to move. Get somewhere safe. Outside the hospital, if I could manage it, but I was in my gown, no socks, no slippers. No wallet. Phone long gone. I'd have to get creative.

Overhead, that same voice, that old litany: *"Priority page. Code green. East building. Second floor. IMCU. Room two-zero-seven."*

When I reached the stairs, I went down. They were solid, no trace of infection or injury. Signs indicated I was starting from the fourth floor. My legs burned as I descended, my knees weak, ankles threatening to roll or simply give out. I clung to the handrail. With every step, I expected one of the doors into the stairwell to open, but none of them did.

I reached the ground floor and kept going. I couldn't go out from there, not as I was. I'd stand out. It was too close to morning, or maybe too far into it; I had no idea how long I'd been unconscious. At any rate, there'd be too many people, and I was too conspicuous.

But the custodian had told me that nobody ever went down. And those rooms we'd passed that night, they'd been offices. Maybe inhabited today, yes, but maybe not. Maybe there'd be somebody's clothing I could take. Was it a weekend? I couldn't remember.

It must have been.

The offices were mostly empty, the windows in the doors closest to me dark. But I could hear voices from farther down. Not much space or time to work in. The first couple doors I tried were locked, but not the third. Inside was an office, paperwork left on the desk, computer quiescent and dark. There was no window, the only light coming in from the hallway. I slipped inside, peering into the shadows. There: a plush sweater hanging from a hook. It was a start. I pulled it on, somebody else's perfume crashing over me.

Before I could find a way to stop it, I was coughing. One of the old fits, the deep ones, and it hurt so much worse with the ragged wound on my chest. I leaned against the wall, then slid down to one knee. Both. I braced myself on the worn, scratchy carpet, coughing into my mask, eyes watering. The world tilted. Slid.

My shoulder hit the ground. I curled up and twitched, unsure of what I was doing, of what I was trying to do. I needed to be somewhere safe. Somewhere protected, where I could rest. I was so tired. I was so *fucking* tired, and the adrenaline was burning off. My hands clutched at my ribs, and I could feel every one of them, jumping beneath my palms. My fingertips were still numb. The joints below burned as if on fire.

When the coughing subsided, I wasn't sure if I could

The Graceview Patient

move. I felt liquid, swollen, and yet so light that I was halfway to dust. My heart beat fast and soft, like it was far away. Or—

No. Those were footsteps.

The noise that escaped me was an animal whine. I rolled myself onto my back, then reached out, scrabbling with unfeeling fingers for the door. The footsteps grew louder, closer. I had no idea what the person who made them could see, but I pushed, slow and steady as I could manage.

The door shut quietly.

I was left in darkness. Not the darkness of my hospital room, where there was always some illumination from outside my window, some light from the medical equipment, the glow of a night-light in the bathroom. This was total and complete, and with it was a silence I hadn't known in weeks. No click of a pump. No murmur of voices in the hall. Nobody would come for me, to take my blood pressure and samples of my body, to measure and evaluate and observe. Nobody knew I was here, if I'd been fast enough to get the door closed.

I could die here, and they wouldn't find me until Monday.

Maybe that's what I'd wanted all along. Maybe that was why I'd hallucinated Isobel. The last little push I needed to go out on my own terms, for all of this to be over. Too cowardly to put the scalpel in my neck, perhaps. But that didn't track, did it, with what I'd managed to do instead. And I wasn't so close to death, wasn't *so* sick, that a day or two alone would finish me off. Right?

The footsteps grew louder. They went right past the door I shivered behind and moved on.

My lungs were mercifully silent.

Slowly, tentatively, I uncurled. My shins stung, and when

I ran my palms over them, I felt torn-up flesh. Not bleeding, just a skinned knee. I was fragile.

Isobel had told me to go somewhere safe. I still had no idea what that looked like. Shakily, I tried to think through what I'd need. Food. Water. Shelter. Some way to keep myself away from other people, so I wouldn't get sick.

So *they* wouldn't get sick.

If Isobel was infected, that meant other people could catch it, too. Other people who weren't me, who weren't Veronica, who weren't artificially burned to the ground. I couldn't inflict it on anybody else, the seizures, the bleeding, the chaos. The roar. And Isobel was so much sicker than I had been, so much faster. Why?

What was different?

The only difference I could see was the obvious one: my immune system had been artificially decimated, hers hadn't. But that was backward. I should have been more at risk than she was. Unless, maybe, she had something else beating down her defenses? Something beyond the burnout, the long nights, the lack of proper meals and breakfasts of energy drinks?

Maybe. Maybe. So many maybes. My brain buzzed with them. My stomach churned. I kept everything in.

Could I go to another hospital, ask for help there? Show up in an ER, feign ignorance of my medical history? But they'd see where the port had been. They'd ask questions. Would they believe me, if I told them what had happened?

Was it worth the risk?

Another hospital wouldn't have Dr. Santos. Wouldn't have whatever approval he'd needed to run the SWAIL trial. No

Dr. Santos, no Adam, no bags of mystery fluid. It had to be better than this.

But...

I'd be leaving Isobel.

I couldn't do that. Not just for her sake, but for mine. She'd been my rock. The one tether to myself, the one *real* thing I'd had. Even after I'd put her in a hospital bed, she'd tried to save me. Tried to warn me.

She understood the trial, had seen this thing kill Veronica. If it had been her here, instead of me, she would have known what to do. I was sure of it.

I couldn't do this on my own, and I couldn't abandon her. Which left me one terrible option:

I had to go back and get her out, too.

· Chapter Thirty-Five ·

Here is what you (I) need to remember: The mind abhors chaos. It cannot abide randomness. It needs a narrative, one event after another, reason and cause and effect. When life is at its most incomprehensible, the mind clings to narrative the tightest.

But the mind is not infallible. It is not rational. It obsesses over what it perceives as sense and order, but when viewed from outside, from after, from far away, that order may only be a momentary trick of perspective.

In that office, I saw the monster.

And I set out to kill it.

I stood. My port was no longer inside me, but the wound was only closed with little butterfly adhesives, and they'd given way when I collapsed. Fresh blood soaked my gown, softening the crusted clot of the initial trauma. In the darkness, it was impossible to see if any had gotten on the sweater. But it didn't matter; when I opened the door, the floor was slick with it, too. A streaked trail, visible in the growing dawn, leading down the hall, in the direction of the fading footsteps. Distantly, I heard the creak of a cart, its wheels squealing for a portion of every revolution.

The air smelled faintly of rot, more strongly of antiseptic. The odor grew as I made my way down the hall.

It was getting worse. The break in the skin that I'd seen in the hallway a few floors up I'd written off to the influence of the drugs still in my system. But the pain was coming back now, and a certain flavor of clearheadedness that was at odds with what my senses were telling me. I saw nobody, and nobody stopped me. It seemed impossible. Hallucinating or not? Dreaming or not?

It didn't matter.

I was on a narrow road, in a slot canyon, with no options but to stop or go forward. Give up, or follow until the end. I hit the west tower end of the office block, back where I'd started. The elevator bank loured, tempting in my infirmity, but impossible. I needed solitude. Secrecy.

So I'd go up instead, and hope I didn't find anybody following my trail.

The climb was worse than the descent. My muscles were atrophied, my skin too delicate to handle the metal caps on the edge of each tread. I couldn't do anything but shuffle, and shuffling pushed the metal into my flesh like a cheese grater. I left scraps of myself behind.

(Who would be sent after me, to clean it up? Would they be safe?)

(I refused to think about it then. It's all I think about now.)

I passed the landing that I thought led back to where I'd escaped from. The fourth floor. Three more to go. The PA system was audible in there, and I heard them calling for me. *"Priority page. Code green . . ."*

One more floor up, and the bones I had rolled over in the

hallway in my half-conscious state were visible here in place of supportive struts. At the sixth-floor landing, jumbled beneath the stairs, was a tangle of lungs, twisted on their bronchi, layered in together. They rose and fell independently, around nodules of scar tissue and pus.

Or maybe those were my own. I was wheezing by then, breath coming in violent little bursts. My skull threatened to split apart, and I wanted to stop. If I could just curl up in a dark corner for a minute, two, then I'd regain a few drops of strength—

No. No, Isobel needed me. I couldn't stop. I couldn't get this far only to fail. If I'd stayed sedated for the new port to be put in, if I hadn't had the chance to slip away, I would have accepted that. I was so tired, so ready to stop trying. But I hadn't stayed sedated. I'd been able to get away, and not just out of the room I'd been in, but down into the bowels of Graceview, and now, here, ascending.

If I'd gotten this far, I had to get that last bit farther. Just in case this was real. Just in case I was right.

I reached the seventh floor. Carefully, I pushed the door open. Or maybe not carefully, but weakly. It moved slowly, either way, and I squinted against the bright light of the hallway beyond. Fluorescent lights at full blast, working light.

And beneath the hum of those lights was the roar.

I could hear the rhythm of it. Tiny independent strains of noise, syncopated, layered on itself, feeding back and back and back—the workings of the pathogen inside me as it grew and spread and extended throughout Graceview.

My own heartbeat settled into time with it. Again the exhaustion swept through me, the longing to rest. I wanted to go to that rhythm, to the wall, press my forehead against the slick surface and sink into it.

The light shone in and pierced my eyes. It cut through, enough that I blinked, squinted, searched. No bodies in the hall beyond. Suppurating flesh walls glistened, not the impression of something alive but the detail of it. Red streaked through it, radiating from the door at the far end. A sign punctured it to my right, a name with an arrow. SEVEN WEST. I was getting closer.

No bodies in the hall, decaying or otherwise. I realized with a sick, strange lurch that there was nobody there. No nurses. No techs. No patients, no visitors. I faltered. Was this real? Could this be real? Could a hospital be so empty?

The roar grew louder. Encouragement or fear? Could the infection hate? Could it scrabble for its own survival? Or was survival different from replication, reproduction? Was *fighting* something it could do, or did it only endure and spread?

Through the organic pulsing, I caught sight of the mundane details beneath. Open patient rooms, empty of equipment. A ladder, lying on its side, flesh growing along it like a trellis. A gap where the nurses' station would have been, the socket of a missing tooth.

The hall was under construction, being taken apart, being rebuilt.

Sudden movement. I froze, huddled by a ridge of scar tissue that arched up the wall, along the ceiling, its ropy furrows providing the barest hint of cover. Down by the exit, I saw a figure peel itself from the flesh. It did not move like a person, but it might have been shaped like one. The lights were so bright that I should have been able to make it out, but it seemed made of incidental shadows, there and gone again as it turned and faded into the door.

The lights just ahead of the door flickered. Dimmed. I looked up in time to see new pink skin growing over the fixture, thickening until I couldn't see anything beneath it. It made a wash of deep shadows by the door, and I approached it unsteadily. Everything in me hurt, hurt to the point where I could barely comprehend it anymore. It was like floating just slightly outside my body, piloting it without feeling. All feeling was erased, subsumed, in the agony.

It was a set of double doors, the kind that could be opened to admit a gurney and a throng of staff if needed. They were heavy, and possibly locked, not the ones I'd been buzzed in and out of before, but very similar. Did they lead to the same place?

Just a little more. Just a little farther. And then—

And then all the way back out.

I wept. My tears burned, and my sinuses raged, and my lungs threatened to burst. I wasn't built for weeping anymore. That took a strength I had already lost. But really, had I ever been strong enough to do this? When I had walked in the doors of Graceview, would I have been able to walk back out, if I had known? I would have had only my own weight to bear, and I wasn't sure I could have done it. How was I supposed to save Isobel, too?

There was a reason she had told me to leave. That she hadn't asked for anything for herself.

But Isobel wasn't like me. She was strong, and she knew the hospital better than I did. If I could just get her out of her room, into these back hallways, she could tell me where to go. I wouldn't be alone anymore.

I could do this. I just needed her help.

Tears slowing, I bent my head to the door. The roar was waiting. It slithered back into my ears, my bones. And this time, I listened. I listened for Veronica's voice, or Isobel's, telling me to go. Telling me it was time, it was safe. They'd helped before. I just needed them to help again.

Please, I thought. *Please, I need you.*

But nobody appeared to me.

Please, I can't do this.

My hands didn't just tremble; they wavered and jerked, uncontrollable. I could force them only to make the broadest gestures. My head swam, lost in the roar, and my vision pulsed with it. In, out, in, out. I felt close to collapse.

There was just this door between me and the ward. A staffed ward, a ward filled with nurses who would recognize me. I could still turn back. I could still leave. I could—

No. I couldn't do any of that. I needed Isobel, or there was no going forward at all.

And then, overhead: "*Priority page. Code blue. Adult. West tower. Seventh floor. Room seven-seven-eight.*"

Not my room. Not Isobel's room. But behind that door, I could hear voices, movement. All headed to room 778, away from this door, away from Isobel.

Beside the door was a key card reader. The light glowed green. No lock. As *"priority page"* repeated overhead, as the sounds from behind the door quieted, I leaned against the door, using all my withered weight.

It eased open. Slowly, slowly. I held my breath, or what was left of it.

Nobody sat at the nurses' station. No Shannon, no Louise, no assistants or runners or even Adam. The ward wasn't deserted; I could hear voices again, voices separate from the roar for just a moment before they, too, were swallowed up. A shrill alarm. Shouting. Somebody dying, or doing their best to. The walls pulsed with it, stretching, reaching.

I had time. Just enough of it, paid in some nameless patient's death. Had I caused that, too? Or was it just heart failure? A stroke? Something entirely normal, half-expected, mortal?

I didn't have time to think about it. I grabbed hold of a wheelchair close to the door and used it as a walker, stumbling across the hall, until I got to room 772.

The roar rose to a crescendo. I could barely think, but I didn't have to.

Same red bar, same unlocked door. Of course they couldn't change that, even with me on the loose: they had to be able to get to Isobel if she, too, started circling the drain.

I abandoned the wheelchair when it became clear I couldn't get the door open enough to maneuver it through. Its wheels were rotting anyway, sagging in deformed circles, trying to merge with the flesh of the floor.

It didn't belong inside, but I'd need it on my way out.

Inside the antechamber, I half expected Mark, the security officer, standing watch. Or some tech, sitting in the antechamber, ready at hand in case of an emergency.

There was nobody.

The vestibule was less rotted than the rest of Graceview, but it was still infected. The floors and walls were the linoleum and drywall they should have been, but patches of peach-pink slime aggregated in the corners. And the room was warm, too warm, febrile and aching.

But quiet. So quiet. I could hear the *click click click* of Isobel's pump and the faintest sound of her breathing, and nothing else. The roar was gone. Even the code blue alert was swallowed by emptiness.

I pushed open the door to the main room.

Isobel lay in the hospital bed, shining with sweat and still tied down in soft restraints. Her eyes were closed. Her breathing was even. Her limbs were limp. I thought of the wheelchair, and how I'd have to bring it in here to have any chance of getting her up and out of bed. The pump, and the likelihood that she needed whatever was being pushed into her veins.

Her room was identical to mine. I knew these floors, these walls, that bed. I knew that pump. Only the view was different, a picture of the east tower and the garden below instead of the mountains. I could feel myself slipping sideways. I hung on to the knob of the door, sagging with the weight of how sick I was, had been, would be—and how much more there still was to do.

And then I saw Isobel, sitting at the window in clean scrubs. She stared at me. And then she said:

"I told you to leave."

· Chapter Thirty-Six ·

I looked between them, uncomprehending: Isobel, dying, and Isobel, alive. The body in the bed was only half-real, wasting away, entirely out of its proper context, while the one by the window looked in every aspect correct.

Except for its impossibility.

For one bright, hysterical moment, I thought, *Twins?* Followed by, *Is that Isobel in the bed or some other unfortunate patient?* And then, when I was truly weeping again, *Am I the one in the bed after all?*

I slid to my knees. My calves were a mottled purple. I brushed at the pigmentation like it was just ink, like it could come off, and saw my hands were the same.

The Isobel by the window had stood and was crossing the floor to me, making a wide circle around the bed. "Meg?"

"I came to take you somewhere safe, too," I said, tearing my attention away from myself, gazing up at her. "I brought—I brought a wheelchair." But she could walk. Or one of her could walk. I felt something wet and hot slide from my nose, around the chapped bow of my lip. It soaked into the fabric of my mask, and I scrabbled, pulling it away from me as it tried to suck in against my mouth. I tossed it aside.

"I can't leave," Isobel said. "Not even with your help. Meg, you shouldn't have come back."

"I couldn't abandon you!" The floor beneath my legs was freezing, and I could feel myself beginning to shiver uncontrollably. My vision shifted in and out, fading and returning, everything dotted with black. But I could see her, crouching beside me. "Come with me, *please*."

"I'm not real, Meg."

"You gave me the scalpel!" I shouted.

She winced at the noise. I made myself take deep, rattling breaths. I wanted her to touch me then. Invalidate her words, prove to me that something about her was concrete. But she didn't. She made no move to wipe my hair off my sweat-soaked forehead, or to guide me up and into a chair. She made no move to clean away the blood beneath my nose.

"Isobel," I whispered.

Footsteps in the hallway. I looked around the room, searching for a place to hide. But there were voices out there, voices growing louder. Somebody had noticed the wheelchair. Or maybe it was just time for shift change, bedside report. The sun was fully risen now.

"There's no time," Isobel said. She sounded so sad. This was it; they were going to find me and take me away. I'd failed.

I couldn't fail.

I forced myself to my feet. "I'll buy us a little more," I said, staggering over to the computer cart. It was heavy but on wheels. I couldn't lift, but I could push. I leaned hard against it, and it moved. Smoothly, slowly for the weight of it, slow enough that I could almost steer it. If I could just get it to the door, I could block it. Block the nurses and the infection both, because in here there was only us. The roar was gone, the walls were no longer flesh. We were both sick, I knew that, but there had to be a reason the room was clean.

I couldn't let either of us be taken back out into that nightmare.

My feet slipped. I felt myself dropping. And then, behind me, around me, Isobel. She braced her arms on either side, hands against the cart bracketing my own. I expected warmth against my back, and it was there, but too warm. Hot. Feverish. And her breath smelled of the same rot as the hallway.

"You're not Isobel," I whispered, not looking at her.

She was the roar.

This close, I could hear it on her breath. Feel it thrumming against my spine. It was quiet, barely more than a whisper, but it came not from the air around us, but from her.

"I'm both," she said into my hair.

She pushed. The cart moved into place. I moved with it. With her. With . . . them.

On the other side of the door, I could hear Louise, exasperated and a little afraid. Somebody else, stridently pissed. And Adam. Adam was saying, "Let me try, let me—she might listen—"

I tried to back away, and Isobel let go, allowing my retreat.

I looked at her, finally. I couldn't see the infection in her. Symptoms were its only footprints, and the version of her now standing by her own bedside was healthy. Her scrubs weren't even wrinkled. She looked at me, then down at her body in the bed. A ripple went through it, spasming, seizing in its sleep.

"Both," I repeated.

"All three," she corrected, softly. "Your nurse. The infection. And Isobel." As she said it, her skin began to shift. Her bones moved. My stomach heaved as her skull rearranged itself, as two more pairs of eyes opened, as two noses joined them, two mouths split through to the surface. It wasn't even or proportional; as her limbs split as well, as her ribs multiplied, her skin sagged and stretched to contain it all.

I wanted to look away. I couldn't.

Her three faces slid one into the other into the last, her varying expressions distorting their neighbors. She looked simultaneously terrified, calm, and hungry. And beneath it all, pain: a begging open mouth, a furrowed brow, grasping hands.

This was what had come to me in my room and given me the scalpel.

This was what had woken me up, had tried to send me out of the hospital.

And it was inside me, too.

"It's difficult to think straight," Isobel confessed, speaking with her central mouth, the one that looked the most like it had before. "Even without the seizures. We must be quick. We need to find some other solution—"

"There is no other solution," whispered the mouth that was in pain. Isobel's voice was so weak and frightened.

And she was right.

There was no other way out of this room. The nurses knew I was here. I could hear a new page going out: *"Code gray. Adult. Room seven-seven-two."* The same code from before, when they'd dragged me away from Isobel's seizing body. It was only a matter of time before somebody got the door open, before they tore us apart again. And they wouldn't see this contorted Isobel; they'd only find me half-dead, ranting and raving.

(And maybe that was the truth.)

"The phone," Nurse Isobel said.

"And call who?" I asked.

She had no answer. No nursing board would take my call, even if she knew the number. No emergency services would believe me.

"Your mother," whimpered the terrified mouth.

"I don't know her number," I said, ashamed.

Adam's voice came from the other side of the door. "Margaret! Margaret, if you can hear me, you need to unblock the door." I jerked where I stood, as if burned. "You aren't in trouble. We just want to make sure you and Nurse Isobel are okay. Can you hear me, Margaret?"

"Another colony," the hungry mouth said, eyes rolling in her lumpen skull. "Growing slowly, quietly."

The pathogen.

And I could hear it, in my voice, saying, *Can we live inside you?*

Its gaze steadied, shifting to one of the cabinets. It pointed. The way it moved its allotment of arms was wrong, too fluid, as if it couldn't figure out the point of osseous joints. I thought I heard something give way with a wet snap. "In there," it said.

The other two faces appeared startled.

I didn't move at first. But then Adam called my name again, and I dragged myself over to the cabinet, opening it. Inside were my laptop and phone, stacked neatly.

"I don't understand," I said, looking frantically between the thing Isobel had become and the immobile body in the bed.

"Hidden," the pathogen mouth said. "To keep you here."

I shook my head but tried to turn my phone on anyway. I was met with only a black screen and my reflection. I threw it away from me, startled by my own gauntness, the filth on my chin, the peeling skin of my cheeks and nose. It slid into the tripartite Isobel's foot.

"Nothing," I said, standing up, trembling, back against the bank of cabinets. "Nothing, it won't turn on. There's nothing left."

The frightened Isobel began to weep. The central arms tried to silence her. I couldn't watch this.

I looked away from those two faces, only to find the pathogen face watching me.

Hungry, I thought again. Strange, to see the face of the mindless thing that was killing me. That was killing both of us. The light in its eyes was so unfamiliar, so alien, even as Isobel's features tried to translate.

I tried, just once, to reason with it. "You can't want this," I said. I gestured to myself. "If you kill us, you die, too, don't you?"

It blinked. "Yes," it agreed. "But first, growth. Spread."

"Not here, not with us, they have us on lockdown."

Its stare was blank.

"It doesn't understand that," the nurse mouth interjected. "It's not— It doesn't *think*. It doesn't plan. It just is. It makes more of itself, it doesn't decide. That's not why we're sick, it didn't target us, do you understand?" Her exhausted, snapping bitterness was so familiar I ached, but it gave me a bit of strength. I crept closer.

"Does it have a name?" I asked.

"Idiogenic collapse disorder," she said with her pathogen mouth. I would have thought it would be mocking when it spoke, but it was strangely toneless. It didn't seem to mind its name at all. "The hospital is a host."

The roar lapped against my eardrums.

"Did you know? This whole time?" I asked Isobel the nurse.

I wanted answers, so badly. But when she said nothing, my heart sank. I knew. I could feel it coming. Whispered in my ear, before she ever spoke.

Eventually, she nodded. "It's—a secondary topic of research, in the SWAIL study. Trying to isolate it, figure out what it is, what to do. Usually it's fugitive, hard to find. Something about patients who have Fayette-Gehret makes them uniquely vulnerable, but only once we start SWAIL. Something about how fast your cells can grow, maybe, or some other mechanism of action that's only uncovered when we take away your immune system. I'm sorry. I'm sorry, Meg. Until Veronica died, I wasn't certain— We didn't know— There are so few cases—"

Adam was pounding on the door again. My throat was clogged with phlegm. I was so tired, I didn't know if I should laugh or scream.

They'd known, all of them; they'd been waiting to see what

it would do. I'd been right, that I was the petri dish, the culturing medium.

Isobel getting sick had just been a tragic accident.

I didn't know, for one brief, violent moment, whether I felt all that bad about it anymore.

· Chapter Thirty-Seven ·

GRACEVIEW MEMORIAL

Room:	772	Phone	XXX-XXX-2772
Date:	??????	\multicolumn{2}{l|}{MON TUES WED THURS FRI SAT SUN}
Patient:	ISOBEL ISOBEL ISOBEL ISOBEL ISOBEL ISOBEL	\multicolumn{2}{l|}{PAIN SCALE}
Doctor:	Can	\multicolumn{2}{l|}{10 10 10 10 10 10 10}
Nurse:	We	Pain medication last given:	help
Charge Nurse:	Live	Next dose:	help
\multicolumn{4}{c|}{Today's Plan! *GROW*}
Diet:	Inside	Fall Risk:	help
Activity Level:	You	Our goal is to have you discharged on:	stay
\multicolumn{4}{c|}{*don't leave me meg*}

"Meg?"

    I stared down at Isobel's body in the bed. I couldn't remember walking there; my brain was on fire, the roar drowned out by my own screaming thoughts. Isobel had known, all along, what was going to happen to me. I'd tried to absolve her of all the guilt she bore, and for what? She'd said she was just burned out, that she felt responsible in some nebulous way, and I'd—I'd reassured her. I'd assumed she was wrong.

But she had been telling me, in her own way. Every time she'd tried to get me to leave. Every time she'd warned me.

It hadn't been enough. And she'd worked here, stayed on this ward, until it had put her in this bed.

Did she deserve it?

(She had told me to run. She didn't want me in that room. Was that pragmatism or self-loathing?)

"Meg, please look at me," the thing behind me said.

I forced myself to straighten. I turned to the abomination wearing my nurse's face. "Did you get me sick? Intentionally?" I asked. I needed to know; it was the only answer that mattered now.

"No," the nurse said. "No, we were just ready when you did get sick. Meg, nothing was withheld from you. You have to understand that. There's nothing we could have done."

"Except warn me," I said.

She looked away.

"Usually," the pathogen mouth said, speaking with a glacial, halting cadence, just learning how to use words, "growth is slow. But not there." It gestured to me. "Delivered, in force."

"Infected, deliberately," the nurse said, and she sounded—surprised. "Are you sure?"

Infected, deliberately.

I couldn't breathe. A performance. This was a pantomime, for my benefit. An attempt to soothe. But even as I had the thought, I registered the horror crossing both the nurse's face and the suffering patient's.

No, Isobel hadn't known. But somebody must have.

With Veronica's voice, the pathogen mouth said, *"He brings you flowers, too?"* And then its face frowned. "No. Not that. Something else."

The faint stench of rot was replaced, for just a moment, with the blooming scent of mango.

All of those meals, with their color-coded containers.

I finally vomited.

Isobel the nurse was there in an instant, but I recoiled, staggering away, colliding with the bed rail. Isobel's body jerked from the force of it. No, not the body, *Isobel*. The real, barely breathing Isobel. She was displaced from her bed, or at least transported, transformed, right behind me—but it wasn't her. I couldn't see it as her, not split as it was. I clung to the railing, staring down at her wan face. I felt blood, my blood, fresh and hot once more. My heaving must have torn open the closures on my chest, or maybe my nose was bleeding again.

Plit plit plit, in time with the pump.

My toes touched something warm and viscous.

I looked down.

Beneath her bed, splattered with my vomit, was the pink-peach biofilm. Compared to my skin, compared to Isobel's, it looked oversaturated. Vivid and vivacious. Alive in a way we weren't. It slicked the floor and was beginning to climb the caster wheels of the bed. But where my blood had fallen, it had retreated, as if burned. I stared at the bare linoleum beneath.

The voices beyond the door were quieting, but the roar rose up to replace them. I struggled to think through it.

"Meg," the tripartite Isobel called. "Meg, come back to me."

Isobel shouldn't have been in that bed. For all her sins, she should have been safe. "Why are you this sick?" I asked. The ground was pulling away beneath me. The world was closing in. But this was important. I could feel it, some missing detail, just beyond my grasp.

"Changing, learning. New patterns, new approaches, new hosts," said the pathogen mouth. And yes, that made sense, pathogens evolve, don't they? And maybe that was how it had jumped to her. Maybe it was the burnout, her own immune system crumpling under the stress heaped upon it. Or maybe—maybe that one dinner, shared with Isobel, maybe that had been the last vector needed.

But it couldn't be why she was dying so much faster than I was. By all rights, I should have been the one in the bed, not her. They'd all but destroyed me.

Except . . . maybe that was it. Maybe that was the difference. Not SWAIL, even if it had left me vulnerable, but *why* I was being put through it in the first place.

I had Fayette-Gehret syndrome.

She didn't.

In her own words, something about Fayette-Gehret made me vulnerable, but only after SWAIL. And while SWAIL had all but hollowed me out, it wasn't finished yet. Isobel had said the next treatment would kill me. Lauren had said there was *almost* nothing left for my body to fix. Louise had called this my last chance.

There was something still in my blood. Something left

over, something SWAIL hadn't gotten rid of, not quite. Something that fought back the biofilm.

Something that, without it, I'd die just like Isobel was dying.

Which meant that with it?

Maybe she could live.

I pushed away from the bed, going to the supply cabinet. I needed—tubing. Some kind of tubing. Maybe a syringe? I didn't know, I didn't have the training. And I didn't have the code I needed to open the drawers, either. I looked over my shoulder, the strain on my neck making the world grow dim for a moment, the floor pitch and yaw. I stood my ground.

I would only have one chance at this. The voices outside the room had quieted, which meant they were preparing some new tactic. Some way in. I met the eyes of the patient aspect of the grotesque amalgamation.

"Give me the code," I said. "I'm going to give you my blood."

"*No*," said the nurse mouth. "Absolutely not, we're not compatible."

"I don't care," I said, and pointed to the film on the floor. "Look. Look, my blood kills it, something in it, my rogue white blood cells, whatever the fuck it is. It's the only useful thing I have left. And I am going to give it to you before it's gone."

I know what I sounded like.

The mind seeks to create a narrative. It keeps trying to exert control over an environment. The only alternative is a damaged passivity, learned helplessness keeping you stuck while the shock comes, again and again.

"Five-seven-two-three," the patient mouth said, and the nurse aspect swore.

The pathogen side, strangely, was quiet.

Of all three of them, I expected it to fight the most. And its lack of reaction made me falter. But what else could it have done? It spoke with Isobel's mouth, but didn't think with her brain. This wasn't battle, not in the way I could understand it. It simply *was*. It lived, it reproduced, it consumed. But it didn't plan or fear.

I punched in the code, then opened the cabinet and drawers. I stared, unsure of what came next.

"Tell me how to do it," I said. "Tell me what I need."

"You'll kill me," the nurse mouth said. She was reaching out, as if to stop me, but the patient's hands grabbed those wrists, held them fast.

"No, no, let her," the patient mouth begged. "I can't do this anymore. I'm going to die."

She sounded so much like me, just then.

But while the nurse in her wavered, it also wasn't enough. She'd seen so many people sick, so many people die. My throat was so dry, but I managed one last plea.

"*Other people could die.* If you're sick, other people could get sick, too." I gestured to the bed. "And if this works—if I can save you—"

Maybe it could end with us.

That was enough. She came to my side, the whole misshapen bulk of her, and she pointed to each thing I would need. Tubing, gloves, Vacutainer needle, scalpel, tape, a prepackaged saline flush, antiseptic wipes, a tourniquet.

"Thank you," I said. I don't know why; I was saving *her*,

not the other way around, and she had done so much to me, put me at such risk. But I needed her, even in this. We needed each other.

I took everything to the bedside. I stepped onto the film and shuddered, but I kept going, dumping everything onto the sheets and then undoing Isobel's restraints. Her skin was so damaged. It was like I could feel it, all that raw, sore skin. "What next?"

The creature loomed over the bed, gazing down at Isobel's shivering, sweating body. She had another IV port in her far arm, not connected to the pump, but even from where I stood, I could see discoloration. Not available.

"Gloves first," she said. When I'd complied, she continued, "Wipe everything down. Remove the hub at the end of your IV tubing—yes, that. Now attach the Vacutainer needle." The plastic cylinder had a bright blue lock on one end, and it screwed on seamlessly. "Now cut off the spike on the new tubing, that's right. Careful. Insert it into the Vacutainer . . . add tape. Should be a good enough seal."

Isobel was so steady, so patient. And that, in turn, made me steady enough to manage the fiddly work despite my numb fingertips and the strange interference of the gloves.

With the tape in place, I looked up and met her eyes. I could see the panic in them, just below the surface. I looked away.

"Now: you'll need to turn off everything in the pump except for the saline."

Isobel's pump wasn't locked down.

My hands shook as I followed the nurse's instructions. The machine was as slow and unresponsive as I remembered, but it was simple to pause everything aside from the one she pointed out. We waited for the line to run a little longer, the air quiet, hushed, impossible.

Then something hit the door.

I flinched but didn't look. "Hurry," I said. "Hurry, they're coming."

"Move me to the floor," the thing said. "Quickly."

"Help me?" I asked, breathless, but the tripartite creature shook her head.

I reached into the bed. Isobel's body was so light, but my muscles were far weaker than they needed to be, and she slipped from my arms. I heard the *thunk* of her head hitting the ground, but I didn't have time. I left her there. Her hand was in the slime. I could feel myself starting to hyperventilate.

Another slam against the door, then another. I clambered back onto the gurney. The nurse hands reached for mine but didn't touch. She mimed for me how to massage the tubing until my blood oozed through the four-foot length of it. I fumbled through it, struggling to manage everything on my own, but she never stabilized a thing. Unable or unwilling? I could still see in that central set of eyes a banked anger, mistrust, fear.

When the blood ran through, she pointed to the stopcock in the line below the pump. "You shouldn't do this," she warned.

"Please," the patient mouth begged.

The pathogen side just observed.

It would have been—not easier, but more understandable, if it had fought.

I connected my blood to Isobel's IV and watched it flow

into the pulses of saline. Down, down, into her vein. The first bloom of red disappeared beneath her skin.

I held my breath. It burned in my ravaged lungs, but I held it, and watched, and waited. More slams echoed from the antechamber, and I could hear the cart squeaking against the floor. They were close. It wouldn't hold much longer. Was it working? How would I know? Would there be any sign?

The roar exploded inside my skull.

Louder than I'd ever heard it, it obliterated all other thought. My eyes were open, and there was light to see by, but the onslaught was so terrible, so all-consuming, that I couldn't tell you what was happening around me. If the pathogen aspect fought, finally, I couldn't see it. Couldn't understand it. There was just me, in the bed, once more a patient; Isobel, on the floor, relegated to nothing. It wasn't supposed to be like that.

And I felt nothing. No mystical connection, no flash of triumph. I could barely feel the blood leaving me at all and had no way of knowing what it felt like as it entered Isobel's veins. Not cold, like my transfusions had been, I suppose, but beyond that—nothing. Nothing but the roar, and the burn of withheld oxygen.

I felt like I was falling. The world began to fade. The roar softened. And, as sight returned, as I watched, the pathogen limbs stopped moving. It didn't go limp, but stiff, as if frozen in place. As if a connection had been cut.

I began to breathe again.

And then the first alarm went off. I couldn't see the screen from where I was, didn't know what had gone wrong, but the sound pierced my brain, ramified down my spine. I wanted to cover my ears but couldn't, not without pulling too hard on the tubing.

"Stop!" the nurse mouth yelled. Her arms, still capable of movement, grabbed for the IV pole. I realized too late that she had half a chance of moving it; nonliving objects had been fair game in the past. The scalpel, the cart.

Before she could get hold of it, Isobel's patient aspect had tangled herself around the nurse's arms once more.

But the patient face was shifting, receding, as if the bone beneath her skull was beginning to fall away. I tore my gaze from her and looked at the real Isobel, sprawled helpless on the floor. Her skin was breaking out in red patches, welts and hives, and as I stared, she began to twitch. Her breathing sounded—wrong.

Then she began to scream.

It hit her and the creature behind me simultaneously, a great wave breaking. Louder than the alarm, louder than the renewed pounding on the door and the motion of the cart. They were breaking in. I had minutes left, seconds. And all I could do was stare down at what I had done.

Her eyes opened, sightless, as she thrashed. The creature construct collapsed into itself, disappeared into nothingness. There was just me, in the bed, blood running into Isobel, on the floor, and we were so sick, so sick, and she was dying.

I was killing her.

I scratched at my arm, desperate to tear the tubing away, but I was so clumsy. *Click click click* went the pump, and my blood kept inching down the line, dumping into her veins again, again, again. I sobbed, wishing her skin would balloon with blood, the IV shot, the vein ruptured. Anything to keep it from moving, anything to stop it.

The cart spun away from the door. I gave up on my own IV and heaved myself to the edge of the bed. I hit the ground beside her, a new blur of pain added to the rest. I couldn't understand the voices behind me, above me, and I reached for her IV.

I never got it free.

They pulled me away from her. I didn't see their faces, still don't know who was there to witness everything, who knows exactly what I did. They disconnected us, moved Isobel back into her bed, took her out of the room. There was so much shouting. Adam stood above me, staring down in horror, and I stared back up at him. His eyes were the only thing keeping me there, keeping me in my body, as I sobbed and fought and begged.

"Please," I whispered, my throat so hoarse, my lungs so tired. "Please, please. I only wanted to save her. Tell me she's going to be okay. She's going to be okay. Is she going to be okay?" I babbled: about the blood, about the roar, about how I'd just wanted to give her a weapon.

They brought a gurney for me. They moved me into it. I never felt the push of drugs, but I felt their effect. Absences, spots in my mind, there and gone, there and gone.

I never saw Isobel again.

Chapter Thirty-Eight

I can still hear the roar.

Most of the time, it's distant. Just another sound of the hospital, almost lost behind the beeping monitors, the movement of equipment, the voices of the living. Everything is louder now, and I cling to it all. Try to anchor myself to what is real.

I'm no longer in the room I started in. The room with the growth in the floor, the room that Adam decorated with flowers, the room where Isobel gave me the scalpel—it houses somebody else now. After a stint in the ICU to treat the sepsis I gave myself, ripping out my port and wandering through the bowels of the hospital, I'm back on the seventh floor, back in an isolation room, but it isn't as large. The computer cart is gone, along with the easy-access supplies. And the door opens directly to the nurses' station.

I only go through that door in a wheelchair or on a gurney. They walk me to the bathroom on occasion, but generally I stick to the commode. Most of the time, I'm not aware enough to care.

When I am, or when the roar grows loud, sometimes I still want to fight. I want to dig my nails and teeth into my nurse, or the sitter that now watches me day in, day out. I want to bite and claw and hit Adam, when he comes to see me. I am desperate, desperate to know if Isobel is doing better—if she is still alive. If I was right. If what I did was worth it.

But I don't ask. I've lost the right to ask. And they would only lie, anyway.

Sometimes I can't control myself, and they fasten soft restraints around my wrists and ankles. My skin is red and raw. They don't let me fight for long, though. It's not safe—for me. I'm so weak, after the fever, after the quiet hell that was the ICU. I spend a lot of time sedated.

It's for my health, they tell me. And perhaps they're right, because I'm not dead yet. Isobel was wrong. The carousel of multihued IV bags continues, and after each one, I am still alive.

They even brought in a psychiatrist, finally. They added an antipsychotic to the mix. I couldn't tell you yet if it's helping; it blunts everything, which is probably for the best anyway.

Today, the new nurse is on shift again. I still don't know her name. I don't care. She isn't Isobel. She will do her job, and she will be kind or she will be remote, she will be competent or she'll hurt me, and I don't care. I can't care, not anymore. The only thing I have left is what Louise told me, before Isobel gave me the scalpel: to let it wash over me.

Today, Adam comes, too. They both stand by my bedside. They talk to me, slow and steady, and none of it pierces through the miserable fog I float in, trying to organize what has happened to me, trying to form it into some kind of narrative so that I can chase absolution in it.

I don't like listening to him. I don't like when he touches my hand. I am only grateful that he no longer brings me flow-

The Graceview Patient

ers or food, no longer tries to win me over. He doesn't have to. He's won.

Except then he says her name.

Isobel.

He tells me that she will make a full recovery. He tells me that it's thanks to me, to what I did, to what I risked. That I was right: there's something in my blood that can fix her. Can fix me, too. That they have some of my blood in storage from when I was first admitted, and they're using my tissue to engineer a cure, and I can't listen. I turn away, because lies are worse than absence. And he is lying, isn't he? I can hear the whispering. The roar is building. It will crash over me soon. In it is Isobel's voice, begging, pleading.

And Veronica, saying, *Can you hear it?*

Either he is lying, or my brain is lying. Saying what I so desperately want to hear. But if I still had my phone, if I looked her up, what would I find?

She hasn't come to see me. That is the only truth I have. I haven't seen her since that last day in her room, I haven't seen her since she was carted away screaming, and all I have left is the sound of her shrieks, deep in the roar.

A part of me is inside her. Will be buried with her.

Crying hurts in new ways. My tears scour me, my throat closes up. The new nurse takes my other hand, and I can't tell if she means to offer comfort, or only to make sure I don't flail around.

Adam says my name, and I look at him at last. I do not trust him, with his perfect suit, his beautiful eyes. I can still see him changing my whiteboard, taking samples of my body, leaving food for me to eat. He'd cared for me, too, kept me company, listened to me, sympathized—but that means nothing if he's also the reason I'm here.

He brings you flowers, too, Veronica had said. And I was so focused on the flowers that I invited Isobel to eat his other gift.

He gazes back at me, steady, sure. I can't tell if my brain is my enemy, or he is. I've never been able to tell. Louise told me it's my brain. That what I think is real *is* real, but not true, not necessarily true. Strength, if I believe her, is inaction. Choosing to endure. Endure, not fight. I can't fight anymore. Fighting killed Isobel. Or, maybe, fighting saved Isobel. But fighting now does nothing.

There are no choices left.

Today, Adam says, *we begin to rebuild you. Today we start making you better. Today we start cultivating your recovery.*

But I'd like your permission to use what we've learned to try something new.

And he places paperwork on my tray.

A pen.

Eventually, I sign.

X—*Margaret Culpepper*

Acknowledgments

First and foremost, this book would not exist without my mother, Betsy. I grew up alongside her eventually fatal illness, and accompanied her to hospitals and HIV clinics. I knew her home nurses and her doctors. Without her, I may still have come to my fascination with medicine, but I suspect the tone would have been very different. She was braver than I hope I ever need to be, and possibly more than I can understand, though I had an inkling one day driving to the NICU to visit my son, and realizing for just a moment what it must have been like for her to raise me knowing she wouldn't live to see me become an adult.

Fayette-Gehret syndrome is named after her, though it doesn't have much in common with HIV besides immune system dysfunction, and I owe a thank-you to my aunt Carolyn, who not only okayed the name but checked in at every step in this book's development to make sure I hadn't changed it.

I was also fortunate enough to reconnect with one of my mother's nurses, Michael Chance, while in the process of fact-checking the medical aspects of this book. Michael, thank you so much for walking me through not only your relationship with my mother, but also the work you did helping to develop

Acknowledgments

drug trials for HIV treatment and your expertise on hospital functioning.

To my wonderful friend and nursing consultant, Kathleen—thank you, forever, for the work you did not only correcting medical errors (any remaining are entirely my fault), but for helping me build out the hospital of Graceview as its own character and culture. Thank you for telling me, "Isobel's a better nurse than that," when I had her make weaker choices in earlier drafts. And thank you for walking me through exactly how to MacGyver that transfusion rigging in the second to last chapter.

David, Alex, Integra—as always, I'm not sure how I'd get through drafting a book without you three. Your constant support, your willingness to listen to me ramble while I troubleshoot plot issues, your excitement for each new project, all of it keeps me going. Thank you, and here's to another one for the (hah) books.

Finally, to my publishing family—Caitlin McDonald, Michael Homler, Maddie Alsup, Rivka Holler, and the rest of the SMP team—it has been a joy to build this book alongside you. And Xe Sands, I will never forget that *this* was the book that made us actually do something about always wanting to work together again.

I want to close out by saying: This is not a book meant to make you fear the science of medicine or the practitioners. The drug trials my mother participated in had their ups and downs; she weathered them to help other people as much as to buy herself more time. My own hospitalization that led to the inspiration for this book was potentially traumatizing, but the guidance and care of my nurses and physicians made

Acknowledgments

all the difference. Medicine, and medical research, are both so, so important, and I hope that if you ever get the chance, you'll consider participating yourself.

And please, do not try to autotransfuse your blood into your nurse. Nurses deal with more than enough as it is.

About the Author

Beth Olson Creative

CAITLIN STARLING is the national bestselling author of *The Death of Jane Lawrence*, the Bram Stoker Award–nominated *The Luminous Dead*, and *Last to Leave the Room*. Her newest novels, *The Starving Saints* and *The Graceview Patient*, epitomize her love of genre-hopping horror; her bibliography spans besieged castles, alien caves, and haunted hospitals. Her short fiction has been published by *Grimdark Magazine* and *Neon Hemlock*, and her nonfiction has appeared in *Nightmare*, *Uncanny*, and *Nightfire*. Caitlin also works in narrative design and has been paid to invent body parts. She's always on the lookout for new ways to inflict insomnia.